William Dunn Macray

The Pilgrimage to Parnassus

with the two parts of The return from Parnassus

William Dunn Macray

The Pilgrimage to Parnassus
with the two parts of The return from Parnassus

ISBN/EAN: 9783337288198

Printed in Europe, USA, Canada, Australia, Japan

Cover: Foto ©Andreas Hilbeck / pixelio.de

More available books at **www.hansebooks.com**

The Pilgrimage to Parnassus

WITH

The Two Parts of

The Return from Parnassus

London

HENRY FROWDE

OXFORD UNIVERSITY PRESS WAREHOUSE

AMEN CORNER, E.C.

THE PILGRIMAGE TO PARNASSUS with THE TWO PARTS OF THE RETURN FROM PARNASSUS. Three Comedies performed in ST. JOHN'S COLLEGE CAMBRIDGE A.D. MDXCVII – MDCI. Edited from MSS. by the REV. W. D. MACRAY, M.A., F.S.A.

OXFORD AT THE CLARENDON PRESS

MDCCCLXXXVI

PREFACE.

THE present volume contains a trilogy of dramas which, although known to have once existed, has lain *perdu* to the world from the time of its composition, except with regard to the third part. That third part was twice printed in 1606, rather more than four years after the date of its first representation; was reprinted in the last century; was included a few years ago in Mr. W. Carew Hazlitt's edition of Dodsley's *Select Plays*; and in 1879 obtained a place in Prof. Arber's *English Scholar's Library*. But why this third part should alone have been published by its author does not clearly appear; it was described by its eighteenth-century editor, Thos. Hawkins, in somewhat exaggerated terms, as being 'perhaps the most singular composition in our language,' but its singularity of design and character is shared equally by the earlier parts, which display also as much humour and are fuller of illustrations of the academic life of the period. They have, unhappily, as much too of that coarseness which is such a blot on the popular literature of the time, but they have no such pages of repulsive rant as are assigned at the close of the third part to the extravagant characters *Furor Poeticus* and *Phantasma*. Probably the secret of the greater popularity of the third part may be found in the personal satire expressed in the character of the *Recorder*. In him is personified Francis Brackyn, who in his office as Recorder of Cambridge incurred extreme unpopularity in the

b

University by maintaining the right of the Mayor to
precedency over the Vice-Chancellor in certain cases.[1] He
had already been satirized in *Club-Law*, a play acted at
Clare Hall in 1597-8; and it is possible that he may also
be the lawyer who at a later date figures as *Ignoramus* in
Ruggles' famous comedy. It may well be that it was on
this account that the last part of our trilogy won the
greater popularity amongst the academic auditors to
whose sympathies it appealed; and the prominence
given through its second title, *The Scourge of Simony*, to
that portion of the play which represents the lawyer's
co-operation with a patron in the sale of an ecclesiastical
benefice, makes it also probable that the latter greedy
reprobate, called by the different names of Sir Frederick,
Sir Raderick, and Sir Randall, may have been some other
easily recognised and notorious character of the time. It
was only some twenty-five years before that a statute had
been passed (13 Eliz. *cap.* 6) forbidding the taking money
for presentation to a vacant benefice, and making that an
offence by civil law which had before been only cognizable
under canon law, but no doubt unscrupulous patrons and
lawyers had already begun to find ways for driving the
proverbial coach and horses through the technicalities
of the enactment.

The first two comedies are now printed from a MS.
preserved in one of Thomas Hearne's volumes of miscellane-
ous collections in the Bodleian Library. With a true sense
of the possible value to others, if not to himself, of all
remnants of earlier times, of the very rags of writings,
Hearne (who, in the words of his self-written epitaph,
'studied and preserved antiquities' in a way for which we
of the later generations can never be too grateful) stored up

---

[1] See Mr. James Bass Mullinger's *University of Cambridge* 1535-1625,
published in 1884, p. 526. An abstract of the third play is there given at
pp. 522-526.

all kinds of papers, binding them together just as they came
to his hands, in most admired confusion. His MSS. now
form part of Dr. Richard Rawlinson's vast collection; and
there, in one of his mixed volumes numbered Rawlinson D
398, I met with these lost plays. The MS. consists of
twenty folio leaves (besides one outside leaf) written
evidently by a copyist, who, as evidently, has sometimes
been unable to read, or too careless to read, his original
correctly. The stage directions are written in pale red ink.
There is a curious peculiarity in the scribe's spelling, which
may perhaps help to determine his provincial locality; words
ending in *ce*, such as 'once,' 'fence,' 'hence,' are written
without the final *e*, 'onc,' 'fenc,' 'henc.' And 'they' is
frequently used for 'the.' On the outside leaf is written, as
an owner's name, 'Edmunde Rishton, Lancastrensis.' It is
possible that, as the plays were acted at St. John's College,
this person was a member of the College; but as unfortunately the registers there only reach back to the year
1634 (as I am informed by Mr. J. B. Mullinger), there
are no means of tracing him through College records. Nor
has Mr. J. Eglington Bailey, whose knowledge with respect
to the families and worthies of Lancashire is extensive and
well known, been able to identify him by this his short
local description of himself. And while this mark of ownership connects this MS. with a northern county, it is worthy
of notice that the second MS., to be described further on,
came to its present possessor's hands from a library in the
north.[1] We should be prepared therefore to look thither
for the author; and in the prologue to the second play we
seem to find some evidence that he was a native of Cheshire.
The two lines in the professed description of the author,

'Hee never since durst name a peece of cheese,
Though Chessire seems to priviledge his name,'

---

[1] The provincial philologist will, I believe, find words of northern use not
infrequent; *e.g.* 'sooping.'

appear to connect him with that county, although the allusion is one which, in our ignorance of the author, defies explanation. If the lines preceding these are to be taken *au sérieux*, and not simply as jocular, he was one who had failed to secure his B.A. hood at Cambridge, and had migrated thence to Germany, where he had at last obtained some 'silie poore degree'; and then, it would seem, had returned to his Alma Mater.

The plays were all of them 'Christmas toys.' The date of the third has been proved from internal evidence (see Prof. Arber's Introduction to his reprint) to be December, 1601. The fresh readings in the prologue to that play, which have been gained from Mr. Halliwell-Phillipps' MS., show us that the first part (which was written in three days) was acted four years before, *i.e.* in December, 1597, and that the third was the final conclusion of the series. That prologue tells us also that the author and a friend, described as the *Philomusus* and *Studioso* of the comedies, had meanwhile been to Italy, which we learn also from the fourth scene of the first act. The two friends represent themselves as having contemplated, in the mercenary hope of profitable preferment, secession abroad to that Roman Faith for which many others had at that time abandoned both Cambridge and Oxford, but finding that 'discontented clerks' could not get a cardinal's cap as easily as they expected, they preferred want at home to mendicancy at Rome or Rheims; in this, no doubt, satirizing the supposed motives of some of the Roman converts. We learn too that the earlier plays had been acted more than once at Cambridge, although some of the allusions which appear to imply this, viz. those to the 'sophisters' knocks' and the 'butler's box,' are by no means clear.

In the former printed texts of the third play there are frequent passages which are unintelligible from errors of the press. These are now rendered clear by readings

gained from a MS. in the possession of Mr. Halliwell-
Phillipps, for the use of which I am greatly indebted to that
gentleman. The new readings show how fair a field is
really open to conjecture in the attempted correction of old
texts for which no MS. authority exists, and justify much
of the conjectural criticism which is applied to Shakespearean
difficulties.[1] They prove also the critical acumen and
ingenuity of Edm. Malone, since several of the corrections
are found to correspond with emendations noted by him, as
apparently his own guesses, in the margins of one of his
printed copies.[2] The MS. in question forms a small
quarto volume, in a parchment cover, and is written by
a contemporary hand. There is no trace of authorship
or ownership; but it came to its present possessor's hands
from an old family library, where it may well have been
from the days of James I.

It has already been mentioned that this third play was
twice printed in the year 1606. Both the editions were
printed at London by G. Eld for John Wright, and are
exactly similar in title-page and appearance. But there are
frequent verbal variations in their texts. The one which
is here designated in the foot-notes as 'B' is that which
was used by Mr. Arber for his reprint. Unfortunately this
is by far (as the notes show) the less correct of the two.
The other, designated as 'A,' has been adopted in the
main for the text here given, with the corrections of the
MS. (enclosed in brackets) and occasionally a few corrections also from 'B.' Of both these editions there are
copies in Malone's collection in the Bodleian Library.

For illustrations of University life and scholars' struggles

---

[1] It is needless here to point out to those who will examine text and notes
the many corrections which are gained from the MS. It is enough to refer to
p. 87 for the important correction in the first of the lines upon Shakespeare,
and to p. 139 for the reading of 'size que' for 'sice kne.'

[2] These places are pointed out in the footnotes of the various readings.

the newly-recovered plays will be found very curious and interesting. Very witty and amusing, too, and full of real life-like character, are the pictures of the carrier Leonard and the tapster Simson, and the village churchwarden Perceval. But the chief interest lies in the fresh notices afforded of Shakespeare, of so early a date as 1600. The quotations with which Gullio interlards his discourse, and which he appropriates as his own, the respect with which he speaks of the poet as ' Mr. Shakspeare,' his declaration that he will have his picture in his study and keep his *Venus and Adonis* under his pillow, and the preference which he gives at once to lines that profess to imitate Shakespeare before those which imitate Chaucer and Spenser, are all signs of the popularity which had already been won. But it is popularity only with a certain class. The notices in the third play seem (as Mr. Mullinger has remarked, *Univ. of Cambr.* p. 524 *n.*) ' to convey the notion that Shakespeare is the favourite of the rude half-educated strolling players, as distinguished from the refined geniuses of the University.' And those in the second play, which all come from the mouth of Gullio, the arrant braggart, the empty pretender to knowledge, and the avowed libertine, and from his page, tend to show that while the *Venus and Adonis* was the best known of the already published writings, this in the esteem of Cambridge scholars made Shakespeare to be re-garded as specially being the favourite of the class which that character represents. Certainly the popularity assigned to him is not of a sort to be desired; but the popularity itself is indisputable.

A comparison with Bishop Hall's *Satires* brings to view a great similarity alike in subjects and in language. The second book of the Satires deals, in fact, with many of the abuses of which our unknown author treats. The second satire in that book is a complaint of the poverty of scholars;

the third deals with lawyers ; the fourth with doctors [1];
the fifth with the growing sin of simony, in relation to which
we meet with the same term of 'steeple-fair' which is used
infra at p. 137 ; the sixth is respecting the engagement of
a tutor, in which the conditions are very nearly identical,
and the payment wholly so, 'five marks and winter livery.'
The *Satires* were first printed in 1597 ; and the coincidences
are so many and striking that it is plain that the writer of
the plays had them at least freshly in remembrance, and
may even have been consciously borrowing ideas from
them.

It may be well to mention that in the first two plays I
have supplied the punctuation, the MS. itself being but
scantily pointed. In regard to the third I have followed the
example of previous editors, and have left the punctuation
as it is found in the edition of 1606 noted as A, bad and
irregular as that often is, and have also retained capital
letters as there given, in order that the text of that edition
may be correctly represented.

---

[1] By both writers the medical consultation-fee is said to be a groat ; to which
in the play the patient of his bounty adds eight pence.

CONTENTS.

PILGRIMAGE TO PARNASSUS.

Actors.

CONSILIODORUS.	AMORETTO.
PHILOMUSUS.	INGENIOSO.
STUDIOSO.	CLOWNE.
MADIDO.	DROMO.
STUPIDO.	

PROLOGUE.

SPECTATORS, take youe noe severe accounte
Of our twoo pilgrims to Parnassus' mount.
If youle take three daies studie in good cheare,
Our muse is blest that ever shee came here.
If not, wele eare noe more the barren sande,   5
But let our pen seeke a more fertile lande.

ACTUS I^{us}.

Enter CONSILIODORUS *with* PHILOMUSUS *and* STUDIOSO.

Consil.   Now, Philomusus, doe youre beardless years,
Youre faire yonge spring time, and youre budded youth,
Urge mee to advise youre younge untutord thoughte,
And give gray-bearded counsell to youre age.   10
Unto an ould man's speache one minute give,
Who manie years have schooled how to live;

B

To an advisinge tounge one halfe houre tende;
Whatsoere I speake experience hath pend.
Perhaps this tounge, this minde-interpretor,　　　15
Shall never more borrowe youre lisninge eare;
Eare youe returne from greene Parnassus' hill
My corps shall lie within some senceless urne,
Some litel grave my ashes shall inclose.
My winged soul 'gins scorne this slimie jayle　　　20
And thinke upon a purer mansion.
Elde summons mee to appeare at Pluto's courte,
Amonge the shadie troups of aerie ghostes.
Ile therefore counsell youe while I have time,
For feare youre faire youth wither in her prime.　　　25
Take good advise from him who lovs youe well;
Plaine dealing needs not Retoricks tinklinge bell.

 Philo. Father, what ere youre lovinge tounge shall utter,
Ile drinke youre words with an attentive eare.
Age in his speach a majestie doth beare.　　　30

 Stud. I love to heare love play the oratoure.
Younge men's advise can beare but litell swaye,
Counsell comes kindlie from a heade thats graye.

 Consil. What wisedom manie winters hath begott
Tyme's midwifrey at length shall bringe to light.　　　35
Youe twoo are pilgrims to Parnassus' hill,
Where with sweet nectar you youre vaines may fill;
Wheare youe maye bath youre drye and withered quills
And teache them write some sweeter poetrie
That may heareafter live a longer daye.　　　40
There may youe bath youre lipps in Hellicon,
And wash youre tounge in Aganippe's well,
And teache them warble out some sweet sonnete
To ravishe all the filde and neighboure-groves;
That aged Collin, leaninge on his staffe,　　　45
Feedinge his milkie flocke upon the downs

May wonder at youre sweete melodious pips,
And be attentive to youre harmonie.
There may youre templs be adornd with bays ;
There may youe slumber in sweet extasies ;   50
There may you sit in softe greene lauriate shade,
And heare the Muses warble out a laye,
And mountinge singe like larke in somer's daye.
There may youe scorne each Mydas of this age,
Eache earthlie peasant and each drossie clowne,   55
That knoweth not howe to weigh youre worthiness,
But feedeth on beste corne, like a stall fed ass,
Whose statelie mouth in scorne by wheate doth pass.
I doe comende youre studious intent
In that youe make soe faire a pilgrimage.   60
If I were younge who nowe am waxen oulde,
Whose yonts[1] youe see are dryde, benumd and coulde,
Though I foreknewe that gold runns to the boore
Ile be a scholler, though I live but poore.
If youe will have a joyfull pilgrimage   65
Youe muste be warie pilgrims in the waye,
Youe muste not truste eache glozinge flatteringe vaine ;
Ofte when the sunn shins bright it straight will raine.
Consorte not in the waye with graceless boys,
That feede the taverne with theire idle coyne   70
Till their leane purses starve at last for foode.
O why shoulde schollers by unthriftiness
Seeke to weaken theire owne poore estate !
Let schollers be as thriftie as they maye,
They will be poore ere theire last dyinge daye ;   75
Learninge and povertie will ever kiss.
Each carter caries fortune by his side,
But fortune will with schollers nere abide.
Eschew all lozell, lazie, loiteringe gromes,
All foggie sleepers and all idle lumps,   80

[1] joints?

B 2

That doe burne out theire base inglorious days
Without or frute or joye of theire loste time.
Let lazie grill snorte till the midst of the day,
Be you industrious pilgrims in the way.
There is another sorte of smooth-faced youthes,   85
·Those Amorettoes that doe spend theire time·
In comminge of their smother-dangled heyre,
The[1] court a lookinge glass from morne till nighte.
Theise would entise youe to some curtezan,
And tell youe tales of itchinge venerie ;   90
But let not theire entisemente cause youre falls,
Esteeme them as faire, rotten, painted walls.
Nore will I have you truste each rugged browe,
Each simple-seeminge mate, eache hearie chin ;
Crafte ofte in suche plaine cottages doth in[n].   95
Associate yourselvs with studious youthes,
That, as Catullus saith, devours the waye
That leads to Parnassus where content doth dwell.
Happie I wish maye be youre pilgrimage!
Joyfull maye youe returne from that faire hill,   100
And make the vallies heare with admiration
Those songs which youre refined tounge shall singe.
But what? doe I prolong my studious speache,
Hindringe the forwarde hastninge of youre steps?
Goe happilie with a swifte swallowes winge   105
To Hellicon faire, that pure and happie springe!
Returne triumphant with your laurell boughes,
With Phoebus' trees decke youre deservinge brows!
Haste, haste with speed unto that hallowed well!
Soe take from mee a lovinge, longe farewell.   110

   Philom.   Farewell, good father! and youre counsell sage
Be my safe guide in this my pilgrimage!

   Stud.   Farewell, good uncle! and youre wise-said says
Keepe mee from devious and by-wandringe wayes!

<hr>

[1] *Read* 'That.'

Consil. Farewell! Farewell! to parte with youe is paine,
But haste! let not the sunn-lighte burne in vain!   116

Philom. Come, Studioso, shall wee gett us gone?
Thinks thou oure softe and tender feet canne bide
To trace this roughe, this harsh, this craggie waye
That leadeth unto faire Parnassus' hill?   120

Stud. Why, man! each lazie groome will take the paine
To drawe his slowe feete ore the clayie lande,
Soe he maye reste upon a faire greene banke.
Theise pilgrims feete, which nowe take wearie toile,
Maie one day on a bedd of roses rest   125
Amidst Parnassus' shadie laurell greene.

Philom. But cann we hit this narowe curious waye.
Where are such by wayes and erronious paths?
Saye, whate the firste ile wee muste travell in?   129

Stud. The firste lande that wee muste travell in (as that
oulde Hermite toulde me) is *Logique.* I have gotten Jack
Seton's mapp to directe us through this cuntrie. This
island is, accordinge to his discription, muche like Wales,
full of craggie mountaines and thornie vallies. There are
twoo robbers in this cuntrie caled *genus* and *species*, that take
captive everie true mans invention that come by them;
Pacius in his returne from Parnassus hadd beene robt
by these twoo forresters, but for one Carterus a lustie club-
man, muche like the Pinder of Wakfield, that defended him.

Philom. Come let us jorney on with winged pace; 140
Rough way shall not dismay our studious mindes.
Let us then hasten to our wished port,
Longe is our jorney and the way[1] is short.
Then, Phoebus, guide us to thy Hellicon,
And when our ruder pipes are taught to singe   145
The eccoinge wood with thy praise shall ringe.

----

[1] *Read 'day'?*

ACTUS II^us.

Enter MADIDO *alone, reading Horace Epistles.*

Madi. O pocet Horace! if thou were alive I woulde
bestowe a cupp of sacke on thee for theise liquid verses;
theise are not drie rimes like Cato's, *Si deus est animus,*
but the true moist issue of a poeticall soule. O if the
tapsters and drawers knewe what thou sayest in the
commendačon of takinge of liquoure, they would score
up thy prayses upon everie but and barrell; and, in faith,
I care not if I doe for the benefite of the unlearned
bestowe some of my English poetrie uppon thy Latin
rimes, that this Romane tonge maye noe longer outface
our poore Englishe skinkers. Ile onlie rouse up my muse
out of her den with this liquid sacrifice, and then, have
he drinks amongste youe, poets and rimers! The common people will
now thinke I did drincke, and did nothinge but conferr
with the ghostes of Homer, Ennius, Virgill, and they[1] rest
he reads that dwell in this watterie region. Marke, marke! here
Horace's springs a poeticall partridge! Zouns! I want a worde
verses miserablely! I must looke for another worde in my dic-
againe tionarie; I shall noe sooner open this pinte pott but the
he drinks worde like a knave tapster will crie, *Anon, Anon, Sir!*
Ey marye Sir! nowe I am fitt to write a book! Woulde
anie leaden Mydas, anie mossie patron, have his asses
ears deified, let him but come and give mee some prettie
sprinkling to maintaine the expences of my throate, and
Ile dropp out suche an encomium on him that shall imor-
talize him as long as there is ever a booke-binder in
he trans- Englande. But I had forgotten my frind Horace. Take
lates not in snuffe (my prettie verses!) if I turne you out of
youre Romane coate into an Englishe gaberdine.   175

¹ *sic.*

[*Enter* PHILOMUSUS *and* STUDIOSO.]

Philom. In faith, Madido, thy poetrie is good;
Some gallant Genius doth possess thy corps.

Stud. I think a furie ravisheth thy braine,
Thou art in such a sweet phantasticke vaine.
But tell mee, shall wee have thy companie   180
Throughe this craggie ile, this harsh rough waye?
Wilt thou be pilgrime to Parnassus' hill?

Madi. I had rather be a horse to grinde in mill.
Zouns! I travell to Parnassus? I tell thee its not a pilgrimage for good wits. Let slowe-brainde Athenians travell
thither, those drie sober youths which can away to reede
dull lives, fustie philosophers, dustie logicians. Ile turne
home, and write that that others shall reade; posteritie
shall make them large note books out of my writings.
Naye, there is another thinge that makes mee out of love
with this jorney; there is scarce a good taverne or ale-
house betwixte this and Parnassus; why, a poeticall spirit
muste needs starve!

Philom. Naye, when thou comes to high Parnassus' hill
Of Hellicons pure stream drincke thou thy fill.   195

Stud. There Madido may quaff the poets boule,
And satisfie his thirstie dryed soule.

Madi. Nay, if I drinke of that pudled water of Hellicon
in the companie of leane Lenten shadowes, let mee for a
punishement converse with single beare soe long as I live!
This Parnassus and Hellicon are but the fables of the
poets: there is noe true Parnassus but the third lofte in a
wine taverne, noe true Hellicon but a cup of browne bastard.
Will youe travell quicklie to Parnassus? doe but carie
youre drie feet into some drie taverne, and straight the
drawer will bid youe to goe into the Halfe Moone or the
Rose, that is into Parnassus; then call for a cup of pure
Hellicon, and he will bringe youe a cup of pure hypocrise,

that will make youe speake leapinge lines and dauncinge
periodes. Why, give mee but a quart of burnt sacke by
mee, and if I doe not with a pennie worth of candles make
a better poeme then Kinsaders *Satyrs*, Lodge's *Fig for
Momus*, Bastard's *Epigrams*, Leichfild's *Trimming of Nash*,
Ile give my heade to anie good felowe to make a *memento
mori* of! O the genius of xij^d! A quart will indite manie
livelie lines in an houre, while an ould drousie Academicke,
an old Stigmaticke, an ould sober Dromeder, toiles a whole
month and often scratcheth his witts' head for the bringinge
of one miserable period into the worlde! If therefore you
be good felowes or wise felowes, travell noe farther in the
craggie way to the fained Parnassus; returne whome with
mee, and wee will hire our studies in a taverne, and ere
longe not a poste in Paul's churchyarde but shall be
acquainted with our writings.   224

Philom. Nay then, I see thy wit in drincke is drounde;
Wine doth the beste parte of thy soule confounde.

Stud. Let Parnass be a fond phantasticke place,
Yet to Parnassus Ile hould on my pace.
But tell mee, Madido, how camest thou to this ile?   229

Madi. Well, Ile tell youe; and then see if the phisicke
of good counsel will worke upon youre bodies. I tooke
shippinge at *Qui mihi discipulus*, and sailed to *Propria
quae maribus*; then came to *As in praesenti*, but with great
danger, for there are certaine people in this cuntrie caled
schoolmaisters, that take passingers and sit all day whippinge
pence out of there tayls; these men tooke mee prisoner,
and put to death at leaste three hundred rodes upon my
backe. Hence traveled I into the land of *Sintaxis*, a land
full of joyners, and from thenc came I to *Prosodia*, a litell
iland, where are men of 6 feete longe, which were never
mentioned in Sir John Mandefilde's cronicle. Hence did I
set up my unluckie feete in this ile *Dialectica*, where I can

see nothinge but idees and phantasmes; as soone as I came
hither I began to reade Ramus his mapp, *Dialectica est
&c.*; then the slovenlie knave presented mee with such an
unsavorie worde that I dare not name it unless I had some
frankensence readie to perfume youre noses with after.
Upon this I threw away the mapp in a chafe, and came
home, cursing my witless head that woulde suffer my headless feete to take such a tedious journey.   250

 Philom. The harder and the craggier is the waye
The joy will be more full another day.
Ofte pleasure got with paine wee dearlie deeme;
Things dearlie boughte are had in great esteeme.

 Madi. Come on, Come on, Tullie's sentences! Leave
youre pulinge of prouerbs, and hearken to him that knowes
whats good for youe. If you have anie care of youre eyes,
blinde them not with goinge to Parnassus; if you love youre
feete, blister them not in this craggie waye. Staie with
mee, and one pinte of wine shall inspire youe with more
witt than all they nine muses. Come on! Ile lead you
to a merie companie!

 Stud. Fie, Philomusus! 'gin thy loitringe feet
To faint and tire in this so faire a waie?
Each marchant for a base inglorious prize   265
Fears not with ship to plowe the ocean;
And shall not wee for learnings glorious meede
To Parnass hast with swallowe-winged speede?

ACTUS 3us.

PHILOM. STUDIO. STUPIDO.

 Philom. I'faithe, Studioso, I was almost wonne
To cleave unto yonder wett phantasticke crewe!   270
I see the pinte pott is an oratoure!
The burnt sacke made a sweet oration

Againste Appollo and his followers;
Discourste howe schollers unregarded walke,
Like threedbare impecunious animals,   275
Whiles servinge men doe swagger it in silks,
And each earth-creepinge peasant russet-coate
Is in requeste for his well-lined pouche:
Tolde us howe this laborious pilgrimage
Is wonte to eate mens marrowes, drye there bloude,   280
And make them seem leane shadowles pale ghostes.
This counsell made mee have a staggeringe minde,
Untill I sawe there beastlie bezolinge,
There drowned soules, there idle meriment,
Voyde of sounde solace and true hartes content: 285
And now I love my pilgrimage the more,
I love the Muses better than before.
But tell mee, what lande do wee travell in?
Mee thinks it is a pleasante fertile soile.

    Stud. Let idle tongues talke of our tedious waye,   290
I never sawe a more delicious earth,
A smoother pathwaye, or a sweeter ayre,
Then here is in this lande of *Rhetorique.*
Hearke howe the birds delight the moving ayre ·
With prettie tunefull notes and artless lays!   295
Harke shrill Don Cicero, how sweete he sings!
See how the groves wonder at his sweet note,
And listen unto theire sweet nightingale!
Harken how Muretus, Bembus, Sadolet,
Haddon and Ascham, chirpe theire prettie notes,   300
And too good ears make tunefull melodie!
Theire chirping doth delight each mounte, each dale,
Thoughe not so sweet as Tullie's nightingale.

    Philom. Indeed I like theire sugred harmonie;
I like this grassie diapred greene earth.   305
Heare tender feete maye travell a whole daye,
And heare with joy the aerye people's laye.

Enter STUPIDO.

But who is yonder? Stupido I see!
The earth hath ten times binne disrobbed quite
Of her greene gowne and flowric coveringe,   310
Since Stupido began his pilgrimage
Unto the place where those nine Muses dwell;
And now our swifter feet have overtooke him!

　　Stud. It is not our swifte feet but his slowe pace,
That makes us overtake him in this race.   315
Ile interrupt his graver meditations,
Kindlie salutinge my friende Stupido.
Well overtaken, Mr Stupido!
I hope wee shall have youre good companie
To travell, and directe us in the waye   320
That leads us to that laureat twoo-topt mounte.

　　Stup. Welcome, my welbeloved brethren! trulie (I
thank God for it!) I have spent this day to my great
comfort. I have (I pray God prosper my labours!)
analised a peece of an hommelie according to Ramus,
and surelie in my minde and simple opinion Mr Peter
maketh all things verie plaine and easie. As for Setons
Logique, trulie I never looke on it but it makes my head
ache! And now not having anie serious business to goe
aboute, least the bad-disposed people shoulde corrupte and
contaminate my pure thoughts by there ungodlie con-
versations, I am goinge abroad to take the benefite of the
aire, and contemplate, whiles they play the reprobate at
home, some persecutinge poore creaturs, cattes, others
spendinge theire moste precious time in card plaie. But
whither are you going? to Parnassus?   336

　　Stud. Eye! and wee hope to have youre companie.

　　Stup. You speake like a younge man indeede! I have
beene to vaine and forwarde this way, but now that I am
come into this *Rhetorique,* and see the follie of theise

vaine artes, I will not travell a foot further. I have
a good man to my uncle, that never wore capp nor surples
in his life, nor anie suche popishe ornament, who sent mee
yesterday a letter and this mandition, and a frize coate
for a token, and the same counsell that he gave mee I,
as I am bounde in charitie, will give you. 'Studie not
these vaine arts of Rhetorique, Poetrie and Philosophie;
there is noe sounde edifying knowledg in them.' Why,
they are more vaine than a paire of organs or a morrice
daunce! If you will be good men indeede, goe no further
in this way; follow noe longer these profane artes that
are the raggs and parings of learning; sell all these books,
and by a good Martin, and twoo or three hundreth of
chatechismes of Jeneva's printe, and I warrant you will
have learning enoughe. Mr Martin and other good men
tooke this course.   356

Philom. Are then the artes foolish, profane and vaine,
That gotten are with studie, toile and paine?

Stud. Artistes belike then are phantastique fools,
That learne these artes in the laborious schools.   360

Stup. Artistes, fools; and that you may knowe by
there undecent apparell. Why, you shall not see a Rhe-
torician, a rimer (as[1] poet as you call it) but he wears such
diabolicall ruffs and wicked great breeches full of sin, that
it would make a zelous professor's harte bleed for grife.
Well, Mr Wigginton and Mr Penorie never wore such profane hose, but such plaine apparell as I doe. Goe with
mee, and you shall heare a good man exercise. I will
get him to handle for youre better direction this pointe
by the way; I would gladlie doe some good of you if I
coulde.   371

Philom. I' faith, *etc.*

Stup. O sweare not, sweare not!

---

[1] *Read* 'or.'

Stud. With thee, my loving Stupido, weele wende,
And to thy counsell listning ears will lende.   375

Stup. Folowe mee; Ile bringe youe into a sober
companie.

ACTUS 4US.

Enter AMORETTO *alone, reading these* 2 *verses out of Ovid.*

Amor. *Oscula qui sumpsit, qui non et coetera sumpsit,*
Oscula quae sumpsit perdere dignus erat;
Who takes a kiss and leaves to doe the rest,   380
Doth take the worse and doth neglect the beste.
Zouns! What an honest animal was I
To part with my Corinna with a kiss!
Yet doe I wronge her devine tempting lipps
To name her kiss with noe more reverence.   385
One touch of her sweete nectar-breathinge mouth
Would ravishe senceless Cinicks with delight,
And make them homage doe at Venus' shrine.
All books are dull which speake not of her praise;
Hange ploddinge doultes, and all there dulled race!   390
True learninge dwels in her faire beautuous face.
I love thee, Ovid, for Corinna's sake,
Thou loves, Corinna, as turtle loves her make.
Of my Corinnaes haire love makes his nett
To captivate poore mortall wandringe hartes.   395
Love keeps his revels in Corinna's browes,
Daunces levaltoes in her speaking eye,
Dyes and is buried in her dimpled cheeke,
Revives and quickens in her cherie lipps,
Keeps watch and warde in her faire snowie chin   400
That noe roughe swaine approach or enter in.
Loves cradle is betwixte her rising brest,
Her[e] sucking Cupid feedes and takes his rest.

Touch not her mount of joy! it is devine;
There Cupid grazes or els he would pine.   405
Expect, the world, my poesie ere longe,
Where Ile commende her daintie quivering thighe,
Sing of her foot in my sweet minstralsie.

Enter PHIL. *and* STUDIOSO.

But who comes yonder?   Philomusus and Studioso!
I saw them latelie in the companie   410
Of stricte Stupido, that pulinge puritane,
A moving peece of clay, a speaking ass,
A walking image and a senceless stone!
If they be of his humor I care not, I,
For such pure honest-seeminge companie.   415

Philom.   Fye, Studioso! what nowe almost caught
By Stupido, that plodding puritane,
That artless ass, and that earth-creeping dolt,
Who, for he cannot reach unto the artes,
Makes showe as though he would neglect the artes,   420
And cared not for the springe of Hellicon?

Stud.   Who can resist seeminge devotion,
Or them that are of the reformed world?
A flintie harte muste needes relent to see
A puritane up-twinckling of his eye,   425
Muche like a man newlie cast in a traunce,
Or like a cuntrie fellowe in a daunce.

Philom.   Eye! these doe norishe a neglected bearde,
Much like a grunting keeper of a hearde;
Speake but a fewe wordes, because the[y] would seeme
    wise ;
Weare but a plaine coate after the wonted guise.   430
Thou owest mee thanks, for but for mee I wis
Thou hadest beene a plaine puritane ere this!

Stud.   I kept thee, Philomusus, from moiste Madido;
Thou savest mee latelie from dull Stupido.   435

Amor.   And are they parted from strict Stupido?
Then are they fit for my societie!
What, Philomusus and Studioso! well met in faith in the
land of poetrie! how doe you away with this aire?

Philom.   Well met, Amoretto! I did longe   440
To meet some poet of a pleasante tounge.

Stud.   It argueth the goodnes of the aire
Because here breathes full manie a cruell faire!

Philom.   Indeede this lande hath manie a wanton nymphe
That knowes alwayes all sportfull dalliance.   445
Here are soe manie pure brighte shininge starrs,
That Cynthiaes want theire faire Endimions
Wherewith to pass away the loittring nighte ;
Here are Corinnaes, but here Ovids wante.
Saye, will you staye with mee in poetrie?   450
Why shoulde you vainelie spende your bloominge age
In sadd dull plodding on philosophers,
Which was ordained for wantone merrimentes?

Stud.   Yea, but our springe is shorte and winter longe :
Our youth by travelling to Hellicon   455
Must gett provision for our latter years.

Amor.   Who thinks on winter before winter come
Maks winter come in sommers fairest shine.
There is noe golden minte at Hellicon!
Cropp you the joyes of youth while that you maye,   460
Sorowe and grife will come another daye.

Philom.   I alwayes was sworne Venus' servitoure ;
I have a wantone eye for a faire wenche.
Hee is noe man but a rude senceless ass
That doth not for refined beautie pass.   465
Perswade thou Studioso if thou can,
And Ile be Cupides loyall duteous man.

Stud.   I am not suche a peece of Cinicke earthe
That I neglect sweete beauties deitie.

I reverence Venus, and her carpet knights 470
That in that wanton warfarre weare theire lipps:
Yet loth I am our pilgrimage to staye
In wanton dalliance and in looser playe.

Amor. Tushe! talk not of youre purposed pilgrimage,
Nor doe forsake this poets' pleasant lande 475
To treade upon philosophers' harshe grounde.
Taste but the joyes that poetric affordes,
And youle all crabbed solaceis forsweare,
Ile bringe you to sweet wantoninge yonge maides
Wheare you shall all youre hungrie sences feaste, 480
That they, grow[n]e proude with this felicitie,
Shall afterwarde all maner object scorne.
Nor are they puling maides, or curious nuns
That strictlie stande upon virginitie;
Theile freelie give what ere youre luste shall crave, 485
And make you melte in Venus' surquerie.
These joyes, and more, sweete poetric affordes:
Let not youre headless feete forsake this lande
Till you have tasted of this joyisance.
Come to my sweet Corinna! Ile you bringe, 490
And bless youe with a touch of her softe lipps.
Then shall you have the choice of earthlie starrs
That shine on earth as Cynthia in her skye;
There maye youe melte with solled sweet delighte,
And taste the joyes of the darke gloomie night. 495

Stud. Well said the poet that a wantone speache
Like dallyinge fingers tickles up the luste.
Chast thoughtes can lodge no longer in that soule
That lendes an eare to wantone poesie.
Well, Ile staye somwhat longer in this lande 500
To cropp those joyes that Amoretto speakes of.
If in them anie sounde contente I finde,
Ile leave Parnassus waye that is behinde.

Philom. Let not thenvious time hinder that joye
That wee shall tast in this thy poetric;　　　　505
Luste is impatient of all slack delaye.
Come, Amoretto, lette's noe longer staye:
Phoebus hath laid his golden tressed locks
In the moist cabinet of Thetis' lapp;
Now shadie night hath dispossest the daye,　　　510
Providing time for maides to sporte and playe.

　Amor. Come haste with mee unto faire beauties
　　beddes,
On Venus' pillow shall you laye youre heades.

　Philom. Luste's wonte to ride on a faire winged steede.

　Stud. Noe marvell, when he lookes for suche a meede.

ACTUS 5us.

PHILOMUSUS. STUDIOSO.

　Stud. Howe sourelie sweete is meltinge venerie!　516
It yealdeth honie, but it straighte doth stinge.
I'le nere hereafter counsell chaster thoughtes
To travell through this lande of poetrie.
Here are entisinge pandars, subtile baudes,　　　520
Catullus, Ovid, wantone Martiall.
Heare them whilest a lascivious tale they tell,
Theile make thee fitt in Shorditche for to dwell,
Here had wee nighe made shipwracke of our youthe,
And nipte the blossomes of our buddinge springe!　525
Yet are wee scaped frome poetric's faire baites,
And sett our footinge in philosophie.

　Philom. Noe soure reforminge enimye of arte
Coulde doe delightfull poetric more wronge
Than thy unwarie sliperie tongue hath done.　　530

C

Are these the thankes thou givest for her mirthe
Wherewith shee did make shorte thy pilgrim's waye,
Made monthes seeme minutes spente in her faire soile?
O doe not wronge this musicke of the soule,
The fairest childe that ere the soule broughte foorthe,
Which none contemn but some rude foggie squires   536
That knowe not to esteeme of witt or arte!
Noe epitaphe adorne his baser hearse
That in his lifetime cares not for a verse!
Nor thinke Catullus, Ovid, Martiall,   540
Doe teache a chaste minde lewder luxuries.
Indeede if leachers reade a wantone clause,
It tickles up each lustfull impure vaine;
But who reades poets with a chaster minde
Shall nere infected be by poesie.   545
An honest man that nere did stande in sheete
Maye chastlie dwell in unchaste Shordiche streete.
Take this from mee; a well disposed minde
Shall noe potato rootes in poets finde.

   Stud. I doe not whet my tongue againste poetrie,
Yet maye youe give a looser leave to talke.   551
Longe have wee loitred idle in [t]his lande,
Her joyes made us unmindfull of our waie.
Our feet are growne too tender and unapte
To travell in the roughe philosophie.   555
Nowe cheare thyselfe in this laborious facte,
Nor like a sluggarde fainte in the laste acte.

   Philom. Indeede, the pleasure poetric did yelde
Made further harshnes to philosophie;
Yet havinge skilful! Aristotle our guide   560
I hope wee soone shall end our pilgrimage.

Enter INGENIOSO.

   Ingen. A plague on youe, Javel, Tollet, Tartare!
they have poysned mee with there breathes!

Philom. Why, how nowe, Ingenioso, shewinge philosophie a faire paire of heeles?   565

Stud. Why, whiter nowe in a chafe, Ingenioso?

Ingen. What, Philomusus and Studioso? well met, ould
schoolefelowes! I have beene guiltie of mispending some
time in philosophie, and nowe, growinge wiser, I begin to
forsake this cuntrie as faste as I can ; and can youe blame
mee? whie, I have bene almoste stifled with the breath
of three Barbarians, Tollet, Javel, Tartarett. They stande
fearefullie gapinge, and everye one of them a fustie, moulie
worde in his mouthe that's able to breede a plague in
a pure aire; they breede suche an ayre as is wonte to
proceede from an evaporatinge dunghill in a summer's
daye. But what doe youe twoo here, in this griggie barbarous cuntrie?

Philom. Wee pilgrims are unto Parnassus hill,
At Hellicon wee meane to drinke our fill.   580

Ingen. What, goe soe farr to fetche water? goe 'to
Parnassus to converse with ragged innocentes? If youe be
wise and meane to live, come not there ; Parnassus is out
of silver pitifullie, pitifullie. I talked with a frende of mine
that latelie gave his horse a bottell of haye at the bottome
of the hill, who toulde mee that Apollo had sente to Pluto
to borowe twentie nobles to paye his commons : he added
further, that hee met comming downe from the hill a
companie of ragged vicars and forlorne schoolemaisters, who
as they walked scrached there unthriftie elbowes, and often
putt there handes into there unpeopled pockets, that had
not beene possessed with faces this manie a day. There,
one stoode digginge for golde in a standishe ; another looking for cockpence in the bottome of a pue ; the third
towling for silver in a belfree : but they were never soe
. happie as Esope's cocke, to finde a precious stone : nay,
they coulde scarce get enoughe to apparell there heade in

an unlined hatt, there bodie in a frize jerkin, and there feet
in clouted paire of shoes. Come not there, seeke for
povertie noe further ; it's too farr to goe to Parnassus to
fetche repentance.   601

   Philom. Thoughe I foreknowe that doults possess the
      goulde,
Yet my intended pilgrimage I'le houlde.

   Stud. Within Parnassus dwells all sweete contente,
Nor care I for those excrements of earthe.   605

   Ingen. Call youe gold and silver the excrements of
earthe ? If those be excrements, I am the cleanest man
upon the earth, for I seldome sweate goulde.

   Philom. Yes, they are excrements ; and hence a man
that wants money is caled a cleane gentleman.   610

   Ingen. If that be to be cleane, then the water of
Hellicon will quicklie make youe cleane : it is an excellent
good thinge to make a man impecunious.

   Stud. Come, shall wee have youre companie on the
      waye ?   614

   Ingen. What, I travell to Parnassus ? why, I have burnt
my bookes, splitted my pen, rent my papers, and curste the
coosceninge harts that brought mee up to noe better fortune.
I, after manie years studie, havinge almoste brought my
braine into a consumption, looking still when I shoulde
meete with some good Maecenas that liberallie would rewarde
my deserts, I fed soe long upon hope, till I had almoste
starved. Why, our emptie-handed sattine sutes doe make
more account of some foggie faulkner than of a wittie
scholler, had rather rewarde a man for setting of a hayre
than a man of wit for makinge of a poeme ; eache long-
eared ass rides on his trappinges, and thinkes it sufficiente
to give a scholler a majesticke nodd with his rude nodle.
Goe to Parnassus ? Alas, Apollo is banckroute, there is .
nothing but silver words and golden phrases for a man ;

his followers wante the goulde, while tapsters, ostlers,
carters and coblers have a fominge pauch, a belchinge bagg,
that serves for a cheare of est[ate] for *regina pecunia*.
Seest thou not my hoste Johns of the Crowne, who latelie
lived like a moule 6 years under the grounde in a cellar,
and cried *Anon, Anon, Sir,* now is mounted upon a horse
of twentie marke, and thinkes the earth too base to beare
the waighte of his refined bodie. Why, woulde it not greeve
a man of a good spirit to see Hobson finde more money in the
tayles of 12 jades than a scholler in 200 bookes? Why,
Newman the cobler will leave large legacies to his haires
while the posteritie of *humanissimi auditores,* and *esse
posse videaturs* must be faine to be kept by the parishe!
Turne home againe, unless youe meane to be *vacui viatores,* and to curse youre wittless heades in youre oulde age
for takinge themselves to no better trades in there youthe.

Stud.   Cease to spende more of thy id[l]e breathe,
Effecting to divert us from our waye.   647
I knowe that schollers commonlie be poore,
And that the dull worlde there good parts neglecte.
A scholler's coate is plaine, lowlie his gate;   650
Contente consists not in the highest degree.

Philom.   I thinke not worse of faire Parnassus' hill
For that it wants that sommer's golden clay,
The idol of the foxfur'd usurer.
Though it wants coyne it wants not true contente,   655
True solace, or true happie merrimente.
If thou will weende with us, plucke up thy feete;
If not, farewell, till next time wee doe meete.

Ingen.   Farewell, and take heede I take youe not
napping twentie years hence in a viccar's seate, asking for
the white cowe with the blacke foote, or els interpretinge
pueriles confabulationes to a companie of seaven-yeare-
olde apes.   663

Philom. Farewell, Ingenioso, and take heede I finde not
a ballet or a pamphlet of thy makinge.   665

Stud. Come, Philomusus, chearfullie let's warke;
Our toiling day will have a night to rest,
Where wee shall thinke with joy on labors past.
Leade on apace; Parnassus is at hande;
Nowe wee have almost paste this wearie lande.   670

Enter DROMO, *drawing a clowne in with a rope.*

Clowne. What now? thrust a man into the common-
wealth whether hee will or noe? what the devill should
I doe here?

Dromo. Why, what an ass art thou! dost thou not
knowe a playe cannot be without a clowne? Clownes have
bene thrust into playes by head and shoulders ever since
Kempe could make a scurvey face; and therefore reason
thou shouldst be drawne in with a cart-rope.   678

Clowne. But what must I doe nowe?

Dromo. Why, if thou canst but drawe thy mouth awrye,
laye thy legg over thy staffe, sawe a peece of cheese
asunder with thy dagger, lape up drinke on the earth, I
warrant thee theile laughe mightilie. Well, I'le turne thee
loose to them; ether saic somwhat for thy selfe, or hang
and be *non plus.*   [*Exit.*

Clowne. This is fine, y-faith! nowe, when they have noe-
bodie to leave on the stage, they bringe mee up, and, which
is worse, tell mee not what I shoulde saye! Gentles, I dare
saie youe looke for a fitt of mirthe. I'le therfore present
unto you a proper newe love-letter of mine to the tune of
Put on the smock o' Mundaye, which in the heate of my
charitie I pende; and thus it begins :—   692

'O my lovely Nigra, pittie the paine of my liver! That
litell gallowes Cupid hath latelie prickt mee in the breech

with his great pin, and almoste kilde mee thy woodcocke
with his birdbolte.   Thou hast a prettie furrowed forheade,
a fine leacherous eye ; methinks I see the bawde Venus
keeping a bawdie house in thy lookes, Cupid standing like
a pandar at the doore of thy lipps.'   699

How like you, maisters? has anie yonge man a desire to
copie this, that he may have *formam epistolae conscribendae* ?
Now if I could but make a fine scurvey face, I were a
kinge ! O nature, why didest thou give mee soe good a
looke?   704

Dromo.   Give us a voyder here for the foole! Sirra, you
muste begone ; here are other men that will supplie the
roome.

Clowne.   Why, shall I not whistle out my whistle? Then
farewell, gentle auditors, and the next time you see mee
I'le make you better sporte.   710

Philom.   Nowe ends the travell of one tedious daye.
In 4 years have wee paste this wearie waye.
Nowe are wee at the foote of this steepe hill,
Where straght our tired feet shall rest there fill.

Stud.   Seest thou how yonder laurell shadie grove
Is greene in spite of frostie Boreas,   716
Scorninge his roughe blasts and ungentle breath
That makes all trees mourne in a mossye ragg?
Nere let the pilgrims to this laurell mounte
Fainte, or retire in this theire pilgrimage,   720
Through the misleading of some amorous boye,
Some swearinge unthrifte, or some blockishe dolte,
Or throughe the counsell of some wilie knave.
Nowe let us boldlie rushe amonge theese trees,
And heare the Muses' tunefull harmonie.   725

Philom. Let vulgar witts admire the common songes,
I'le lie with Phoebus by the Muses' springes,
Where wee will sit free from all envie's rage,
And scorne eache earthlie Gullio of this age.

Stud. Haste hither all good witts, with winged speede,
Where youre faire browes shall have a laureat meede!
And youe that love the Muses' deitie
Give our extemporall showe the *Plaudite*!   733

THE

RETURNE FROM PARNASSUS.

Actors.

CONSILIODORUS.
PHILOMUSUS.
STUDIOSO.
INGENIOSO.
LUXURIOSO.
GULLIO.
LEONARDE, a carier.

DRAPER }
TAYLER } townsmen.
SIMSON, an inne keeper.
PARCEVALL, a clowne.
Boy unto Luxurioso.
Boy unto Studioso.

PROLOGUE.

"Gentle"—

    Stage Keeper. Howe gentle? saye, youe cringinge parasite,

That scrapinge legg, that doppinge curtisie,

That fawninge bowe, those sycophant's smoothe tearmes,

Gained our stage muche favoure, did they not?

Surelie it made our poet a staide man,   5

Kepte his proude necke from baser lambskins weare,

Had like to have made him senior sophister.

He was faine to take his course by Germanie

Ere he coulde gett a silie poore degree.

Hee never since durst name a peece of cheese,   10

Thoughe Chessire seems to priviledge his name.

His looke was never sanguine since that daye;

Nere since he laughte to see a mimick playe.
Sirra, begone! you play noe prologue here,
Call noe rude hearer *gentle, debonaire.*   15
We'le spende no flatteringe on this carpinge croude,
Nor with gold tearmes make each rude dullard proude.
A Christmas toy thou haste; carpe till thy deathe!
Our Muse's praise depends not on thy breathe!

ACTUS PRIMUS. SCOENA PRIMA.

CONSILIODORUS. LEONARDE.

Consil. Leonarde, I have made thee staye somwhat longe for my letters, but here they be at laste. I pray thee, deliver them to Studioso and Philomusus; give them some good counsell, I pray thee.   23

Leon. Mass, Mr., and soe I will! I'le tell them what's fit for men of there 'haviour! by that time they have seene as manie winters as I and youe have done, the'le be a litel wiser.

Consil. Eye, well said, Leonarde! manie frosts indeed have made thee wise.   29

Leon. I thanke God, Mr., none of my kinred were fooles. My father (God rest his soule!) was wonte to tell mee (God rest his soule! he was as honest a carier as ever whip horse)—he tolde mee, I saye (I remember at that time he sate upon a stoole by the fire warminge his boots) that these yonge schollers woulde spend God's abbies, if they had them, and then woulde sende there fathers home false notaries. He would tell our neighboure Jenkin that he enquired after his sonn's breeches, and tooke them nappinge but with one pointe, and tooke him to the next shopp and bought him a dozen of good substantiall lether points. He woulde counsell them, yea (—and which is more; marke you

mee Sir?—) he woulde advise them, to turne there ould
jerkings, and keepe a good housholde loafe in there cheste,
to save charges; nay, and which is more, he woulde have
rounded them in the eare, and wished them to provide a
nall, and he woulde bring them some hempe from home, to
the good husbaning of there shoes. Oh! he was a wise
man! he coulde give such fine rules concerning the liquor-
ing of boots for the houlding out of water (nay, list you
Sir?); he coulde have tolde by a cowe's water how manie
gallons of milke shee woulde have given, foretolde by the
motion of his dun horse his taile the change of the weather,
insomuche that he was supposed amonge his neighboures to
have gathered up some art in the Universitie. Well, this
bagg was his, and I meane for his sake to leave it to my
sonne. But I thinke by this time, Tib and Cutt have eaten
the provender I gave them; I'le sadle them, and be jogging
forwarde.

 Consil. He was a good man, and thou followes his
steps, Leonarde. I'le holde thee noe longer; farewell, good
Leonarde.   [*Exit.*
Seaven times the earth in wantone liverie
Hath deckt herselfe to meete her blushinge love,
Since I twoo schollers to Parnassus sent,
The place of solace and true merimente.   65
There tender yeare, much like a frutefull springe,
Promised a plenteous harvest shoulde ensue,
Where I mighte gather store of golden frute.
But nowe, when I shoulde reape what I had sowne,
Ther's nought but thornes and thistles to be mowne. 70
My poore smale farme, my litell, litell, store,
Hath yealded fuell for so longe expence;
Whatever nowe is left muste serve to warme
My live's December, age's chillie froste.
Sufficeth it I cared for there springe,   75
In hope ther somer woulde a harvest bringe.

If they have lived by a watchinge lampe,
Prysinge each minute of a flyinge houre,
If they have spent there oyle, there strength, there store,
In art's quicke subtelties and learninge's lore,   80
Then will god Cynthius (if a god he be)
Keepe these his sonns from baser povertie.
But if they have burnt out the sun's faire torch
In foolish riot and regardless plaie,
Then lett them live in want perpetuallie;   85
As they have sowne soe let them reape for mee.
Noe care for them shall rouse mee out of bedde;
I knowe this well, arts seldome beg there breade. [*Exit.*

Enter STUDIOSO, *reading a letter.*

Stud. Fie coosninge arts! is this the meede you yelde
To youre leane followers, youre palied ghosts?   90
Hencfoorth youre shrines be worshipt by noe knee,
Noe foolish tonge adore youre deitie!
Wee, foolish wee, have sacrificed our youth
At youre coulde altars everie winter's morne.
Our barckinge stomacks have had slender fare,   95
Our eyes have bene deluded of there sleepe;
Yet all this while noughte els to us doth gaine
But onlie helps our fortunes to there waine.

Philom. What! I leave Parnassus and these sisters Nine,
These murmuringe springes, this pleasant grove, this ayre?
What greater ills hath fortune then in store   101
Then to expose my state to miserye?
The partiall heavens doe favoure eche rude boore,
Mackes droviers riche, and makes each scholler poore.
Well may my face weare sorowe's liverie   105
Whiles angry I do chide this luckless ayre,
Where I am learninge's outcast, fortun's scorne.
Nowe, wandring, I muste seeke my destinie,
And spende the remnante of my wretched life

'Mongst russet coates and mossy idiotts.   110
Nere shall I heare the Muses sing againe,
Whose musicke was like nectar to my soule.

Stud. How now, Philomusus? what, singinge *Fortune
my foe?*

Philom. If sorowe laye on mee her worst disgrace,
Give sorowe leave sadd passions to embrace.   115

Stud. Fortune and vertue jarred longe agoe,
Foule fortune ever was faire vertue's foe.

Philom. Th'arts are unkinde that doe theire sonns
neglect.

Stud. Unkinder frendes, that schollers doe rejecte.

Philom. Dissemblinge arts lookt smoothlie on our
youth.   120

Stud. But loade our age with discontent and ruthe.

Philom. Frends foolishlie us to this woe doe traine.

Stud. Fick[l]e Appollo promised future gaine.

Philom. Wee want the prating coyne, the speaking
golde.

Stud. Yea, frends are gained by that yellow moulde.

Philom. Adew, Parnassus! I must pack away.   126

Stud. Fountaines, farewell! where beautuos nimphes
do plaie.

Philom. In Hellicon noe more I'le dipp my quill.

Stud. I'le sing noe more upon Parnassus' hill.

Philom. Let's talke noe more, since noe relife wee finde.

Stud. In vaine to skore our losses on the winde.   131

Philom. Let us resolve to wander in the worlde,
And reape our fortunes whersoe're they growe.
Some thacked cottage or some cuntrie hall,
Some porche, some belfry, or some scrivener's stall,   135
Will yealde some harboure to our wandringe heades.

Stud. Be merie then in spite of Fortun's change!
We'le finde some lucke, or throughe the worlde we'le range.
But, Philomusus, I here that Ingenioso is in towne followinge a goutie patron by the smell, hoping to wringe some
water from a flinte.　　　　　　　　　　　　　141

Philom. Faith, coulde wee meete that ladd of 'jollitie
This duller discontent woulde quicklie die.
And here he comes!

Stud. What? Ingenioso come to Parnassus to fetche
water? or to looke for a ragged coate? I thought thou
hadest forsworne this starved aire! How goes the worlde
with youe?　　　　　　　　　　　　　148

Philom. Give mee that hand of thine that's not acquainted with the corrupting mettall! say, how hath thy
pocket fared since our laste partinge?

Ingen. What? Philomusus and Studioso? have no hungrie
schools swallowde youe up before this time? yt's merie
y-faith when *vacui viatores* meete! As for my state, I am
not put to my shiftes, for I wante shiftes of shirtes, bandes,
and all thinges els; yet I remaine thrise humblie and most
affectionatelie bounde to the right honourable printing
house for my poore shiftes of apparell.

Stud. But, I pray thee, how haste thou fared since I
sawe thee laste?　　　　　　　　　　　　　160

Ingen. In faith, I have bene posted to everie poste in
Paules churchyarde *cum gratia et privilegio*, and like Dicke
Pinner have put out *newe books of the maker, new books of
the maker.*

Philom. I am glad, y-faith, thy father hath lefte thee
suche a good stocke of witt to set up withall! Why,
thou cariest store of landes and livinges in thy heade! 167

Ingen. But the'le scarse pay for the cariage! I had
rather have more in my purse and less in my heade! I see

wit is but a phantasme and idea, a quareling shadowe that
will seldome dwell in the same roome with a full purse, but
commonly is the idle folower of a forlorne creature. Nay,
it is a devill, that will never leave a man till it hath brought
him to beggerie; a malicious spirit, that delights in a close
libell or an open satyre. Besides, it is an unfortunate
thinge; I have observed that that heade where it dwelleth
hath seldome a good hatt, or the back it belonges unto a
good sute of apparell.   178

Stud. Soe thou wilt make an ass the most fortunate
creature that lives! Indeede, the time was when long ears
and gould dwelt together, and so they doe still: but if
nature had given thee noe more wit than wealth, thou
migh[t]st betake thyselfe in *forma pauperis* to a boxe and
a passporte. But husbande thy witt, if thou beest wise; it's
all the goods and cattels thy father lefte thee. Nourishe it
with oyles and waters; if that be gone one, ther's noe waye
but thou muste either plaie the counterfeit criple or else
beare a parte in the consorte of *Three blinde beggars.* 188

Ingen. That I may doe nowe, for my purse wants these
gray silver eyes that stande idlelye in the face of a citizen's
daughter, and those silver noses that stande out daringe
mee in the face of everie base broker. And yet I was even
with one of them verie latelie; for I tell youe what, it was
my chance in a taverne to light on the companie of a knave
seargaunt with a silver nose; the villaine woulde not parte
with a denaire; the drawer came making of curtesies, and
had an eye to my worshipps purse, litell knowing what
solitarines was there; my companions were as impecunious
as myselfe; I had noe devise therfore but to call for more
wine; while, wee had drunke him deade, and then I tooke
his nose, and paide the reckoninge. How he did, when he
wakt, to purg the rheume, I know not, but I thinke if ever
he purchase a new nose againe, he were best entertaine

some caste boy to wach his fugitive nose while he sleepe! But to the pointe; for the husbanding of my witt I put it out to interest, and make it returne twoo phamphlets a weeke. 207

Philom. If thou haste stuft thy pocket with ere a pamphlet, lett's see one, to make our worshipps laughe!

Stud. Indeede, Ingenioso, thou was wonte to carie some dissolute papers in thy bosome, that a man which hadd not knowne thy witt would have thought they had bene licences that the constables of sundrye townes had subscribed unto. But if thou haste ere an *omne tulit punctum*, ere a *magister artium utriusque academiae*, ere an *opus* and *usus*, ere a needie pamphlet, drincke of a sentence to us, to the healthe of mirth and the confusion of melancholye. 218

Ingen. I have indeede a pamphlet here that none is privie unto but a pinte of wine and a pipe of tobacco. It pleased my witt yesternighte to make water, and to use this goutie patron instead of an urinall, whome I make the subject and content of my whole speache. 223

Stud. What patron is that youe speak of? Art thou traveling towarde a Mæcenas?

Ingen. In faith, laying a snare to catche a dottrell! Why, her's Midas his grandchilde, one that will put him downe in a paire of long eares and a rude witt, braggs, when he comes abroade, of his liberalitie to schollers and what a rewarder he is of wittie devises : but indeed he is a meere man of strawe, a great lumpe of drousie earth. Yet I have better hope of him now that he is sicke, that the divell and his conscience betwixt them will let him bloude in the liberall vaine ; however it happeneth, I'le to him, and trie if there be ere a dropp of Mæcenas his bloude in his whole bodie. 236

Stud. Well, Ingenioso, we will trouble youe noe longer.

Wee shall meete anon at the signe of the Sunn, and make
some good jeste of it.   [*Exeunt.*

Ingen. Crowes flie to carion, and good witts to dyeng
churles. The carle lyeth here, att the house of this *Phar-
macopola,* this seller of dreggs and potions. I'le marche
on with a light purse and a nimble tonge, and picke a
quarell with his doore.   [*He knocks.*

Enter SERVING-MAN.

Serving-man. Fellowe, youre too saucye! youre rude
knockinge hath wakened my maister out of a napp, that he
prisde at an hundret pounde!   247

Ingen. Saucie? no, my good frende, unless thou takest
hunger to be a sauce, as wee schollers say, *optimum condi-
mentum fames.* I would thy father had brought thee up to
learninge, then woulde I make thee mends for my knockinge
with an hundreth Latin sentences, which thou migh[t]est
make use of in the elevation of the serving-man's blacke
Jacke or the confusion of a mess of brewes; but, frend, for
thy better instruction, answerr not a man of art so churl-
eshlye againe while thou livest. Why, man, I am able
to make a pamphlet of thy blew coate, and the button in
thy capp, to rime thy bearde of thy face, to make thee a
ridiculous blew-sleevd creature while thou livest. I have
immortalitie in my pen, and bestowe it on whome I will.
Well, helpe mee to the speache of thy maister quicklie, and
I'le make that obscure name of thyne, which is knowne
amongst none but hindes and milkmaides, ere longe to
florishe in the press and the printer's stall!   264

Serving-man. Faith, thou seems a mad Greeke, and I
have lovd such ladds of mettall as thou seems to be from
mine infancie; and wheras thou proferest such favours,
I will but demande this onlie, that thou wilte make mee a
love letter in elegant tearmes to our chambermaide.   269

D

Ingen. Give mee but a taste of thy love, and I'le so fitt thy fancie that the litell god Cupid shall put on his pumps, and caper it on a paper stage to please thy lovinge wenche!　　　　　　　　　　　　　　　　　　273

Serving-man. Give mee thy hande! faith, I am sorie I shewed my selfe so unmanered, but I hope we shall be better acquainted hereafter! well, I'le bringe my maister downe to youe presentlie.　　　　　　　　　[*Exit.*

Ingen. O fustie worlde! were there anie commendable passage to Styx and Acharon I would go live with Tarleton, and never more [b]less this dull age with a good line. Why, what an unmanerlie microcosme was this swine-faced clowne! But that the vassall is not capable of anie infamie, I would bepainte him; but a verie goose quill scornes such a base subject, and there is no inke fitt to write his servill name but a scholeboye's, that hath bene made by the mixture of urin and water. Yet must I forsooth sooth upp this bearded point-trusser, this cursie creator, this ingrosser of cringers, this *ante-ambulo* of a clokbagge, this great hilted dagger! But 'st! I heare his worshipp's fleame stirringe.　　　　　　　　　　　　　　　　　　290

Enter PATRON.

Patron. How nowe, felowe? have you anie thinge to saye to mee?

Ingen. Pardon, Sir, the presumpsion of a poore scholler, whose humble devoted ears being familiar with the commendacions that unpartiall fame bestoweth upon youre worship, reporting what a free-harted Mæcenas you are unto poore artists, that other favorers of learninge in comparison of youre worship are unworthie to untie youre worship's purse-stringes, that it hath beene youre ancient desire to get wittie subjects for youre liberalitie, that you coulde never endure the seven liberall sciences to carie there fardles on

there backes like footemen, but have animated there poore
dyinge pens, and put life to there decayed purses; here-
uppon I, unfurnished of all thinges but learninge, caste
myselfe downe at your worship's toose, resolving that
liberalitie sojourneth here with you or else it hath cleane
lefte our untoward cuntrie.   Take in good part, I beseech
youe, youre owne eternitie, my pains, wherin in the ages
to come men shall reade youre prases and give a shrewde
gess at youre vertues.   310

Patron, reading in the epistle dedicatorie this sentence,

'Desolat eloquence and forlorne poetric, youre moste
humble suppliant[s] *in forma pauperum*, laye prostrate at
youre daintie feete and adore youre excellencie,' &c.

I doe in some sorte like this sentence, for in my dayes *He nods*
I have bene a great favorer of schollers, but surelie of *his head.*
late the *utensilia* of potions and purges have bene verie
costlie unto mee.   For my owne part I had not cared for
dying, but when I am deade I know not what will become
of schollers; hitherto I have bespringled them pritilie with
the drops of my bountie.   320

Ingen.   O youre worshippe may be bolde with youre
selfe!   Noe other tong will be soe nigarde as to call those
dropes which indeede are plentuous showres, that so often
have refreshed thirstie brains and sunburnt witts; and
might it nowe please the cloude of youre bountie to breake,
it never founde a drier soile to worke upon, or a grounde
that will yealde a more plenteous requitall.   327

Patron.   Indeed these lines are pritie, and in time thou
maist doe well.   I have not leasure as yet to reade over
this booke, yet, howsoever, I doe accept of thy dutie, and
will doe somthinge if occasion serve; in the meane time, *He gives*
houlde, take a rewarde.   I tell thee Homer had scarse soe *him twoe*
groats.
much bestowed upon him in all his lifetime; indeede, our
countinance is enough for a scholler, and the sunshine of

our favoure yealdes good heate of itselfe ; howesoever, I am
somwhat prodigall that waye, in joyninge gifts to my
countenance ; yet it is fitt that all suche younge men as
you are should knowe that all dutie is farr inferiour to our
deserts, that in great humilitie doe vouchsake to reade
your labours. Well, my phisicke workes ; I cannot stay to
take a full sight of youre pamphlet ; hereafter I will look
on it, and at my better leasure, and in my good discretion,
favoure you accordinglie.   [*Exit.*

Ingen. Goe in a poxe and necre returne againe,   344
Thou lave-car'd ass, that loves dross more than arts !
Thinkest thyselfe liberall, if thy mule's dull heade
Give a poore scholler a ungratious nodd ?
Our lives are bounde unto thy churlishe eyes,
If thou bestowest on them a squintinge glanse,
If thou givest three dayes housroome to a booke,   350
Reprivinge it from thy unsavorie stoole.
Yet afterwarde, in Mounsier's Ajax vaine,
With poesie thou doest a coursie straine.
Foole I, to angell in a miser's mudd !   354
But hope of goulde did make mee guilde this woode.
Farewell, gross peece of earth, base braginge dunge ;
Soone maist thou grovell in the lowlie duste,
And nere be spoken of but in obloquie :
And if I live, I'le make a poesie
Shall loade thy future's yeares with infamie.   360

　　　　　Enter Philomusus *and* Studioso.

Philo. Howe now, Ingenioso ? what, well relived ?

Ingen. Slender relife I can assure youe in the predicament of privation ! yonder's a churle thinkes it enough for
his favoure like a sunn to shine on the dunghill of learning !
I came to the apothecarie's dore by the smell ; his worshipp
perfumde through five dores ; outsteps the yeoman of his
privie chamber, and with the face of an Iseland curr grind

upon mee. I was faine to take paines to washe his doges
face with a few good tearmes, and then he steps, and
bringes out signiour Barbarisme in a case of nightcapps,
in a case of headpeeces all-to-be wrought, like a blocke
in a seamster-shopp, who, with a camelion's gape an a
verie emphaticall nodd of the heade, solemlye strokinge
his lousie bearde, asked my errand; and when I had pro-
nounsed my litell speach, with a hundred damnable lies, of
his liberalitie, he puts his hande into the pocket of a paire
of breeches that were made in William the Conquerour's
dayes, groping in his pocket with greate deliberation, and
while I stoode by dreaminge of the goulde of India, he
drew mee out twoo leane faces, gave mee fidler's wages,
and dismiste mee.   381

Stud. Well, Ingenioso, the worlde is badd, and wee
schollers are ordayned to be beggars.

Philom. But, Ingenioso, how doest thou meane to shifte
for thy livinge?

Ingen. To London I'le go; I'le live by the printinge
house, as I have done hitherto.

Stud. Nay then, take us with thee; for wee muste
provide us a poore capp of mantenance.   389

Ingen. Well then, let's launch forwarde; if wee can get
noe livinge wee'le dye learned beggars.

Philom. Naye, staye awhile; wee'le take Luxurio with
us, for he is in the same predicament.

Enter LUXURIOSO.

Lux. O brave witts of mine acquaintance, howe doe
yee? howe doe yee? what, Ingenioso? how haste thou
helde out rubbers ere since thou wentest from Parnassus?

Ingen. What, oulde pipe of Tobacco! why, what's to
paye? give mee thy liquid hande! How haste thou
mantained thy nose in that redd sute of apparell ere since

I lefte thee? as for my holdinge out rubbers, I have ruled
so longe in apparell that my clothes cannot be taken
nappinge.   402

Lux. Why, youe whoreson *Opus* and *usus*, you! Be it
knowne unto all people that the bearer hereof, you tattered
prodigall, thou enviest that a man's nose shoulde be better
apparelled than thy backe! Were thy disapointed selfe
possest with such a spirit as inhabiteth my face, thou
wouldest never goe fidlinge thy pamphlets from doore to
dore, like a blinde harper, for breade and chease, present-
inge thy poems like oulde broomes to everie farmer.   410

Ingen. Spirit calest thou it? it shoulde seeme by the
fier ther's a divell! But I pray thee, Luxurio, how meanest
thou to bestowe thy waterie witt?

Lux. My waterie wit shall dwell in a waterie region.
And yet thou doest abuse my witt to call it waterie: much
have I spente in rare Alcamie, in brewinge of wine and
burninge sackes to make my witt a philosophers stone,
when I shoulde make use of it. And now the time is
come, I hope, whatere I make will beare marmelett and
sacket in the mouthe, and savore of witts that have bene
familiar with the other quart and a reckoninge.   421

Ingen. Let it be a French wit for mee! Tell me howe
thou meanest to bestowe it.

Lux. To London I'le goe, for there is a great nosde
balletmaker deceaste, and I am promised to be the rimer
of the citie. Ile fit them for a wittie in Creete when
Daedalus. I have alwaies more than naturallie affected
that poeticall vocation.

Ingen. Wilt thou leave Parnassus then?   429

Lux. Is it not time thinkest thou? I have served here
an apprentishood of some seaven yeares, and have lived
with the Pythagorean and Platonicall Διακας, as they call

it; why, a good horse woulde not have endured it! Adew
single beare and three qus of breade! if I converse with
you anie longer, some sexton must toll the bell for the
death of my witt. Here is nothing but levelinge of colons,
squaringe of periods, by the monthe. My sanguin scorns
all such base premeditation; I'le have my pen run like a
spigot, and my invention answerr it as quick as a drawer.
Melancholick art, put downe thy hose; here is a suddaine
wit that will lashe thee in the time to come!   441

Stud. Luxurio, wee are not disposed to laugh anie
longer; we'ele make more use of youre merrie vaine in our
jorney.

Philom. Thy mirth helps to drowne that melancholicke
that our departure from Parnassus doth create. Longe for
a rewarde may youre witts be warmde with the Indian
herbe! Nowe it's time for us to provide for our jorney, and
closly convey ourselves away, least *aes alienum* be knockinge at our doores.   450

Lux. Marrye, all my debts stande chaukt upon the
poste for liquor! Mine hostis may cross it if shee will, for I
have done my devotion! Farewell, mine alone hostis, thou
shalt heare newes of thy ale-knighte!

Stud. Muses, adewe! longe may youre groves growe
   greene,   455
Though you to us too too unkinde have beene!

Philom. Farewell, Apollo! e're will I adore thee,
Though thy poore hande's not able to relive mee!

Ingen. Youe beautuous nimphes of Hellicon, adew!
However poore, yet I will worship youe!   460

Lux. Farewell, the Sisters nine! the truth for to saye,
Luxurio will youre goodchilde be, and love youe everie
   daye!
Why, here's poetrie hath a foot of the twelves! why, I
cannot abide these scipjake blanke verses!   464

Ingen. Peace! what musicke is this? Marrye, I thinke the Muses bestowe a fitt of mirth upon there poore attendants at our departure! [*The Muses playe.*

Lux. Good wenches! y-faith, the'le scrape where ther's no hops of silver! This is for the love of there loving Luxurio. 470

Stud. Thanks, gentle nimphes, for this sweete harmonie! Soe musick yealdes some ease to miserie.

Philom. Thanks, sweet Apollo, for this smoother strayne!
To dwell with thee is joy, to part is paine. 474

Ingen. Thanks, Muses, that a part in sorrowe beare! Longe may youre musick bless ech listninge eare!

Lux. Thankes to the Muses majestic of Parnass pro-pertie!
For they have eased my carefull hart that I may tell no lie.

Ingen. Why, thou beginest to practise alreadie! but let's begone? 480

Stud. Fairewell, Parnassus! farwell, faire content!

Philom. Welcome, good sorowe! farewell, meriment!

Lux. Hange sorow! care will kill a catt!

ACTUS 2^(*us*). *SCAENA* 1^(*a*).

Enter DRAPER *and* TAYLER.

Draper. Neighboure Birde, wee townsmen have such kinde harts that it will goe neare to undoe us! Why, who woulde thinke that men in such grave gownes and capps. and that can say soe bravlye, woulde use honest men soe badlie? Philomusus and Studioso hath not beene ashamed to run 20 nobles in my debt for apparell, and after theire departure abuse mee with a letter, and also my neighboure

Giles, recantinge in the colde of his feare for preachinge on
his shopborde againste organs, in the heat of his choller,
was laught at by them, though he spake verie wiselie, as
became a man of his clothe.   494

Tayler. Fye, neighboure! if they had our wisdome
joyned to theire learninge they woulde prove grave men.
Well, God forgive them! They shoulde shewe good
examples to others, as our towne clarke shewed verie
learnedly in an oration he made, and they are the worste
themselves. They came to mee, and were as curteous as
passeth; I doe not like they shoulde put of theire hatts so
much to mee; well, they needs upon oulde acquaintance
woulde borowe 40*s* for three dayes; I (as I had alwayes
bene a kinde man to schollers) lent it them, and delivered
them theire breeches new turned and there stockings new
footed, even as thoughe I had bene privie to there runninge
awaye.   507

Draper. Well, whersoever they be they are a couple of
my men, they weare my clothe; for there sakes I'le truste
but few, unless I knowe them well, and those shall be none
of these fine youthes that have their apparell in printe, there
treble cypresses, double ruffs, silke stockings. I have
gotten thus much by my owne experience that the more
willinge[1] he is that trustes, the slower he'le be to paye; a
note, neighboure, worthy thy retention, for (marke you
mee!) if wee will needs be trustinge, let us truste honest,
simple, plaine felowes, such as ourselves, that weare foure-
pennie garters, and winter shoos that have kept the cobler's
companie; but as for those neat youths they are out of my
books; and yet I lie, for they are more in them than the'le
pay in haste.   521

Tayler. Nay, that grives mee moste of all. When I
came to enquire for them, out steps a leane-faced scholler

---

[1] willninge MS.

(surlie I thinke he was well learned, for he was redinge a
great booke with a smale printe), he stept out, I saye, and
told mee they were not within; which answerr when I
woulde not take (for it urged my conscience somwhat when
I remembered my money) he cald me 'Pagan, Tartarian,
heathen man, base plebeian,' and (which grived mee most
of all) he caled mee 'simple animal.' Well, saide I, simple
may I be, but animal was I never; and I added that
Philomusus and Studioso were rather animals, to use an
honest, simple, plaine man so as they have not bene
ashamed to doe. 534

Draper. Why, I thinke it was the same scipjacke that
when I knockt at the dore asked what clothwritt was there?
and said he was makinge an oration which everie scurvey
vulgar felowe, everie measuringe pesante, must not interrupt;
he said he was about a sentence that was worth all the
cloth in my shopp. So these schollers use as long as they
have anie cloths on there backs; and when the knaves
begin to be ragged, then they scrape acquaintance to be
trusted, and give us an *Ita est*, with a scurvey coozeninge
name, and ther's all the paiment wee can gett. 544

Enter SIMSON *the Tapster speaking alone.*

Simson. O my frozen balderkine of stronge ale! well
might I have foretold by the burninge of a pot of youre
liquor that some dry lucke hunge over my moiste heade!
And is Luxurio gone? the answer is, he is gone! Ey, but
one will say, Will not Luxurio returne againe? I answer, I
knowe not. Ey, but some will object and saye, Did not
Luxurio strike of the score before he wente? I answer, he
did not. 552

Draper. Good morow, good man Simson! how goes the
world with youe?

Tayler. Good morow, neighboure, good morowe! 555

Simson. O, good morowe, my good neighbours! by

cocke, the worlde squints upon mee! it hath not lookt straight upon mee this good while, but nowe it hath given mee a bob will stick by mee! Wott yee what? Luxurio, as they say, a man of God's makinge, as they saye, came to my house, as they saye, and was trusted by my wife, a kinde woman, as they saye, for a dozen of ale, as they saye, and he a naughtie felowe, as they saye, is run away, as they saye; for even as an emptie barrell soundeth moste, as they saye, even so Luxurio came to my house and was welcom, as they saye, and even as a pot of ale and a puddinge are good in a frostie morninge, even soe Luxurio hath betaken himselfe to his heels, and hath overrune the reckoninge. My wife and I, twoo honest folkes, as they saye, ment no harme, but even as the ape wanteth a tale, as they saye, even so wee wanted all malice, as they saye; but nowe I finde, I finde at length t[h]roughe much experience, that, even as wishers and woulders are never good housholders, soe trusters and lenders are never good housholders. Well, neighbours, I have it here in white, as they saye; my ale had alwayes a verie good name, and Luxurio was a good drinker, for even as a changlinge the more hee eats the more he maye, even soe Luxurio the more he drancke the more he mighte, which I founde, as they saye.   580

Draper. Well, for all this, good man Simson, you have it in youre cellar that will kill care and hange sorowe.

Tayler. Nay then, let's in and be merie.

Simson. Neighbours, I have as good a cupp of ale as ere was turnde over tonge, as they saye; it's it will do the deede, as they saye.   [*Exeunt.*

Enter PHILOMUSUS *with a blacke frise coate, solus.*

Philom. Come, black frise coat! become my sable minde! Helpe me to painte forth blackefaced discontente!

Come, keyes and spade! the ensigns of my state,
That treads the ragged stepps of fortun's race.   590
My fortune, that whilcome did seeme to floate,
Is now at length brought to the lowest ebb,
And I that lately in Parnassus sunge,
And consort kept in Muses' melodye,
Doe live moste baselie now 'mongst russet coats   595
And earns my livinge here moste painfullie.
Thus am I nipt by winter's chillie froste
That seemd of late to florish in my Maye.
I mighte have learnde to see by risinge morne
This cloudie daye that threatens now to poure   600
Both storms and tempests on my beaten barke,
That faine woulde a[n]chor upon vertue's shore,
Where I might staye untill some warblinge winds
Might drive my shipp unto my wished porte.
But why doe I prolonge my tedious speeche?   605
Studioso promisd to be here ere longe
To beare a parte in this our mournfull songe.
And here he comes.

Enter STUDIOSO.

  Stud. What, Philomusus? thou art well mett!
I have oft heard that to have companie   610
Hath alwayes bene an ease to miserie.
Thus farr hath fortune plagued us equallie,
And caused us both to weare her servile yoke;
And now mee thinks shee 'gins to leade the chase,
And here hath given to us a baitinge place.   615

  Philom. True, Studioso, she needs to doe noe more,
For wee have yealded to her conqueringe hande,
And wilninglie goe captives in her bande.
But saye, canste thou endure this servile life?
What shall wee doe in this adversitie?   620

  Stud. We muste make profit of necessitie.

Philom. When thinkest thou better fortune will begin?

Stud. I nere sawe winter but a springe came in.

Philom. Get I my pence by digginge of the earthe?

Stud. Ey! so the planets raigned at thy birthe.　625

Philom. Banisht am I from Phoebus lovely bowrs?

Stud. The Muses dwell as oft in woods as towres.

Philom. The cuntrie moss noe true contente here yelds.

Stud. Apollo once did dwell in cuntrie fildes.

Philom. Noe fairies dance upon this ruder greene.

Stud. By ruder springes oft beautous nymphes are
seene.　　　　　　　　　　　　　　　　631

Philom. I'faith, Studioso, this dull patience of thine
angers mee! Why, can a man be galde by povertie, free
spirits subjected to base fortune, and put it up like a
Stoick? But saye, I pray thee, upon what condition art
thou intertayned to thy ould master and ould mistris? to
thy yonge master and yonge mistris?　　　　　637

Stud. Marrie, I had like have missed of this preferment
for wante of one to be bounde for my truthe! Mistris
Mincks, with a tonge as swifte as a swalowe, cride, 'The
world's nought, the worlde's noughte!' whiles her husbande
like a phisiognomer put on his spectacles, and gasde me in
the face as thoughe he woulde have tolde my fortune.
Well, the conclusion was this; they indented with mee;
ether I muste set my hande to the conditions followinge, or
els I muste take up my staffe and be packinge. The
conditions were these :—　　　　　　　　　647

1. That I shoulde faire no worse than there owne housholde servants did; have breade and beare and bacon
enoughe, whils my mistris, mincinge Avaritia, sayde, 'there
was not such a house within fortie miles.'

2. I shoulde lye cleane in hempen sheets and a good
mattress, to keepe mee from growinge pursic.　　　653

3. That I shoulde waite at meals.

4. That I shoulde worke all harvest time. And upon this pointe the olde churle gave a signe with a 'hemm!' to the whole householde of silence, and began a solem senc[e]less oration againste Idlenes, noddinge his head, knockinge his hande on his fatt breste, shakinge the hayrie attire of his chin, usinge the verie grace of Dametas.   660

5. That I shoulde never teache my yonge master his lesson without doinge my dutie as becometh mee to the offspringe of such a scholler.

6. That I shoulde complane to his mother when he coulde not say his lesson. And lastlie, for all this, my wages muste be five marke a yeare, and some caste out of his forlorne wardropp that his ploughmen woulde scarse accept of. And now let mee heare of thy promotion, what thy rents are that come in by thy spade and thy church dore keyes.   670

Philom. I am double benefisde with my sextonshipp and my clearkeshippe! a faire age when a scholler must come to live upon carions, and a voice that was made to pronounce a poet or an oratour be imployed, like a belman, in the inquirie of a strayed beaste ; yet the beste is, I meete nowe and then with a clown's heade that is as good to one as the poesie '*ut hora sic vita*,' ready to putt mee in minde of the end of this my miserie. For my conditions, the hoydons, for want of further rhetorique, made them but few, and contained them in these twoo, '*Digg well and Ring well*,' 'and in soe doinge,' quoth our churchwarden, ' thou shall gaine not onlie our praise but also our commendations.'   682

Stud. Well, Philo, we'le meete once a weeke and laughe at our fortuns! Fortie pounde to a pennie, ere this th'ould churle hath swore manie an othe, and asked for the knave scholler!

Philom. Then wee may fitlie parte, for here comes a rusticke knave will interrupte us.   688

Stud. Farewell, Phil.   [*Exit.*

Percev. Nowe good man Sexton, I sende our maide
Johne to youe even now to bid you toll for my good ould
father, that God hath taken full sore againste my will, and
I pray you, good man Sexton, make him a good large
grave, that he may lie easilie ; he coulde never abide to be
crouded in his life time, and therfore he was wonte to chide
with a good oulde woman my mother for takinge soe muche
roome in the bed, more than was fit for a woman of her
condition and place. I will see him as well as I can brought
to his grave honestlie ; he shall have a faire coverlet over
him, and lie in a good flaxon sheete, and youe and the reste
of my good neighbours shall have breade and cheese
enoughe. And I pray youe, good man Sexton, laye twoo or
three good thick clods under his heade, for I'le tell youe, of
a cuntrie felowe he was as sqemish in his bed as ye woulde
wonder at, he coulde not abide to lie lowe, insomuche that
he was wonte to put his lether breeches and his cotton
dublet under his boulster.   707

Philo. Surelie, good man Percevall, the towne shall have
a great miss of him ; he was as honeste a cunstable as ever
put beggar in stocks. But saye, good man Percevale, where
will youe have youre father lie ?

Perce. Marrie, I coulde be contente to be at coste to
burie him in the churche, but that I will not bringe up
newe customs ; he shall lie with his posteritie in the churchyarde, and I that am the aire of the house may about twoo
hundred years hence lie by him. But harke you, Sexton, I
pray you burie him quicklie ; for he was a good man, and
I knowe he is in a better place, that's fitter for him than
this scurvey worlde, and I woulde not have him alive againe
to his hindrance : it will be better for him and mee too,
for ther's a greate change with mee within this two hours,
for the ignorant [1] people that before calde mee *Will* nowe

---

[1] ingorant MS.

call mee *William,* and you of the finer sorte call mee *good man Percevall.*　　724

Philom. Well, good man Percevall, you speake like a wise yonge man. Why, if death shoulde repente him, and give youre father his life againe, then were youe but plaine *Will.* Dispache him, man, dispache him quicklie ; bringe him to the grave, and for thy sake I'le make him sure.　　729

Perce. Goodlic Lorde, howe sen youe? howe sen youe? Nay, I woulde not wish my father soe muche hurte as to live againe! But harke you, good man Sexton, they saie you can write and reade ; I'le please youe for youre paines if youe will write out my father's will : ther's as good matter in it as ere youe sawe, howe he is well in minde and sicke in bodie, and a hundreth such prettie thinges. He gave all to mee but the lambs that 2 or 3 ewes will ayne at the nexte ayninge time, and a drye cowe shall be 7 years oulde at the nexte roode daye, and a pann, all which he gave to his base daughter. O good man Sexton! that was a foule facte, to be soe wilde ; if he remember it in the other worlde it will goe harde with him.

Philom. I'le doe a greater matter for youe than this comes too, good man Percevalle.　　745

Perce. Marrie, I thanke youe and you shall have my carte to carrie home a jagg of haye when you wonn. I pray let the grave be readie quicklie ; its time my father were takinge his reste.

Philom. It shall, good man Percevall.　　750

Perce. I'le goe home to get my neighbours carrye him to churche. Fare well.　　[*Exit.*

Philom. Woulde I were laide upon a balefull beare, Toste longe enoughe with fortun's mockeries! Yet this the comforth for all miserie,　　755 Who findes not where to live findes where to dye.

Enter STUDIOSO *with his scholler.*

Stud. Ey, her's a true Pedantius, and yet no truculent
Orsylius[1], one that can heare a boy speake false Lattin
without stampinge of his feete, can looke on a false verse
without wrincklinge of his browe, one that will give his
scholler leave to prove as verie a dunce as his father and
nere commaunde the untrussinge of his points. My hands
are bounde to the peace, and his wit is bounde to the good
bearinge, for it will not beare. I have in the bottom of my
dutie broughte my yonge master a stoole and a boss, a boss
for his worship's feete and a stoole for the yonge foole to
speake false Lattin on. Well, here comes the dandipratt!

Boy. Schoolmaister, cross or pile nowe for 4 counters?

Stud. Why cross, my wagg! for thinges goe cross with
    mee,
Els woulde I whipp this childishe vanitie.   770

Boy. Scholmaster, it's pile.

Stud. Well may it pile in suche a pilled age,
When schollers serve in such base vassalage.

Boy. I muste have 4 counters of youe.

Stud. Full manie a time Fortune encounters mee;
More happie they that in the Counter be.   776

Boy. You'le paye them, I hope?

Stud. Fortune hath paide mee home, that I may pay;
And yet, sweet wagg, I hope you'le give mee daye.

Boy. What day will you take to paye them?   780

Stud. That day I'le take when learninge florisheth,
When schollers are esteemde by cuntrie churles,
When ragged pedants have there pasports scalde
To whip fonde wagges for all there knaverie,
When schollers weare noe baser liverie   785
Nor spend there dayes in servile slaverie.

Boy. But when will this be, scholmaister?

---

[1] *Sic. Read* Orbilius.

Stud. When silie shrubs th'ambitious cedars beate,
Or when hard oakes softe honie 'gins to sweate.
   But wilt please you to goe to youre booke a litell?

Boy. What will you give mee then?   791

Stud. A resin, or an aple ; or a rod if I had authoritie.
Wilt please you, Sir, to sit downe and repeate youre lecture?

Boy. *Quamquam te, Marce fili*, etc.

Stud. *Quae pars orationis, Athenis?*   795

Boy. I'le speake English todaye.

Stud. What parte of speache is it then?

Boy. A nowne adjective.

Stud. Noe ; it's a nowne substantive.

Boy. I saye it's a nowne adjective, and if I feche my
mother to youe I'le make you confess as muche.   801

Stud. I woulde thy mother coulde stande as well by
herselfe as this worde doth !
Then shoulde thy sire have a more naked heade,
And less shame waitinge on his jaded bedd.   805

Boy. I am wearie of learninge : I'le goe bowle awhile,
and then I will goe to my booke againe.   [*Exit.*

Stud. Doe what thou wilt, starve thou thy minde for
   me,
I'le never frett to see thy vanitie.
If thou prove sottish in the after time   810
Thy parents beare the shame ; their's is the crime.
Fonde they to thinke that this child's waxen daye
Will be well spente when maister beares no swaye.
That tender sprig must timely bended be
Which will hereafter prove a stately tree.   815
For my base usage this is tolde by mee,
The sire a clowne, the sonne a foole shall bee.

Enter LUXURIO *and his* BOY.

Lux. Come boy, if thou chante it finely at the fayre
wee'll make a good markitt of it.   I will put thee into
a new sute of apparell, and thy nose into that sanguin
complexion which it hath loste for wante of good companie and good dyet.   I am sure I have done my parte,
for I am sure my pen hath sweated through a quire of
paper this laste weeke ; and they are noe small verses like
‘ *Captaine couragious, whome death coulde not daunte,*’ but
verses full of a poeticall spirit, such that if Elderton were
alive to heare (happie is he that is not alive to heare them,
els !) his blacke potts shoulde put on mourninge apparell,
and his nose for verie envie departe out of the worlde.

Boy.   I warrante youe I'le purchase suche an auditorie
of clowns that shall gape, nodd and laughe ! one shall crye
‘a goodlie matter,’ another ‘bravely wanton,’ and a thirde
‘commende the sweet master.’   I'le make every hoydon
bestowe a fairinge on his dore, his wall, his windowe.

Lux.   Then *ficus pro diabolo*—Kinge Harrie loved a man !
Take heede youe clowns ! here comes a juggling rimester
that will pull you by the rude ears with a ballet !   my
father's sonne might have had a better trade if it had pleased
Fortune ; but shee is a drab, and Luxurio will drinke to her
confusion !   Exercise thy voice, boy, in some of my prettie
sonnets, while wee go on.   841

Boy.   ‘Nowe listen all good people
         Unto a strange event
         That did befall to two yonge men
         As they to market went.   845
         The one of them height Richarde,
         The truthe for to saye,
         The other they cal'd him Robert,
         Upon a holiday.

And are not the Spaniards knaves　　850
To put us to this paine?
They woulde have conquered Englande once,
But nowe we'le conquer Spaine!

ACTUS 3. SCOENA 1.

INGENIOSO. GULLIO.

Ingen. Nowe, gentlemen, youe may laughe if you will,
for here comes a gull.　　855

Gul. This rapier I boughte when I sojourned in the
universitie of Padua. By the heavens, its a pure Tolledo; it
was the death of a Pollonian, a Germaine and a Ducheman,
because the[y] woulde not pledge the health of Englande.

Ingen. (He was never anie further than Flushinge, and then
he came home sicke of the scurveys.) Surely, Sir, a notable
exploite worthy to be cronicled! but had you anie witness
of youre valiancie?　　863

Gul. Why, I coulde never abide to fighte privatelie, because I woulde not have obscuritie soe familiar with my
vertues. Since my arrivall in Englande (which is nowe 6
months, I take, sithens) I had bene the death of one of our
pulinge Liteltomans[1] for passinge by mee in the Moore
Fildes unsaluted, but that there was noe historiographer by
to have recorded it.　　870

Ingen. Please you now, Sir, to lay the rayns on the necke
of youre vertuous disposition; you have gotten a suppliant
poet that will teach mossy posteritie to know howe that
this earthe in such a raigne was blest with a yonge Jupiter.

Gul. I'faith I care not for fame, but valoure and vertue
will be spoken of in spite of oblivion. Had I cared for that
pratinge eccho, fame, my exploits at Cosmopolis, at Cals,
at Portingall voyage, and nowe verie latelie in Irelande,
had bene gettinge ere this throughe everie by-streete, and

---

[1] (Qu. 'Liteltonians'?)

talk[ed] of as well at the wheele of a cuntrie maide as the
tilts and turnaments of the courte.   881

Ingen. I dare sweare youre worship scapt knightinge
verie hardly.

Gull. That's but a pettie requitall to good deserts! He
that esteems mee of less worth than a knight is peasande
and a gull. Give mee a new knight of them all, in fenc-
schoole, att a Nimbrocado or at a Stocado! Sir Oliver, Sir
Randal, base, base chamber-tearmes! I am saluted every
morninge by the name of 'Good morow, Captaine, my
sworde is at youre service!'   890

Ingen. Good faith, an honorable title! Why, this is the
life of a man, to commande quick rapier in a taverne, to
blowe two or three simple felowes out of a roome with a
valiant othe, to bestowe more smoke on the worlde with
the draught of a pipe of tobacco than proceeds from the
chimnie of a solitarie hall! But say, Sir, you were tellinge
me a tale even nowe of youre Hellen, youre Venus, that
better parte of youre amorous soule.   898

Gull. Well remembred. *Etas prima canit venerem,
postrema tumultus.* Since souldierye is not regarded, I'le
make the ladies happie with enjoyinge my youth, and
hange up my sworde and buckler to the behoulders.
Amonge manie daintie court nymphes that with petition-
inge looks have sued for my love, it pleased mee to bestowe
love, this pleasinge fire, upon Lady Lesbia: manie a
health have I drunke to her upon my native knees, eating
that happie glass in honour of my mistris!   907

Ingen. Valiantlie done! admirable, admirable!

Gull. And for matters of witt oft have I sonnetted it in
the commendačons of her sqirill; and verie latelie (I
remember) that time I had a muske jerkin layde all with
golde lace, and the rest of my furniture answerable, pretty
sleightie apparell, stood mee not paste in twoo hundred

pounds, they frowarde fates cut her munkey's threed
asunder, and I in the abondance of poetric bestowed an
Epitaphe upon the deceased litell creature.   916

Ingen. I 'faith, an excellent witt that can poetize upon
such meane subjects! everie John Dringle can make a
booke in the commendacions of temperance, againste the
seven deadlie sinns, but that's a rare wit that can make
somthinke of nothinge, that can make an Epigram of a
Mouse and an Epitaphe on a Munkey. But love is very
costlie, for I have hearde that you were wonte to weare
seven sundry sutes of apparell in a weeke, and them no
meane ones.   925

Gull. Tushe. man! at the courte I thinke I shoulde
growe lousie if I wore less than two a daye.

Ingen. The divell of the sute hath he but this, and
that's not payd for yet (*aside*).

Gull. I am never scene at the courte twise in one sute
of apparell; that's base! as for boots, I never wore one paire
above two hours; as for bands, stockings, and handcher-
chiefs, myne hostes, where my trunkes lye, nere the courte,
hath inoughe to make her sheets for her housholde.

Ingen. I wonder such a gallante as you are scaps the
marriage of some Countess.   936

Gull. Nay, I cannot abide to be tide to Cleopatra, if
shee were alive. It's enough for me to crop virginitie, and
to take heed that noe ladies dye vestalls and leade aps in
hell. But seest thou this? O touche it not! it is divine!
why, man. it was a humble retainer to her buske. And
here is another favoure, which I snached from her as I was
in a gentleman-like curtesie tyinge of her shooe stringes.
It is my nature to be debonaire with faire ladies, and
vouchsake to employ this happie hande in anie service
ether domesticall or private.   946

Ingen. Amonge other of youre vertues I doe observe

youre stile to be most pure; youre English tonge comes
as neere Tullie's as anie man's livinge.

Gull. Oh, Sir, that was my care to prove a complet
gentleman, to be *tam Marte quam Mercurio;* insomuche
that I am pointed at for a poet in Paul's church yarde,
and in the tilte-yarde for a champion; nay, every man
enquires after my abode.　　　　　954

> Gnats are unnoted where soe ere they flie,
> But Eagles waited on with every eye.

I had in my dayes not unfitly bene likned to Sir Phillip
Sidney, only with this difference, that I had the better
legg, are[1] more amiable face: his Arcadia was prettie, soe
are my sonnets: he had bene at Paris, I at Padua: he
fought, and so dare I: he dyed in the Lowe Cuntries, and
soe I thinke shall I: he loved a scholler, I mantaine them,
witness thyselfe nowe. Because I sawe thee haue the
wit to acknowledge those vertus to be mine which indeede
are, I have restored thy dylaniated back and ruinous estate
to those prittie clothes wherin thou now walkest.　　　966

Ingen. (Oh! it is a moste lousie caste sute of his that he
before bought of an Irish souldier!) Durste envie otherwise reporte of youre excellencie than I have done, I would
bob him on the pate, and make forlorne malice recante. If
I live, I will lim[n]e out your vertues in such rude colours
as I have, that youre late nephewes may knowe what good
witts were youre worshipp's most bounden!　　　973

Gull. Nay, I have not onlie recreated thy could state
with the warmth of my bountie, but also mantaine other
poetical spirits, that live upon my trenchers, insomuche that
I cannot come to my inn in Oxforde without a dozen
congratulorie orations, made by *genus* and *species* and his
ragged companions. I reward the poore *ergoes* most
bountifullie, and send them away. I am verie latelie

---

[1] *Read* and.

registered in the roules of fame in an Epigram made by
a Cambridge man, one weaver fellow I warrant him, els
coulde he never have had such a quick sight into my
vertues; however, I merit his praise: if I meet with him
I will vouchsafe to give him condigne thankes.   985

Ingen. Great reason the Muses shoulde flutter about
youre immortall heade, since youre bodye is nothinge but
a faire inne of fairer guests that dwell therin. But you
have digrest from your mistris, for whose sake you and I
began this parley.   990

Gull. Marrie, well remembred! I'le repeat unto you an
enthusiasticall oration wherwith my new mistris' ears were
veric lately made happie. The carriage of my body, by
the reporte of my mistriss, was excellent: I stood stroking
up my haire, which became me very admirably, gave a low
congey at the beginning of each period, made every
sentence end sweetly with an othe. It is the part of an
Oratoure to perswade, and I know not how better than to
conclude with such earnest protestations. Suppose also
that thou wert my mistris, as somtime woodden statues
represent the goddesses; thus I woulde looke amorously,
thus I would pace, thus I would salute thee.   1002

Ingen. (It will be my lucke to dye noe other death than
by hearinge of his follies! I feare this speach that's a
comminge will breede a deadly disease in my ears.)   1005

Gull. Pardon, faire lady, thoughe sicke-thoughted Gullio
maks amaine unto thee, and like a bould-faced sutore
'gins to woo thee[1].

Ingen. (We shall have nothinge but pure Shakspeare
and shreds of poetrie that he hath gathered at the theators!)

---

[1] 'Sick-thoughted Venus makes amain unto him,
And like a bold-faced suitor 'gins to woo him.'
            Venus and Adonis, st. 1.

Gull. Pardon mee, moy mittressa, ast am a gentleman, the moone in comparison of thy bright hue a meere slutt, Anthonie's Cleopatra a blacke browde milkmaide, Hellen a dowdie.   1014

Ingen. (Marke, Romeo and Juliet! O monstrous theft[1]! I thinke he will runn throughe a whole booke of Samuell Daniell's!)

Gull. Thrise fairer than myselfe (—thus I began—)
The gods faire riches, sweete above compare,
Staine to all nimphes, [m]ore lovely the[n] a man,
More white and red than doves and roses are!   1021
Nature that made thee with herselfe had[2] strife,
Saith that the worlde hath ending with thy life[3].

Ingen. Sweete Mr. Shakspeare!

Gull. As I am a scholler, these arms of mine are long
     and strong withall,   1025
Thus elms by vines are compast ere they falle.

Ingen. Faith, gentleman! youre reading is wonderfull in our English poetts!

Gull. Sweet Mistris, I vouchsafe to take some of there wordes, and applie them to mine owne matters by a scholasticall invitation.   1031
Report thou, upon thy credit; is not my vayne in courtinge gallant and honorable?

Ingen. Admirable, *sanes* compare, never was so mellifluous a witt joynet to so pure a phrase, such comly gesture, suche gentlemanlike behaviour.   1036

Gull. But stay! it's verie true good witts have badd memories. I had almoste forgotten the cheife pointe. I cal'd thee out for new year's day approcheth, and wheras

---

[1] *Cf.* Romeo and Juliet, ii. 4.   [2] *sic: for* at.
[3] *Venus and Adonis.* st. 2.

other gallants bestowe jewells upon there mistrisses (as I have done whilome) I now count it base to do as the common people doe; I will bestowe upon them the precious stons of my witt, a diamonde of invention, that shall be above all value and esteeme; therfore, sithens I am employed in some weightie affayrs of the courte. I will have thee, Ingenioso, to make them, and when thou hast done I will peruse, pollish, and correcte them.   1047

Ingen. My pen is youre bounden vassall to commande. But what vayne woulde it please you to have them in?

Gull. Not in a vaine veine (prettie, i'faith!): make mee them in two or three divers vayns, in Chaucer's, Gower's and Spencer's and Mr. Shakspeare's. Marry, I thinke I shall entertaine those verses which run like these;

Even as the sunn with purple coloured face

Had tane his laste leave on[1] the weeping morne, &c. O sweet Mr. Shakspeare! I'le have his picture in my study at the courte.   1055

Ingen. (Take heed, my maisters! he'le kill you with tediousness ere I can ridd him of the stage!)

Gull. Come, let us in! I'le eate a bit of phesaunte, and drincke a cupp of wine in my cellar, and straight to the courte I'le goe. A Countess and twoo lordes expect mee to day at dinner; they are my very honorable frendes; I muste not disapointe them.   [*Exeunt.*

Enter LEONARDE *and* CONSILIODORUS.

Leon. Mr. Consiliodorus, are you within? God be here!

Consil. What, Leonarde? fill us a cupp of beare for Leonard! what good news, Leonarde?   1065

Leon. Oh, I have had great affliction since I sawe you laste. Tib is fallen sore sicke of the glanders, and Dun, poore jade, I thinke he hath eaten a feather. But I have

---

[1] 'of': *Venus and Adonis*, l. 2.

letters for youe, and as manie commendacions as there are
greene grass betwixt you and them. I told them of there
'havioure, I warrant youe ; I tolde them howe costlie there
nutreringe was, and they might by this time if they had
bene good boyes have learned all there bookes. I chid
them roundlie, without bawking, for blowing at tabecca;
I toulde them plainely it was nothing but a docke leafe
stept in a chamber pott ; and by cocke ! Mr. Consiliodorus,
I did such good upon them, that I thinke by this time they
are gone into the cuntrie to teache. I warrant Mr. Philomusus will prove a greate clarke, he is such a ready man of
his tongue ; yet I thinke Mr. Studioso is as well book-
learned as he is.   1081

Consil.   I pray thee, Leonarde, goe in, and eate a bit of
meate. I'le followe thee straighte.

Leon.   God thanke youe, Mr., wee that are stirringe
betimes have good stomackes ; but I'le firste leade my
horses to the hay racke ; they, poore jades, are as shallowe
as a cloakbagg.   [*Exit.*

Consil.   Henceforthe let none be sent by carefull syres,
Nor sonns nor kinred, to Parnassus hill,
Since waywarde fortune thus rewardes our coste   1090
With discontent, theire paines with povertie.
Mechanicke arts may smile, there followers laughe,
But liberall arts bewaile there destinie,
Since noe Mæcenas in this niggard age
Guerdons they sonns of Muses and of skill.   1095
My joyless minde foretells this sad event,
That learning needs muste leave this duller clime
To be possest by rude simplicitie,
And thither hasten with a nimble winge
Where arts doe florishe like the gaudy springe.   1100
Too longe sweet birds have carrolde in our woodes,
Too longe they nightingales have jo[y]de our groves,

If thus they be rewarded with disdayne.
Hencfoorth night-ravens nessle in our trees,
And scrichinge owles dwell in those leavie cages   1105
Where erst did chaunt they springtime's prettie pages!
Never dare anie boulde attemptinge pen
Seeke to expell the Tyrant of the northe,
Rough Barbarisme, that in those ackhorns[1] times
Commanded our whole ilande as his owne.   1110
But stay, my tounge! too lavish of her tearmes!
Pray God the times be faultie of this ill!
I feare mee, I, the times be innocent,
While guile doth cleave to theire unstayed youthe,
In trewantinge there time, wastinge whole years,   1115
Without or feedinge time or harvest hope.
Howe ere it be, blameworthy am not I,
That cared for them with a wakefull eye.
Litell I have; that litell muste mantaine
That litell scene of life which doth remaine.   1120
My soule ere longe will leave this house of clay,
Death's nighte will come, and ende my livinge daye.

Exit.

ACTUS 4. SCOENA 1.

GULLIO. INGENIOSO.

Gull. The Countess and my lorde entertayned mee veric honorablely. Indeede they used my advise in some state matters, and I perceyved the Earle woulde faine have thruste one of his daughters upon mee; but I will have noe knave priste to medle with my ringe. I bestowed 20 angells upon the officers of the house att my departure, kist the Countess, tooke my leave of my lorde, and came awaye. 1129

Ingen. (I thinkes he meanes to poyson mee with a lie! Why he is acquainted with nere a lorde except my lorde

---

[1] *Qu.* Acheron's?

Coulton, and for Countesses, he never came in the cuntrie
where a Countess dwells!) Faith, Sir, I must needs commende youre generous high spirit that cannot endure to be
stinted to one, though shee were a goddess, consideringe
that there are soe manie ladies that sue for youre favoure.

Gull. I thinke there is such a sayinge in Homer—*ut
ameris amabilis esto,* that is, be a complet gentleman, and
they ladies will love thee ; howsoever prating Tullie in his
poem saith, *Cum amarem eram miser,* when I loved I was
a drivell ; yet he was well taunted by another poet in this
goulden sayinge, *vir sapit qui parum loquitur,* that is,
Tullie might have houlde his peace with more honestie.
True it is that Ronzarde spake—*Thi pecora si pha illupola
mangia,* which I thus translated—*Quisquis amat ranam,
ranam putat esse Dianam,* and thus extempore into Englishe,   1147
     What man soever loves a crane
     The same he thinkes to be Diane.
A dull universitie's heade woulde have bene a month
aboute thus muche !

Ingen. Is it possible you should utter such highe
spirited poettrie without premeditation?   1153

Gull. As I am a gentleman and a scholler, it was but a
suddaine flash of my invention. It is my custome in my
common talke to make use of my readinge in the Greeke,
Latin, French, Italian, Spanishe poetts, and to adorne my
oratorye with some prettie choice extraordinarie sayinges.
But have youe finished those verses in an ambrosiall
veyne that must kiss my mistris' daintie hande? I'le nowe
steale some time from my weightie affayres to peruse
them.   1162

Ingen. Yes, Sir, I have made them in there severall
vaynes. Lett them be judged by youre elegante cares, and
soe acquitted or condemned.

Gull. Lett mee heare Chaucer's vaine firste. I love antiquitie, if it be not harshe.

Ingen. Even as the flowers in the coulde of night
    Yclosed slepen in there stalkes lowe,
    Red ressen them the sunne brighte   1170
    And spreaden in theire kinde course by rowe,
    Right soe mine eyne, when I up to thee throwe
    They bene yclear'd; therfore, O Venus deare,
    Thy might, thy grace, yheried be it here.

    Nor scrivener nor craftilie I write,   1175
    Blott I a litell the paper with my tears,
    Nought might mee gladden while I endite
    But this poore scroule that thy name ybears.
    Go, blessed scroule! a blisfull destinie
    Is shapen thee,—my lady shalt thou see.   1180

    Nought fitteth mee in this sad thinge I feare
    To usen jolly tearmes of meriment;
    Solemne tearmes better fitten this mattere
    Then to usen tearmes of good content.
    For if a painter a pike woulde painte   1185
    With asse's feet and headed like an ape,
    It cordeth not; soe were it but a jape.

Gull. Noe more! nowe, in my discreet judgment, this I judge of them, that they are dull, harshe and spiritless; my mistris will soone finde them not to savoure of my sweet vayne. Besides, thers a worde in the laste canto which my chaste Ladye will never endure the readinge of. Thou shouldest have insinuated soe much, and not toulde it plainlye. What is becomne of arte? Well, dye when I will, I shall leave but litell learninge behinde mee upon the earthe! Well, those verses have purchast my implacable anger; lett mee heare youre other vayns.   1197

Ingen. Sir, the worde as Chaucer useth it hath noe unhonest meaninge in it, for it signifieth a jeste.

Gull. Tush! Chaucer is a foole, and you are another for defendinge of him.

Ingen. Then you shall heare Spencers veyne.
A gentle pen rides prickinge on the plaine,
This paper plaine, to resalute my love. 1204

. *Gull.* Stay, man! thou haste a very lecherous witt; what wordes are these? Though thou comes somwhat neare my meaninge yet it doth not become my gentle witt to sett it downe soe plainlye Youe schollers are simple felowes, men that never came where ladies growe; I that have spente my life amonge them knowes best what becometh my pen and theire ladishipps ears. Let mee heare Mr. Shakspear's veyne. 1212

Ingen. Faire Venus, queene of beutie and of love,
Thy red doth stayne the blushinge of the morne,
Thy snowie necke shameth the milkwhite dove,
Thy presence doth this naked worlde adorne;
Gazinge on thee all other nymphes I scorne.
When ere thou dyest slowe shine that Satterday,
Beutie and grace muste sleepe with thee for aye! 1219

Gull. Noe more! I am one that can judge accordinge to the proverbe, *bovem ex unguibus*. Ey marry, Sir, these have some life in them! Let this duncified worlde esteeme of Spencer and Chaucer, I'le worshipp sweet Mr. Shakspeare, and to honoure him will lay his Venus and Adonis under my pillowe, as wee reade of one (I doe not well remember his name, but I am sure he was a kinge) slept with Homer under his bed's heade. Well, I'le bestowe a Frenche crowne in the faire writinge of them out, and then I'le instructe thee about the delivery of them. Meanewhile I'le have thee make an elegant description of my mistris; liken the worste part of her to Cynthia; make also a familiar dialogue betwixt her and myselfe. I'le now in, and correct these verses. [*Exit.*

Ingen. Why, who coulde endure this post put into a sattin sute, this haberdasher of lyes, this bracchidochio, this ladyemunger, this meere rapier and dagger, this cringer, this foretopp, but a man that's ordayned to miserie! Well, madame *Pecunia*, one more for thy sake will I waite on this truncke, and with soothinge him upp in time will leave him a greater foole than I founde him.   [*Exit.*

Enter WARDEN.

Warden. Mass, maisters! the case is alterd with mee since I was here laste. They call mee noe more plaine 'Will,' nor 'William,' nor 'goodman Percevall,' but 'Mr. Warden,' at everye worde. Well, if yee please mee well you may happ make the bells speake sometime for this. But stay, I seeke our Sexton, and yonder he is. Now good Sexton, I am tirde as anie of my plage jades with enquiringe you. You shoulde have 'pearde 'fore Mr. Maior his maistershipp, for, wott you what? The parish have put up a subligation against you, and say you are the moste unnegligent Sexton that ever came these forty years and upwarde, for in Jenkin's dayes (well may the bons rest of the good ould Sexton!) the chauncell was kept in order, the church swept, and the bords rubde that thou mightest have scene youre face in them, and for my parte I never used other lookinge glass; well he woulde have gott our prelate hadle up service! Moreover they saye the bells are never tunge [1], and they complaine youe are too proude to whipp they doggs out, as youre predecessours have done. Thus much can I saye of mine owne knowledge, that since you were Sexton, the parish doggs have not been ashamed to beraye mine owne pue.   1262

Philo. But I pray youe, in breefe, what did they magistrats conclude of Philomusus?

---

[1] *Sic.*

Warden. Faith, Philomusus, ways mee for yee, gud ladd! ther's sorowfull tydings; you are out of office, and I was readie to crye to heare the sentence pronounced. Yet thus much of frenshipp, I bespoke you a pasport, least the clarigols att some town's ende catche you. Well, give mee upp youre keys, for I must begone. [*Exit.*

    Philom. Take them, for the[y] are better lost than
      founde!
That day I tooke them dyd my fortune frowne,
Yet may I see fortuns inconstancye
As well in this as in some dignitie.
Longe since I gave a farewell to good haps,   1275
And bade them cozen whom they woulde for mee;
I longe had bene there faithfull follower,
Yet reapt noe guerdon but disgrace of them.
Come, colde and scarcitie! for youe have bene
My faithfull bedfelowes this manie a yeare,   1280
And kept mee companie in sorrowe's bedd,
Where care hath chased slumbers quite away
That would have ceas'd upon my watchfull eyes.
Longe since my fortun's sunshine's bene eclypst
With foggie clouds and made as black as piche;   1285
Soe that I see my mournfull funerall
Of all good happs and faire felicitie.
My thoughts like mourners follow this my hearse,
My sobbs resounde like to a passinge bell,
And drearie sighes ring out my dolefull knell.   1290

            Enter STUDIOSO.

    Stud. And is it soe? will fortune nere have done?
Longe since I thought that shee had left mee quite
When shee had brought mee to this slaucrie,
But nowe I see shee hath more whipps in store
To scourge my corps and lash my galled sides.   1295
My bloominge flowers, which did daylie waite

            F

To be refreshed with an Aprill shower,
And promised some frutes in latter years,
Are nowe quite nipt with the chillie froste,
And blasted by the breath of Boreas.   1300
Thus, thus, alas! my winter now is come
Ere I had thought the springe time had bene done!
But who is this? Philomusus I see? he carries the oulde
characters of Melancholy in his face; I'le put him out of
his dumps! howe now, Philomusus, howe goes the worlde
with youe?   1306

Philo. Nere worse, and seldome better; one againe
I muste goe wander nowe from place to place,
Till it please Fortune take mee to her grace.

Stud. Art thou to seeke thy fortuns new againe?
And soe am I; Ile keepe thee companie,   1311
Till Fortune give us one a restinge place.
I thinke it is ordayned by destinie
That wee shoulde still match in adversitie.
But I pray thee, Philomusus, how did the parish fall out
with thee?   1316

Philom. I was put out by a stuttringe churchwarden
because I woulde not be a dogg whipper. The clowne
toulde mee suche an absurde tale, howe since I was Sexton
they doggs have not bene ashamed to bewray his seate.
But why shoulde I recite this drivell's speches? To
conclude, I am put out, and am sent away with a pasporte.
But tell mee, art thou put away nowe for whippinge thy
yonge M^r?   1324

Stud. Noe, not soe. I am putt out for a matter of less
importance; marry, because I would not suffer one of the
blew coates to pearch above mee at the latter dinner. My
yonge maister whome I taughte was verie forwarde to have
mee gone, and toulde his mother he never learned in a
greate booke since I came; my mistris with a shrill voice

cride, 'These schollers are proude, these schollers are
proude,' and sent mee packinge awaye.

Philom. Yea, every tawnye trull, each mincinge dame,
Each ambling minion, may commande the arts,
Kill a poore scholler with a suddaine frowne,   1335
Place or displace him as her humor goes.
Minerva, see! and shame to see thy sonns
Made servile druges to the female sex,
Of less repute than is each whislinge groome,
Each unrefined hinde, each start-upp clowne.   1340

Stud. It heats thy bloude, endeared Philomusus,
To see the happs of thy unhappie frendes.
It grieves my sp'rits to see thy great deserts
Soe litell guerdon'd by this thankless age.
The gapinge grave, they could dead carcasses   1345
Of more humanitie than livinge men,
Seemed alate to paye to thy poore stale
Some tribute pence for meaner mantenance.
Soe learning is of senseless things regarded,
Thoughe scarse of anie living wight rewarded.   1350

Philom. Well, Studioso, better happ befall thee
In whatsoever ayre thou livest or breathest.
I meane to change this heaven for another,
And finde or better happ or kinder grave.
Alter I will my soyle, but not my minde ;   1355
That lives with thee ; soe soules live where they love.
When as I treade upon a stranger earthe
I'le thinke on thee, and with a deepe breath'd sighe,
Recounte our springtime's hapless destinies :
Then straight a smile shall smooth my clouded browe,
Whiles hope perswads mee of thy happiness.[1]   1361

Stud. Nay, where thy happs be nipt my hopes must
    wither !

[1] 'pappiness' MS. !

The ayre that not rewards thee scorneth mee.
Then lett us flye together with a winge
Whither good starrs and happie fates us bringe.   1365

Philom. As I was loath to pull thee from thy frendes,
Distracte thee from thy cuntries sweet embrace,
To robb thy lipps from suckinge of that ayre
Where firste thou sawest the gawdye flatteringe light,
Soe nowe my partinge harte doth leape for joy,   1370
Since I shall have a mate for my longe waye
Whose talke will add winges to the tedious daye.

Stud. Come, let us caste our cards before wee goe,
Summon our losses if wee nere returne,
Cross our oulde cares, and turne the leafe anew,   1375
And, after, give our soyle a longe adewe!

Actus quarti finis.

ACTUS 5.   SCŒNA 1ᵈ.

GULLIO. INGENIOSO.

Gull. Howe nowe, Ingenioso, didest thou accordinge
to my direction deliver my letters?

Ingen. I did, if it please youre worshipp.

Gull. What answerr did faire Lesbia, the mistris of
thoughtes, returne mee?   1381

Ingen. Shee tooke youre letter, and red it over.

Gull. Then surely by this time shee is mightilie
enamour'd of mee.

Ingen. And after shee hadd redd over youre letter,
shee gave it mee againe, as if shee knew you not. 1386

Gull. Not knowe mee? You are a verie Jacke to mistake my mistris in that sorte! Suche an inhumane worde
coulde not proceede from the mouthe of my sweete mistris.

Noe less than a million of times have I participated unto
her both mercuriall and martiall discourses in the active
and chivalrous vaunt of Don Bellerephon! How often of
yore have I sunge my sonnets under her windowe to a consorte of musicke, I myselfe playinge upon my ivorie lute
moste enchantinglie!   1395

Ingen. (The divell of the musition is he acquainted with,
but onlye Jacke fidler!)

Gull. Whenc shoulde this chaunge of hers proceede?
canst thou gess?

Ingen. I cannot imagine, except that younge gallant
that stoode dallyinge with her be some rivall in youre love.

Gull. Have I a rivall? by Bellona my goddess, he
shoulde dye, coulde I meete with anie such audacious puny
longe cloke! I woulde make him not refuse the humblest
vassalage to the soale of my boots! But I warrant my
mistris mistooke! Indeede, I use not to sende on such
messages suche unmanerlye knaves as thyselfe. Thou
shouldst, accordinge to thy portion of witt, have described
unto her the perfections of my minde and bodie.   1409

Ingen. I gave you as sweet a reporte as was possible;
I sayde there is not a more compleat gentleman on the
earth; but all woulde not serve the turne: she gave youe
a *nescio*, and youre letter a scornefull smile.   1415

Gull. True it is that Virgill saithe,
Quid pluma levius? Flamen. Quid flamine? Ventus.
Quid vento? Mulier. Quid muliere? Nihil.   1416
These pulinge minions had rather have a carpett knighte a
capringe page, than a man of warr and a scholler! Ha, Ha,
see thee nowe! I smell it! It was youre duncerie wrought
mee this disgrace, and yet I adorn'd thy seely invention
with a prettie wittie Latinn sentence. Henceforthe I will
not norishe any such unlearned pedants. These universities
send not foorth a good witt in an age! I'le travell to Paris

myselfe, and there commence for *filius nobilis*, and converse
noe more with anie of our base English witts, which have
somwhat corrupped the generous spirit of my poetrie. As
for the sute, thy wittie lines have thus dishonoured mee,
thy Mæcenas here cassceeres thee, and dothe bequeath
thee to the travellinge trade.   1429

Ingen. Sir, it was not my lines but youre Lattin that
spoyled youre love markett. To say the truthe, I deliver'd
youre letter, and was rewarded with the tearmes of 'What,
youe saucye groome, are you bringinge mee such paper
wisps? from what sattin sute I pray you comes this? what
foretopp bewrayed this, this paper?' and when I named
you, 'What, Gullio, that knowne foole?' sayde shee.

Gull. Why, that's verie true, my fame is spread farr and
neare, but why saide shee that shee knew mee not?   1438

Ingen. Belike she was ashamed of you before her
gallant; but interrupt mee not. 'If it be his' (sayd shee)
I am sure not a worde of it proceeds from his pen but a
sentence of Lattin (which I was toulde is false): well, warne
him that hee looke to his rheumeticke witt; that he bespitt
paper pages noe more to mee; if he doe, I'le have some
porter or bearewoode to cudgell the vayne braggadochio.'

Gull. Peace, youe impecunious peasant! As I am a souldier, I was never so abus'd since I firste bore arms! What,
you vassall, if a lunaticke bawdie trull, a pocketinge
queane, detracte from my vertues, will thy audacious selfe
dare to repeate them in the presence of this blade? Were
it not that I will not file my handes upon suche a contemptible rascalde, and that I will not have my name in the
time to come, where myselfe shall be cronicled, disgraced
with the base victorie of such an earth worme, I woulde
prove it upon that carrion of thy witt, that my Lattin was
pure Lattin, and such as they speake in Rhems and Padua.
Why, it is not the custome in Padua to observe such base

ruls as Lilie, Priscian, and such base companions have sett
downe; wee of the better sorte have a priveledge to create
Lattin like knights, and to saye, Rise up, Sir Phrase. But,
Sirra, begone! thou haste moved my chollar; report of my
clemencie that in mine anger, contrarie to my custome,
[I] suffer thy contemptible carcass to possess thy cowadly
ghoste.   1464

Ingen. What, youe whorsonn *tintunabulum*, thou that
art the scorne of all good witts, the ague of all souldiers,
that never spokest wittie thinge but out of a play, never
hardest the reporte of a gun without tremblinge, why,
Mounsier Mingo, is youre asse's heade growne proude with
scratchinge? thinkest thou a man of art can endure thy
base usage?   1471

Gull. Terrence, thou art a gentleman of thy worde:
familiaritas parit contemptum! Sirra, Alexander did never
strive with anie but kinges, and Gullio will fight with none
but gallants. Farewell, base peasante, and thanke God thy
fathers were noe gentlemen; els thou shouldest not live an
houre longer. Base, base, base peasant, peasant! Soe hares
may pull deade lions by the bearde!   [*Exit*

Ingen. Farewell, base carle clothed in a sattin sute,
Farewell, guilte ass, farewell, base broker's poste!   1480
Too ofte have I rub'd over thy mule's dull head,
Fedd like a flie on thy corruption.
Nowe had I rather live in povertie
Than be tormented with the tedious talks
Of Gullio's wench and of his luxuries,   1485
To heare a thousand lies in one short day
Of his false warrs at Portingale or Calls.
My freer spirit did lie in tedious woe
Whiles it applauded bragging Gullio,
Applide my veyne to sottishe Gullio,   1490
Made wanton lines to please lewd Gullio.

Attend henceforth on Gulls for mee who liste,
For Gullio's sake I'le prove a Satyrist.

I heard that Studioso and Philomusus, discontented with
theire fortuns, meane to trye another ayre; they appointed
to call on mee at Gullio's chamber in Shordiche; I'le
thither, and truss upp my trincketts, and enquire after
them, that our fortuns may shake handes before they parte.
Then I'le goe to the press, they to the seas.   1499

SCŒNA 2.

Luxurio. Boy.

Lux. There is a beaste in India call'd a polecatt, that
the further shee is from youe the less she stinks and the
further she is from you the less you smell her. This dry
cuntrie is that polecatt, that creats such an unsavourie smell
in the noistrells of a liquid scholler, it's better nowe adayes
to be a mute than a liquidd, and a consonant cryer than a
voacall academicke.   1506

Boy. Why, Mr., are you growne melancholicke?

Lux. I' faith noe, boy! I have a jollie soule, that scorns
sorow; but I am in some choller with this asshcaded age,
where the honorable trade of ballet makinge is of such base
reckoninge; but soe it hath bene in ancient time, when
Homer first sett up his riminge shopp, one of the firste that
ever was of my trade.

Boy. Why, was Homer of our trade? I tooke him to
have bene a blinde harper.   1515

Lux. Blinde he was indeede, and that is the onlie
difference betwixt us. And ere longe I'le drincke out
mine eyes, and then be as true a Homer as μῆνιν ἄειδε θεά.
He was poore in his life, I was as veric a beggar as hee for
his soule. No man carde for him in his life time, I am sure
I am in as litell reckoninge as he for his life. Scaven

cuntries strove about him when he was deade, and I doubt
not when I am made tapster of the lower cuntries, and the
workes of my witt left behinde mee here upon earthe,
manie a towne will chalenge unto itselfe the creditt of my
birthe. Howsoever now I am a plaine *Si nihil attuleris, ibis,
Homere, foras;* noe pennie, noe pott of ale.   1527

Boy. Indeed, Sir, noe doubt but that cuntries will miss
youe when youe are gone; when they shall have a calfe
with 5 feet, see a hare at a crosslande, here a pye chatter
or a raven sitt uppon the top of a new kitchen, they shall
want there oulde poet to emparte it to the worlde, and
there younge Ismenias to singe it at a stall. They maidens
shall want sonnets at there pales, and they cuntrie striplings
ditties to sing at the maydes windowes; the cart-horses will
goe discontented for want of there wonted musicke, and the
cowes lowe for the want of there Luxurio. But as for
youre tapstershipp in hell, it were a good office in soe
whott a place; and unless youe provide youe some such
place, youre drye soule will quicklie will[1] be out of drincke.

Lux. I' faith, well saide! I meane to drincke the worlde
drye before I leave it, and not leave soe muche as the
element of water for generation. Let us loiter noe longer,
leaste the clarigoles catche us, but travell towards our
frends, to be kept like honeste oulde beggars by the parishe.
Farewell, daintie poetrie, I kiss my hande, and humblie take
my leave of thee; thou art but a ragged patroness, and soe
I leave thee.   1548

Boy. Shee makes her followers ragged, and soe shee
leavs them. But lett us marche forwarde to the confusion
of these cellars, which our thristie[1] soules shall besiege.

Lux. Farewell, thou mustie worlde! I meane to beare
   no coals,   1553
And therfore will I straight drincke out these seeinge holes.

---

[1] *Sic.*

Boy. Farewell, thou impecunious clyme! Luxurio and
　　his page
Will beggars prove elsewheare, and run from thee in rage.

　　　　　　　　　　　　　　　　　　[Exeunt.

　　　　　　　　SCŒNA 3.

　　　　INGENIOSO. STUDIOSO. PHILOMUSUS.

　Ingen. Nay, sighe not, men! laughe at the foolish
　　worlde;
They have the shame, though wee the miserie.
Strange regions well may scoff at our rude clyme,
And other schools laugh at Parnassus' hill,　　　　1560
That better doe rewarde each scrivener's pen,
Each tapster's cringe, each rubbinge ostler,
Than those that live like anchors in a mue
And spend there youthe in contemplation,
Bycause they woulde refine the ruder worlde,　　　1565
And rouse the souls in clayie cottages.

　Stud. Schollars cride longe agoe, the worlde was
　　naught!
And yet, like Marius' mules, they laboure still
To get these arts, these poore contemned arts,
As though they studied with a wakefull eye　　　1570
To goe the nearest way to povertie.

　Philom. I'le spende noe treuan breath in this stale
　　theame!
Full ofte have I chid this unkinder worlde,
Tould groves and murmuringe brooks of this sad tale,
Rated my luck, my thwartinge destinie,
That train'd mee upp in learninge's vanitie.　　　1576

　Ingen. Rayle wee for care, asses will folowe kinde,
A fox may change his heyre but not his minde.

　Stud. Yea, Midas' brood fore care must honoured be,
While Phœbus followers live in miserie.　　　　1580

Philom. Nor envie I each painted dunghill store:
A scholler is alwayes better than a bore.

Ingen. Well, fawne the worlde or frowne, my wit
   mantaine mee;
The press shall keepe me from base beggarie.

Stud. To Rome or Rhems I'le hye, led on by fate,
Where I will ende my dayes or mende my state.   1586

Philom. And soe will I; heard-hearted clyme, farewell!
In regions farr I'le thy unkindness tell.

Ingen. If schollers' wants would end with our short
   scene,
Than should our litell scene end more content.   1590

Stud. But schollers still must live in discontent;
What reason than our scene shoulde end content?

Philom. Till then our acts some happier fortuns see,
We'le banish from our stage all mirth and glee.

Ingen. Whatever schollers

Stud.   discontented be   1595

Philom. Let none but them

All.   give us a *Plaudite.*

PLAUDITE.

THE

RETVRNE FROM PERNASSVS:

OR

THE SCOURGE OF SIMONY.

Publiquely acted by the Students in Saint Iohns Colledge in Cambridge.

———◆— ⋯⋯—

[The bracketed words are the corrections adopted from Mr. Halliwell-Phillipps' MS. The list of characters follows the prologue in the printed copies.]

———◆———

· 𝕿𝖍𝖊 𝕹𝖆𝖒𝖊𝖘 𝖔𝖋 𝖙𝖍𝖊 𝕬𝖈𝖙𝖔𝖗𝖘.

Dramatis Persona.

[Boy, Stagekeeper, and two other in the Prologue.]

INGENIOSO.	AMORETTO.
IUDICIO.	Page.
DANTER.	Signor IMMERITO.
PHILOMUSUS.	STERCUTIO, his father.
STUDIOSO.	Sir FREDERICK [2].
FUROR POETICUS.	Recorder.
PHANTASMA.	Page.
Patient.	PRODIGO.
RICHARDETTO [1].	BURBAGE.
THEODORE, phisition.	KEMPE.
Burgesse, patient.	Fidlers.
IAQUES, STUDIOSO.	Patients man.
ACADEMICO.	

[1] Rhicardetto, *A.*

[2] In the printed text this name is always afterwards given as *Raderick.* "Sir Randall," MS.

THE PROLOGUE.

Boy, Stagekeeper, Momus, Defensor.

Boy.   Spectators we will act a Comedy (*non plus*).

Stage.   A pox on't this booke hath it not in it, you would be whipt, [you[1]] raskall[2]: [you] must be sitting vp all night at cardes, when [you] should be conning your[3] part.   5

Boy.   Its all long [of[4]] you, I could not get my part a night or two before that I might sleepe on it.

Stagekeeper carrieth the boy away vnder his arme.

Mo.   It's euen well done, here is such a stirre about a scuruie English show.   9

Defen.[5]   Scuruy in thy face, thou scuruie Jack, if this company were not, you paultry Crittick,[6] [Gentlemen,[7]] you that knowe what it is to play at primero, or passage, you that haue beene deepe students at post and paire, saint[8] and Loadam. You that haue spent all your quarters reueneues in riding post one night in [9]Chrismas, beare with the weake memory of a gamster.   16

Mo.   Gentlemen you that can play at noddy, or rather play vpon nodies: you that can set vp a icast, at primero[10] insteed of a rest, laugh at the prologue that was taken away in a voyder.   20

Defen.   What we present I must needes confesse is but slubbered inuention: [but] if your wisedome [obserue][11] the circumstance, your kindenesse will pardon the substance.   24

Mo.   What is presented here, is an old musty show, that hath laine this twelue moneth in the bottome of a

---

[1] 'thou,' edits.   [2] 'rakehele,' MS.   [3] 'thy,' B.   [4] 'on,' edits.
[5] *'Defender of the Play was non plus,'* MS.   [6] 'crickhett,' MS.   [7] 'Gentleman,' edits.   [8] 'sanul,' MS.   [9] The last line is lost in the MS.
[10] 'priemero,' B; 'primero or passage,' MS.   [11] 'obscure,' edits.

coalehouse amongst broomes and old shooes, an inuension
that we are ashamed of, and therefore we haue promised
the Copies to the Chandlers to wrappe his candles in.   29

Defen. It's but a Christenmas[1] toy, and [so] may it
please your curtisies to let it passe.

Mom. Its a Christmas toy indeede, as good a conceit
as [stanging[2]] hotcockles, or blinde-man buffe.

Defen. Some humors you shall see aymed at, if not
well resembled.   35

Mom. Humors indeede: is it not a pretty humor to
stand hammering vpon two *indiuiduum vagum*[3] 2. schollers some whole[4] yeare. These same *Phil* and *Studio*:
haue beene followed with a whip, and a verse like a Couple
of Vagabonds through *England* and *Italy*. The Pilgrimage
to *Pernassus*, and the returne from *Pernassus* haue stood
the honest *Stagekeepers* in many a Crownes expence for
linckes[5] and vizards: purchased [many] a Sophister a knock
[with[6]] a clubbe: hindred the buttlers box, and emptied
the Colledge barrells; and now vnlesse you know the
subiect well[7] you may returne home as wise as you came,
for this last is the [last[8]] part of the returne from *Pernassus*,
that is[9] the last time that the Authors wit wil turne vpon
the toe in this vaine, and at this time the scene is not at
Pernassus, that is, lookes not good inuention in the
face.   51

Defen. If the Catastrophe please you not, impute it to
the vnpleasing fortunes of discontented schollers.

Mom. For Catastrophe ther's neuer a tale in sir *Iohn
Mandeuil*, or *Beuis* of *Southampton* but hath a better
turning.   56

---

[1] 'Christmas,' B.   [2] 'slauging,' edits.   [3] *ind. vag.* omitted in MS.
[4] 'foure,' MS.   [5] 'torches,' MS.   [6] 'which,' edits.   [7] 'unless
you have heard the former,' MS.   [8] 'least,' edits.   [9] 'both the first
and,' inserted in edits.

Stagekeeper. What you ieering asse, be gon with a pox.

Mom. You may doe better to busy your selfe in prouiding beere, for the shew will be pittifull drie, pittifull drie.   [*Exit.*

[*Defen*]. *No more of this, I heard the spectators aske for a blanke verse*[1].

What[ear] we shew, is but a Christmas iest,
Conceiue of this and guesse of[2] all the rest :   65
Full like a schollers haplesse fortunes pen'd,
Whose former griefes seldome haue happy end,
Frame[n] aswell, we might with easie straine,
With far more praise, and with as little paine.
Storyes of loue, where forne the wondring bench,   70
The lisping gallant might inioy his wench.
Or make some Sire acknowledge his lost sonne,[3]
Found when the weary act is almost done.
Nor vnto this, nor [that is our scene] bent,[4]
We onely shew a schollers discontent.   75
In Scholers fortunes twise forlorne and dead
Twise hath our weary pen earst laboured.
Making them Pilgrims [to[5]] *Pernassus* hill,
Then penning their returne with ruder quill.
Now we present vnto each pittying eye,   80
The schollers progresse in their misery.
Refined wits[6] your patience is our blisse,
Too weake our scene : too great your[7] iudgment is.
To you we seeke to shew a schollers state,
His scorned fortunes, his vnpittyed fate.   85
To you : for if you did not schollers blesse,
Their case (poore case) were too too pittilesse.

---

[1] The first twelve lines of this speech are in the MS. transposed to the end.
[2] 'at,' MS.   [3] 'Perhaps alluding to *Patient Grissill*, a comedy, 1603.' Malone.   [4] 'nor vnto that our scene is bent,' edits.   [5] 'in,' edits.
[6] 'spirrits,' MS.   [7] 'our.' B.   [8] 'made,' B.

You shade the muses vnder fostering,
And make[1] them leaue to sigh, and learne to sing.

ACTUS 1. SCENA 1.

INGENIOSO, *with Iuuenall in his hand.*

Difficile est, Satyram non scribere, nam quis iniquæ   90
Tam patiens vrbis, tam [*ferreus*[2]] *vt teneat se?*
I, Iuuenall: thy ierking hand is good,
Not gently laying on, but fetching bloud,
So surgean-like thou dost with cutting heale,
Where nought but lanching can the wound auayle.   95
O suffer me, among so many men,
To tread aright the traces of thy[3] pen.
And light my linke at thy eternall flame,
Till with it I brand euerlasting shame
On the worlds forhead, and with thine owne spirit,   100
Pay home the world according to his merit.
Thy purer soule could not endure to see,
Euen smallest spots of base impurity:
Nor[4] could small faults escape thy cleaner hands.
Then foule faced Vice was in his swadling bands,   105
Now like *Anteus* growne a monster is,
A match for none but mighty *Hercules.*
Now can the world practise in playner guise,
Both sinnes of old and new borne villanyes.
Stale sinnes are [stale[5]]: now doth the world begin   110
To take sole pleasure in a witty sinne.
Vnpleasant is[6] the lawlesse sinne has bin,
At midnight rest, when darknesse couers sinne.
It's Clownish vnbeseeming a young Knight,
Vnlesse it dare out-face the [glaring[7]] light.   115

---

[1] 'made,' B.   [2] 'furens,' edits.   [3] 'my,' MS.   [4] 'For,'
MS., incorrectly.   [5] 'stole,' edits.   [6] *qu.* 'as'?   [7] 'gloring,' edits.

Nor can it ['mongst[1]] our gallants praises reape,
Vnlesse it be [y]done in staring Cheape
In a sinne-guilty Coach not cloasely pent,
Iogging along the harder pauement.
Did not feare check my repining sprit,　　　　　120
Soone should my angry ghost a story write,
In which I would new fostred sinnes combine,
Not knowne earst by truth telling *Aretine.*

SCENA 2.

Enter[2] INGENIOSO, IUDICIO.

Iud. What, *Ingenioso*, carrying a Vinegar bottle about thee, like a great schole-boy giuing the world a bloudy nose ?

Ing. Faith, *Iudicio*, if I carry [a[3]] vineger bottle, it's great reason I should confer it vpon the bald pated world : and againe, if my kitchen want the vtensilies of viands, it's great reason other men should haue the sauce of vineger, and for the bloudy nose, *Iudicio*, I may chance indeed giue the world a bloudy nose, but it shall hardly giue me a crakt crowne, though it giues other Poets French crownes.

Iud. I would wish thee, *Ingenioso*, to sheath thy pen, for thou canst not be successefull in the fray, considering thy enemies haue the aduantage of the ground.　　　　　135

Ing. Or rather, *Iudicio*, they haue the grounds with aduantage, and the French crownes with a pox, and I would they had them with a plague too : but hang them swadds, the basest corner in my thoughts is too gallant a roome to lodge them in ; but say, *Iudicio*, what newes in your presse, did you keepe any late corrections vpon any tardy pamphlets ?　　　　　142

Iud. Veterem iubes renouare dolorem. Ingenioso, what ere

---

[1] 'nought,' edits.　　[2] ' Iud.' inserted wrongly in both editions.　　[3] 'the,' edits.

[befall[1]] thee, keepe thee from the trade of the corrector of the presse. 145

Ing. Mary so I will, I warrant thee, if pouerty presse not too much, Ile correct no presse but the presse of the people.

Iud. Would it not grieue any good [spiritt[2]] to sit a whole moneth nitting [over[3]] a lousie beggarly Pamphlet, and like a needy Phisitian to stand whole yeares, tossing[4] and tumbling the filth that falleth[5] from so many draughty inuentions as daily swarme in our printing house? 152

Ing. Come (I thinke) we shall haue you put·finger in the eye and cry, *O friends, no friends*[6], say man, what new paper hobby horses, what rattle babies are come out in your late May morrice daunce?[7] 156

Iud. Slymy rimes[8] as thick as flies in the sunne, I thinke there be neuer an [ale[9]]-house in England, not any so base a maypole on a country greene, but sets forth some poets petternels or demilances to the paper warres in Paules Church-yard. 161

Ing. And well too may the issue of a strong hop learne to hop all ouer England, when as better wittes sit like lame coblers in their studies. Such barmy heads wil alwaies be working, when as sad vineger wittes sit souring at the bottome of a barrell : plaine Meteors, bred of the exhalation of Tobacco, and the vapors of a moyst pot, that [soare[10]] vp into the open ayre, when as sounder wit keepes[11] belowe.

Iud. Considering the furies of the times, I could better endure to see those young Can quaffing hucksters shoot of [ſ] their pellets so they would keepe them from these Eng-lish *flores-poetarum*, but now the world is come to that passe, that there starts vp euery day an old goose that sits hatching

---

[1] 'befalls,' edits.   [2] 'spirits,' edits.   [3] 'out,' edits.   [4] 'tooting,' MS.
[5] 'which hath fallen,' MS.   [6] 'A parody on "O eyes, no eyes"; *Span. Trag.*'
Malone.   [7] 'late morrice edition,' MS.   [8] 'rimers,' MS.; 'Flye my
rimes,' B.   [9] 'All,' A.   [10] 'soure,' edits.   [11] 'witts keepe,' MS.

vp those eggs which haue ben filcht from the nest[s] of
Crowes and Kestrells: here is a booke *Ing*: why to con-
demne it to [*Cloaca*[1]] the vsuall Tiburne of all misliuing
papers, were too faire a death for so foule an offender. 177

Ing. What's the name of it, I pray thee *Iud*.?

Iud. Looke [heere, its cald] *Beluedere*[2].

Ing. What a bel-wether in Paules Church-yeard, so cald
because it keeps a bleating, or because it hath the tinckling
bel of so many Poets about the neck of it ? what is the rest
of the title?

Iud. *The garden of the Muses*.

Ing. ["What have we here? The Poett garish   185
Gayly bedeckt like forehorse[3] of the Parish."]
what followes?

Iud. *Quem referent musæ, viuet dum robora tellus,*
Dum cælum stellas, dum vehit amnis aquas.

[*Ing*.] Who blurres fayer paper with foule bastard rimes,
Shall liue full many an age in latter[4] times :   191
Who makes a ballet for an ale-house doore,
Shall liue in future times for euer more.
Then [Bodenham[5]] thy muse shall live so[6] long,
As drafty ballats to [the paile[7]] are song.   195
But what's his deuise? Parnassus with the sunne and the
lawrel : I wonder this owle dares looke on the sunne, and
I maruaile this go[o]se flies not ; the laurell?[8] his deuise
might haue bene better a foole going into the market place
to be seene, with this motto, *scribimus indocti*, or a poore
beggar gleaning of eares in the end of haruest, with this
word, *sua cuique gloria*.   202

Iud. Turne ouer the leafe, *Ing*: and thou shalt see the

---

[1] 'cleare,' edits.   [2] 'Looke, its here Belvedere,' edits.   [3] 'horses,
edits. The arrangement of the lines is from the MS.   [4] 'after,' MS.
[5] '"Antony," i.e. Antony Mundy, the eulogist of *Belvidere*"; Malone, incorrectly, as the MS. shows.   [6] 'as,' MS.   [7] 'thy praise,' edits
[8] The punctuation is from the MS.

paynes of this worthy gentleman, Sentences gathered out of
all kind of Poetts, referred to certaine methodicall heads,
profitable for the vse of these times[1], to rime vpon any
occasion at a little warning: Read the names.   207

    Ing.   So I will, if thou wilt helpe me to censure them.

Edmund Spencer.	*Michaell Drayton.*
Henry Constable.	*Iohn Dauis.*
Thomas Lodge.	*Iohn Marston.*
Samuel Daniell.	*Kit: Marlowe.*
Thomas Watson.	

Good men and true, stand togither : heare your censure,
what's thy iudgement of *Spencer* ?   215

    Iud.   A sweeter[2] Swan then euer song in Poe,
A shriller Nightingale then euer blest
The prouder groues of selfe admiring Rome.
Blith was each vally, and each sheapeard proud,
While he did chaunt his rurall minstralsie.   220
Attentiue was full many a dainty care.
Nay, hearers hong vpon his melting tong,
While sweetly of his Faiery Queene he song,
While to the waters fall he tun'd [her[3]] fame,
And in each barke engrau'd[4] Elizaes name.   225
And yet for all this, vnregarding soile
Vnlac't the line of his desired life,
Denying mayntenance for his deare releife.
Carelesse [ere[5]] to preuent his exequy,
Scarce deigning to shut vp his dying eye.   230

    Ing.   Pity it is that gentler witts should breed,
Where thick skin chuffes laugh at a schollers need.
But softly may our [Homer's[6]] ashes rest,
That lie by mery *Chaucers* noble chest.

    But I pray thee proceed breefly in thy censure, that I

---

[1] 'this time,' MS.   [2] 'swifter,' B.   [3] 'for,' edits.   [4] 'endore't,' MS.
[5] 'care,' edits.   [6] 'honours,' edits.

may be proud of my selfe, [if] as in the first, so in the
last, my censure may[1] iumpe with thine. *Henry Constable,
Samuel Daniell*[2], *Thomas Lodg, Thomas Watson.*

Iud. Sweete *Constable* doth take the [wandring[3]] care,
And layes it vp in willing prisonment :   240
Sweete hony dropping *Daniell*[4] doth[5] wage
Warre with the proudest big Italian,
That melts his heart in sugred sonneting.
Onely let him more sparingly make vse
Of others wit, and vse his owne the more :   245
That well may scorne base imitation.
For *Lodge* and *Watson*, men of some desert,
Yet subiect to a Critticks marginall.
Lodge for his oare in euery paper boate,
He that turnes ouer *Galen* euery day,   250
To sit and simper *Euphues* legacy.

Ing. Michael Drayton.

[*Iud.*[6]] *Draytons* sweete muse is like[7] a sanguine dy,
Able to rauish the rash gazers eye.   254

How[8] euer he wants one true note of a Poet of our
times, and that is this, hee cannot swagger it well in a
Tauerne, nor dominere in a hot house.

[*Ing.*[9]] *Iohn Dauis.*

[*Iud.*] Acute *Iohn Dauis*, I affect thy rymes,
That ierck[10] in hidden charmes these looser times :   260
Thy plainer verse, thy vnaffected vaine,
Is grac'd with a faire [end and sooping traine[11].]

Ing. Locke and *Hudson.*

---

[1] 'may' omitted in the MS., where the names that follow are given as the
beginning of Judicio's speech.   [2] 'S.D.,' B.   [3] 'wondring,' edits.
[4] 'D.,' B.   [5] 'may,' MS.   [6] Correctly inserted in MS.   [7] 'of,' MS.
[8] Incorrectly in the edits. assigned to Ingenioso.   [9] 'Iud.' edits.
[10] 'jerckt,' MS.   [11] 'Is grac't with a faire and a sooping trayne,' edits. ;
'Martiall and he may sitt upon one bench, Either wrote well, and either lov'd
his wench,' added in MS.

Iud. *Locke* and *Hudson*, sleepe you quiet shauers, among the shauings of the presse, and let your bookes lye in some old nookes amongst old bootes and shooes, so you may auoide [1] my censure.

Ing. Why then clap a lock on their feete, and turne them to commons.

         Iohn Marston.   270

Iud. What *Monsier Kynsader*, lifting vp your legge and pissing against the world, put vp man, put vp for shame.
[2] Me thinks he is a Ruffian in his stile,
Withouten bands or garters ornament,
He quaffes a cup of Frenchmans Helicon.   275
Then royster doyster in his oylie tearmes,
Cutts, thrusts, and foines at whomesoeuer he meets,
And strewes about Ram-ally meditations.
Tut, what cares he for modest close coucht termes,
Cleanly to gird our looser libertines.   280
Giue him plaine naked words stript from their shirts
That might beseeme plaine dealing *Aretine*:
I, there is one [3] that backes a paper steed
And manageth a pen-knife gallantly.
Strikes his poinado at a buttons breadth,   285
Brings the great battering ram of tearmes to towns
And at first volly of his Cannon shot,
Batters the walles of the old fustic world.

     Ing. Christopher Marlowe.

     Iud. *Marlowe* was happy in his buskind [4] muse,   290
Alas vnhappy in his life and end.
Pitty it is that wit so ill should dwell,
Wit lent from heauen, but vices sent from hell,

---

[1] 'may happ to avoyd,' MS.   [2] Assigned to 'Ingen.' in the MS.
'This is a description of Marlowe'; Malone. But *quære?* The lines beginning here are assigned in the MS. to Judicio, and appear to express his opinion of Marston, as in sequence to Ingenioso's.   [4] 'buskine,' B.

Ing. Our *Theater* hath lost, *Pluto* hath got,
A Tragick penman for a driery plot. 295
  Beniamin Iohnson [1].

Iud. The wittiest fellow of a Bricklayer in England.

Ing. A meere Empyrick, one that getts what he hath
by obseruation, and makes onely nature priuy to what he
indites. so slow an Inuentor that he were better betake
himselfe to his old trade of Bricklaying, a bould whorson,
as confident now in making a[2] booke, as he was in times
past in laying of a brick. 303
  William Shakespeare [3].

Iud. Who loues [not *Adons* loue, or *Lucrece* rape?[4]]
His sweeter verse contaynes hart [throbbing line[5]],
Could but a grauer subiect him content,
Without loues foolish lazy[6] languishment.

Ing. Churchyard.
Hath not *Shor's* wife, although a light skirts she, 310
Giuen him a chast long lasting memory?

Iud. No, all light pamphlets [one day[7]] finden shall,
A Churchyard and a graue to bury all.

Inge. Thomas [*Nash* [8]].

I, heare is a fellow, *Iudicio*, that carryed the deadly stock-
[ado] in his pen, whose muse was armed with a gagtooth
and his pen possest with *Hercules* furies[9].

Iud. Let all his faultes sleepe with his mournfull chest,
And [there[10]] for euer with his ashes rest.
His style was wittie, though [it[11]] had some gal[l], 320
Something[s] he might haue mended, so may all.
Yet this I say, that for a mother witt,
Few men haue euer seene the like of it.

[1] 'B.I.,' B. [2] 'of a,' MS. [3] Mis-spelt 'Shatespeare' in A.
[4] 'Who loves Adonis love or Lucre's rape,' edits. [5] 'robbing life,' edits.
[6] 'lazy' omitted in B. [7] 'once I,' edits. [8] 'Nashdo,' edits.
[9] 'the spiritte of Hercules furens,' MS. [10] 'then,' [11] 'he,' edits.

Ing.   *Reades the rest.*   324

Iud. As for these, they haue some of them beene the old hedgstakes of the presse, and some of them are at this instant the botts and glanders of the printing house. Fellowes that stande only vpon tearmes to serue the tearme [1], with their blotted papers, write as men go to stoole, for needes, and when they write, they write as a [boare [2]] pisses, now and then drop a pamphlet.   331

Ing. *Durum telum necessitas*, Good fayth they do as I do, exchange words for mony. I haue some traffique this day with *Danter*, about a little booke [3] which I haue made, the name of it is a Catalogue of *Cambrige* Cuckolds, but [4]this Beluedere, this methodicall asse, hath made me almost forget my time : Ile now to Paules Churchyard ; meete me an houre hence, at the signe of the Pegasus in Cheapside, and Ile moyst thy temples with a cuppe of Claret, as hard as the world goes,   *Ex.* IUDICIO.   340

ACTUS 1. *SCENA* 3.

Enter DANTER *the Printer.*

Ing. *Danter* thou art deceiued, wit is dearer then thou takest it to bee. I tell thee this libel of Cambridge has much [salt [5]] and pepper in the nose : it will sell sheerely vnderhand, when all [6] these bookes of exhortations and Catechismes, lie moulding on thy shopboard.   345

Dan. It's true, but good fayth M. *Ingenioso*, I lost by your last booke ; and you knowe there is many a one that payes me largely for the printing of their inuentions, but for all this you shall haue 40 shillings and an odde pottle of wine.   350

---

[1] 'turne,' B.   [2] 'beare,' edits.   [3] 'a libell,' MS.   [4] The rest of this speech is assigned in the MS to Judicio.   [5] 'fat,' edits. [6] 'when as,' MS.

Inge. 40 Shillings? a fit reward for one of your reuma-
tick poets, that beslauers all the paper he comes by, and
furnishes the Chaundlers with wast papers to wrap candles
in : but as for me, Ile be paid deare euen for the dreggs
of·my wit : little knowes the world what belong[s] to the
keeping of a good wit in waters, dietts, drinckes, Tobacco,
&c. it is a dainty and costly creature, and therefore I must
be payd sweetly: furnish mee with mony, that I may
put my selfe in a new sute of clothes, and Ile sute thy
shop with a new suite of tearmes : it's the gallantest Child
my inuention was euer deliuered off.　The title is, a
Chronicle of Cambrige Cuckolds : here a man may see,
what day of the moneth such a mans commons were in-
closed, and when throwne open, and when any entayled
some odde crownes vpon the heires of their bodies vnlaw-
fully begotten : speake quickly, ells I am gone.　　　366

Dan. Oh this will sell gallantly: Ile haue it whatsoeuer
it cost, will you walk on, M. *Ingenioso*, weele sit ouer a cup
of wine and agree on it.

Ing. A cup of wine is as good a Constable as can be, to
take vp the quarrell betwixt vs.　　　　　　*[Exeunt.*

ACTUS 1.　SCENA 4.

PHILOMUSUS *in a Phisitions habite :* STUDIOSO *that is* IAQUES
man [1], *And patient.*

Phil.　Tit tit tit, non poynte, non debet fieri phlebetomotio [2]
in coitu lunæ : here is a Recipe.

Pat. A Recipe.　　　　　　　　　　　　　374

Phil. Nos [Gallici [3]*] non curamus quantitatem sylla-
barum :* Let me heare how many stooles you doe make.
Adeiu mounseir, adeiu good mounseir, what [4] *Iaques, Ihn'a
personne apres icy ?*

---

[1] 'Studioso like his man,' MS.　　[2] 'phlebotomatio,' MS.　　[3] 'Gallia,'
edits.　　[4] 'what how,' MS.

Stud. Non.

Phil. Then let vs steale time [from[1]] this borrowed
   shape,   380
Recounting our vnequall haps of late.
Late did the Ocean graspe vs in his armes,
Late did we liue within a stranger ayre:
Late did we see the cinders of great Rome.
We thought that English fugitiues there eate   385
Gold, for restoratiue, if gold were meate,
Yet now we find by bought experience,
That where so ere we wander vp and downe,
On the rounde shoulders of this massy world,
Or our ill fortunes, or the worlds ill eye,   390
Forspeake our good, procures our misery.

Stud. So oft the Northe[r]n winde with frozen wings,
Hath beate the flowers that in our[2] garden grewe:
Throwne downe the stalkes of our aspiring youth,
So oft hath winter nipt our trees faire rinde,   395
That now we seeme nought but two bared boughes,
Scorned by the basest bird that chirps in groaue.
Nor Rome, nor Rhemes, that wonted are to giue
A Cardinall['s] cap, to discontented clarkes,
That haue forsooke the[ir] home-bred [thatched[3]] roofes,
Yeelded vs any equall maintenance: 401
And it's as good to starue mongst English swine,
As in a forraine land to beg and pine:

Phil[4]. Ile scorne the world that scorneth me againe.

Stud. Ile vex the world that workes me so much paine.

Phil. [Thy lame reuenging power[5],] the world well
   weenes.   406

---

[1] 'for,' edits.　　　[2] 'one,' A.　　　[3] 'thanked,' edits.　　　[4] This line
is given in the MS. to Studioso, and the names are consequently changed in all
the following lines, and apparently, from the subsequent reference to the
'capping of rimes,' correctly.　　　[5] 'Fly lame reuenging's power,' edits.

Stud. Flyes haue their spleene, each sylly ant his
teenes.

Phil. We haue the words, they the possession haue.

Stud. We all are equall in our latest graue. 409

Phil. Soon then: O soone may we both graued be.

Stud. Who wishes death, doth wrong wise destinie.

Phil. It's wrong to force life loathing men to breath.

Stud. It's sinne for[c] doomed day to wish thy death.

Phil. Too late our soules flit to their resting place.

Stud. Why mans whole life is but a breathing space.

Phil. A painefull minute seemes a tedious yeare.

Stud. A constant minde eternall woes will beare.

Phil. When shall our soules their wearied lodge forgoe?

Stud. When we haue tyred misery and woe.

Phil. Soone [then may fates this gayle deliuery[1]]
send vs. 420
[2]Small woes vex long, great woes [will] quickly end vs.

But letts leaue this capping of rimes, *Studioso*, and follow
our late deuise, that wee may maintaine our heads in
cappes, our bellyes in prouender, and our [hacks[3]] in sadle
and bridle : hetherto wee haue sought all the honest meanes
wee could to liue, and now let vs dare[4], *aliquid breuibus*
[*giaris[5] et*] *carcere dignum* : let vs run through all the lewd
formes of lime-twig purloyning villanyes : let vs proue
Cony-catchers, Baudes, or any thing, so we may rub out ;
and first my plot for playing the French Doctor, that shall
hold : our lodging stand[s] here [fitly[6]] in shooe lane, for if
our commings in be not the better, London may shortely

---

[1] 'may then fates this gale deliuer,' edits. Malone rightly conjectured what
the reading should be. [2] Assigned to 'Phil.' in MS. [3] 'backs,' edits.
[4] 'letts *audere*,' MS. [5] '*gracis*, and,' edits. The correct reading was
conjectured by Malone. [6] 'filthy,' edits. Malone again conjectured
rightly what the reading should be.

throw an old shooe after vs, and with those shredds of
French, that we gathered vp in our hostes house in *Paris,*
wee'l gull the world, that hath in estimation forraine
Phisitians, and if any of the hidebound bretheren of
Cambridge and Oxforde, or any of those Stigmatick
maisters of arte, that abused vs in times past, leaue their
owne Phisitians, and become our patients, wee'l alter quite
the stile of them, for they shall neuer hereafter write, your
Lordships most bounden : but your Lordships most
laxatiue.   442

Stud. It shalbe so, see [how[1]] a little vermine pouerty
altereth a whole milkie disposition.

Phil. So then my selfe streight with reuenge Ile [sate[2]]

Stud. Prouoked patience growes intemperate.

ACTUS 1. SCENA 5.

Enter RICHARDETTO, IAQUES *Scholler learning French.*

Iaq. How now my little knaue, *quelle nouelle mounseir.*

Richard. Ther's a fellow with a night cap on his head,
an vrinal in his hand, would faine speake with master
Theodore.   450

Iaq. *Parle Francoyes moun petit garsoun.*

[[3] *Richard.* *Il y a un home auec le bonnet de*   *la
teste et un urinell en la main qui veult parler Theodore.*

Iaq. *For bien.*

Theod. *Iaques alonus.*   *Exeunt.*]

---

[1] 'what,' edits.   [2] 'seate,' edits. Correctly altered by Malone.
[3] ' *Richard. Ily a vn homme aue le bonnet de*   *et vn vrinell in la mens,
que veut parler.*
Iaq. For bien. (' *Foc beieu,'* A.)   *La teste.*
Theod. Iaques, a bonus.   *Exeunt* THEODORE,' edits.

ACTUS 1. *SCENA* 6.

FUROR POETICUS : *and presently after enters* PHANTASMA.

FUROR POETICUS *rapt within contemplation.*

Fur. Why how now *Pedant Phœbus*, are you smoutching
Thalia on her tender lips? There hoie: pesant avant:
come Pretty short-nosd nimph; oh sweet *Thalia*, I do
kisse thy foote. What *Cleio*? O sweet *Cleio*, nay pray
thee do not weepe *Melpomene*. What *Vrania*, *Polimnia*,
and *Calliope*, let me doe reuerence to your deities.   461

PHANTASMA *puls him by the sleeue.*

Fur.[1] I am your holy swayne, that night and day,
Sit for your sakes rubbing my wrinkled browe,
Studying a moneth for on[e] [fitt] Epithete.
Nay siluer *Cinthia*, do not trouble me: 465
Straight will I thy *Endimions* storye write,
To which thou hastest me on [both] day and night.
You light[2] skirt starres, this is your wonted guise,
By glomy light perke out your doutfull heads:
But when *Don Phœbus* showes his flashing snout,   470
You are sky puppies, streight your light is out.

Phan. So ho, *Furor*.
Nay preethee good *Furor* in sober sadnes.

Furor. *Odi profanum vulgus et arceo.*

Phant. Nay sweet *Furor*, *ipsæ te Tytire pinus*,   475
Ipsi te fontes, ipsa hæc arbusta vocarunt.

Furor[3]. Who's that runs headlong on my quills sharpe
     point,
That wearyed of his life and baser breath,
Offers himselfe to an Iambicke verse.[4]

---

[1] In the MS. the three first lines are given (apparently more correctly) to
Phant., and *Furor's* speech recommences at 'Nay.'   [2] 'like,' MS.
[3] Wrongly placed on the preceding line in the editions.   [4] 'death,' suggested by Malone ; but the MS. has ' verse.'

Phant. *Si quoties peccant homines, sua fulmina mittat*
Iupiter, exiguo tempore inermis erit.   481

Fur. What slimie bold presumtious groome is he,
Dares with his rude audacious hardye chatt,
Thus seuer me from [skybredd[1]] contemplation?

Phant. *Carmina vel cælo possunt deducere lunam.* 485

Furor. Oh *Phantasma*: what my indiuiduall mate?

[*Phant.*] *O mihi post nullos Furor memorande sodales.*

Furor. Say whence comest thou? sent from what
     deytye?
From great *Apollo* or sly *Mercury*?

Phan. I come from [that[2]] litle Mercury, *Ingenioso*. For,
Ingenio pollet cui vim natura negauit.   491

Furor. Ingenioso?
He is a pretty inuenter of slight prose[3] :
But there's no spirit in his groaueling speach.
Hang him whose verse cannot out-belch the wind: 495
That cannot beard and braue *Don Eolus*,
That when the cloud of his inuention breakes,
Cannot out-cracke the scarr-crow thunderbolt.

Phan. Hang him I say[4], *Pendo pependi, tendo tetendi,*
pedo pepedi. Will it please you maister *Furor* to walke
with me? I promised to bring you to a drinking[5] in
Cheapside, at the signe of the nagges head, For,   502
Tempore lenta pati fræna docentur equi.

Furor. Passe the[e] before, Ile come incontinent.

Phan. Nay faith maister *Furor*, letts go togither,
Quoniam Conuenimus ambo.   506

Furor. [Let us[6]] march on vnto the house of fame :

---

[1] 'skibbered,' edits.   [2] 'the,' edits.   [3] 'slight inventor of base
prose,' MS.   [4] These four words are the end of *Furor's* speech in the MS.
[5] 'drinking Inne,' edits.   [6] 'Lett's,' edits.

There quaffing bowles of Bacchus bloud ful nimbly,
Endite a Tiptoe, strouting poesy.

They offer the way one to the other.

Phan. *Quo me Bacche rapis tui plenum,* 510

[*Furor.*] *Tu maior: tibi me est æquum parcre Menalca.*

ACT. SECUNDUS. SCENA 3[1].

Enter PHILOM. THEOD. *his patient the Burgesse, and his man
with his staffe*[2].

THEOD. *puts on his spectacles.*

Mounsciur here are *atomi Natantes*, which doe make shew
your worship to be as leacherous as a bull. *

Burg. Truely maister Doctor we are all men, [all men].

Theod. This vater is intention[3] of heate, are you not
perturbed with an ake in [your vace][4] or in your occiput.
I meane your head peece, let me feele the pulse of your
little finger. 518

Burg. Ile assure you [sir] M. *Theodour*, the pulse of
my head beates exceedingly, and I thinke I haue disturbed
my selfe by studying the penall statutes.

Theod. Tit, tit, your worship takes cares of[5] your
speeches. *O, couræ leues loquuntur, ingentes*[6] *stoupent*, it is
an Aphorisme in Galen.

Burg. And what is the exposition of that? 525

Theod. That your worship must take a *gland, vt emit-
tatur sanguis:* the signe is for[t] exccellent, for excellent.

Burg. Good maister Doctor vse mee gently, for marke
you Sir, there is a double consideration to be had of me:
first as I am a publike magistrate, secondly as I am a
priuate butcher: and but for the worshipfull credit of the

---

[1] *Sic.* [2] 'state,' A. [3] 'intation,' MS. [4] 'you race,' edits.
[5] 'for,' MS. [6] 'ingantes,' MS., apparently continuing to represent the
foreign pronunciation.

place, and office wherein I now stand and liue, I would not [so] hazard my worshipfull apparell, with a suppositor or a glister : but for the countenancing of the place, I must go oftener to stoole, for as a great gentleman told me of good experience [1] that it was the chiefe note of a magistrate, not to go to the stoole without a phisition.   537

Theo.   [2] *A, vous ettes vn gentell home vraiment*, what ho *Iaques, Iaques, don e vous ? vn fort gentel purgation for monsier Burgesse.*

Jaq.   *Vostre tres humble scruiture a vostre commande-ment.*

Theod.   *Donne vous vn gentell purge a Monsier Burgesse.* I haue considered of the crasis, and syntoma of your disease, and here is *vn fort gentell purgation per euacua-tionem excrementorum*, as we Phisitions vse to parlee.   546

Burg.   I hope maister Doctor you haue a care of the countryes officer. I tell you I durst not haue trusted my selfe with euery phisition, and yet I am not afraide for my selfe, but I would not depriue the towne of so carefull a magistrate.   551

Theod.   O monsier, I haue a singular care of your valetudo, it is requisite that the French Phisitions be learned and carefull, your English veluet cap is malignant and enuious.   555

Burg.   Here is maister Doctor foure pence your due, and eight pence my bounty, you shall heare from me good maister Doctor, farewell farewell, good maister Doctor.   559

Theod.   Adieu, good Mounsier, adieu good Sir mounsier. Then burst with teares [3] vnhappy graduate :
Thy fortunes [wayward still[4]] and backward bin :
Nor canst thou thriue by vertue, nor by sinne.

---

[1] 'a gentleman of good experience told me,' MS.   [2] This line is given in the MS. 'donnee vous un gentill purge a mounsieur Burgesse.'   [3] 'teene,' MS. [4] 'still wayward,' edits.

Stud. O how it greeues my vexed soule to see,
Each painted asse in chayre of dignitye :   565
And yet we grouell on the ground alone,
Running through euery trade, yet[1] thriue by none.
More we must act in this liues Tragedy.

  Phi. Sad is the plott, sad the Catastrophe.

  Stud. Sighs are the Chorus in our Tragedy.   570

  Phi. And rented thoughts continuall actors be.

  Stud. Woe is the subiect : *Phil.* earth the loathed stage,
Whereon we act this fained personage.
Mossy[2] barbarians the spectators be,
That sit and laugh at our calamity.   575

  Phil. Band be those houres when mongst the learned
      throng,
By Grantaes muddy bancke we whilome song,

  Stud. Band be that hill which learned witts adore,
Where earst we spent our stock and little store.

  Phil. Band be those musty mewes, where we haue
      spent   580
Our youthfull dayes in paled langu[i]shment.

  Stud. Band be those coesning arts that wrought our
      woe,
Making vs wandring *Pilgrimes* too and fro.

  Phil. And *Pilgrimes* must we be without reliefe,
And wheresoeuer we run there meets vs greefe.   585

  Stud. Where euer we tosse vpon this crabbed[3] stage
Griefe's our companion, patience be our page.

  Phil. Ah but this patience is a page of ruth,
A tyred Lacky to our wandering youth.   589

---

[1] 'but,' MS.   [2] In the margin is printed in italics 'most like,'
as apparently a 'various reading,' but the MS. has 'mossy.'
  [3] 'troubled,' MS.

ACTUS 2. SCENA 2.
ACADEMICO *solus.*

Acad. Faine would I haue a liuing, if I could tel how
to come by it. *Eccho.* Buy it.   591

Acad. Buy it fond Ecc[ho]? why thou dost greatly
mistake it. *Ecc.* stake it.

Stake it? what should I stake at this game of simony?
Ecc. mony.   595

What is the world a game, are liuings gotten by playing?
Eccho. Paying.

Paying? but say what's the nearest way to come by
a liuing?

Eccho. Giuing.[1]   600

Must his worships fists bee needs then oyled with Angells?
Eccho. Angels.

Ought his gowty fists then first with gold to be greased?
Eccho. Eased.

And it is then such an ease for his asses backe to carry
mony?   606
Eccho. I.

Will then this golden asse bestowe a vicarige guilded?
Eccho. Gelded.

What shall I say to good sir *Roderick*, that haue [no[2]]
gold here?   611
Eccho. Cold cheare.

Ile make it my lone request, that he wold be good
to a scholler.

Eccho. Choller.   615

Yea, will hee be cholerike, to heare of an art or a science?
Eccho. hence.

---

[1] The MS. omits the rest of this scene, adding here ' &c. &c. &c.'
[2] Correctly inserted in B.

Hence with liberal arts, what then wil he do with his chancel?

Eccho. sell.   620

Sell it? and must a simple clarke be fayne to compound then?

Eccho. pounds then.

What if I haue no pounds, must then my sute be proroagued?   625

Eccho. Roagued.

Yea? giuen to a Roague? shall an asse this vicaridge compasse?

Eccho. Asse.

'What is the reason that I should not be as fortunate as he?   631

Eccho. Asse he.

Yet for al this, with a penilesse purse wil I trudg to his worship.

Eccho. words cheape.   635

Wel, if he giue me good words, it's more then I haue from an *Eccho.*

Eccho. goe.

ACTUS 2. SCENA 3.

AMORETTO *with an Ouid in his hand.* IMMERITO.

Amor. Take it on the word of a gentleman thou cannot haue it a penny vnder, thinke ont, thinke ont, while I meditate on my fayre mistres.   641

Nunc sequor imperium magne Cupido tuum.

What ere become of this dull[1] thredbare clearke,

I must be costly in my mistresse's eye:

Ladyes regard not ragged company.   645

I will with the reuenewes of my chafred church,

---

[1] 'bare,' MS.

First buy an ambling hobby for my fayre:
Whose measured pace may teach the world to dance,
Proud of his burden when he gins to praunce:
Then must I buy a iewell for her care,   650
A Kirtle of some hundred crownes or more:
With these fayre giftes when I accompanied goe,
Sheele giue *Ioues* breakfast: *Sidny* tearmes it so.
I am her needle, she is my Adamant:
[Shee's a¹] fayre Rose, I her vnworthy pricke.   655

Acad. Is there no body heere will take the paines to
geld his mouth?

Amor. Sh[e]'s Cleopatra, I Marke Anthony,

Acad. No thou art a meere marke for good witts² to
shoote at: and in that suite thou wilt make a fine man
to dashe poore [clownes³] out of countenance.   661

Amor. She is my Moone, I her Endimion,

Acad. No she is thy shoulder of mutton, thou her
onyon: or she may be thy Luna [well], and thou her
Lunaticke.   665

Amor. I her *Æneas*, she my *Dido* is.

Acad. She is thy Io,⁴ thou her brazen asse,
Or she Dame *Phantasy* and thou her gull:
She thy *Pasiphae*, and thou her louing bull.

ACTUS 2. *SCENA* 4.

Enter IMMERITO, *and* STERCUTIO *his father.*

Ster. Sonne, is this the gentleman that sells vs the
liuing?   671

Im. Fy father, thou must not call it selling, thou must
say is this the gentleman that must haue the gratuito?

Acad. What haue we heere, old trupenny come to
towne, to fetch away the liuing in his old greasy slops?
then Ile none: the time hath beene when such a fellowe
medled with nothing but his plowshare, his spade, and
his hobnayles, and so to a peece of bread and cheese,
and went his way: but now these [scurvy] fellowes are
growne the onely factors for preferment.   680

Ster. O is this the grating gentleman, and howe many
pounds must I pay?

Im. O thou must not call them pounds, but thanks,
and harke thou father, thou must tell of nothing that is
done: for I must seeme to come cleere[1] to it.   685

Acad. Not pounds but thanks: see whether this simple
fellow that hath nothing of a scholler. but that the
draper hath blackt him ouer, hath not gotten the stile
of the time.   689

Ster. By my fayth, sonne, looke for no more portion.

Im. Well father, I will not, vppon this condition, that
when thou haue gotten me the gratuito of the liuing. thou
wilt likewise disburse a little mony to the bishops poser, for
there are certaine questions I make scruple to be posed in.

Acad. He meanes any question in Latin, which he
counts a scruple; oh this honest man could neuer abide
this popish tounge of Latine, oh he is as true an English
man as liues.

Ster. Ile take the gentleman now, he is in a good vayne,
for he smiles.   700

Amor. Sweete Ouid, I do honour euery page.

Acad. Good *Ouid* that in his life time, liued with[2] the
Getes, and now after his death conuerseth with a Bar-
barian.

---

[1] 'cleerely,' MS., which has 'you' for 'thou' in Immerito's speeches.
[2] 'among,' MS.

Ster. God bee at your worke Sir: my Sonne told me
you were the grating gentleman, I am *Stercutio* his
father Sir, simple as I stand here. 707

[*Amor.*[1]] Fellow, I had rather giuen thee an hundred
pounds, then thou should[st] haue put me out of my
excellent meditation[;] by the faith of a gentleman I
was [even] rapt in contemplation. 711

Im. Sir you must pardon my father, he wants bringing vp.

Acad. Marry it seemes he hath good bringing vp, when
he brings vp so much mony. 715

Ster. Indeed Sir, you must pardon me I did not
knowe you were a gentleman of the Temple before.

Amor. Well I am content in a generous disposition to
beare with country education, but fellow whats thy name?

Ster. My name Sir, *Stercutio* Sir. 720

Amor. Why then *Stercutio*, I would be very willing to
be the instrument to my father, that this liuing might be
conferred vpon your sonne: mary I would haue you know,
that I haue bene importuned by two or three seueral
Lordes, my Kinde cozins, in the behalfe of some Cambridge
man[2]: and haue almost engaged my word. Mary if I
shall see your disposition to be more thankfull then other
men, I shalbe very ready to respect kind natur'd men:
for as the Italian prouerbe speaketh wel, *Chi ha haura.*[3]

Acad. Why here is a gallant young drouer of liuings.

Ster. I beseech you sir speake English, for that is
naturall to me & to my sonne, and all our kindred, to
vnderstand but one language.

Amor. Why [then] thus in plaine english: I must be
respected with thanks. 735

---

[1] 'Acad.' edits., but evidently a misprint. [2] 'schollers,' MS. [3] The
last three words omitted in the MS.

Acad. This is a subtle tractiue [1], when thanks may be felt and scene.

Ster. And I pray you Sir, what is the lowest thanks that you will take?

Acad. The verye same Method that he vseth at the buying [2] of an oxe.   741

Amor. I must haue some odd sprinckling of an hundred pounds [or [3]] so, so I shall thinke you thankfull, and commend your sonne as a man of good giftes to my father.

Acad. A sweete world, giue an hundred poundes, and this is but counted thankfullnesse.   746

Ster. Harke thou Sir, you shall haue 80. thankes.

Amor. I tell thee fellow, I neuer opened my mouth in this kind so cheape before in my life. I tel thee, few young gentlemen are found, that would deale so kindely with thee as I doe.   751

Ster. Well Sir, because I knowe my sonne to be a [good] toward thing, and one that hath taken all his learning [4] on his owne head, without sending to the vniuersitye, I am content to giue you as many thankes as you aske, so you will promise me to bring it to passe.   756

Amor. I warrant you for that : if I say it once, repayre you to the place, and stay there, for my father, he is walked abroad [into the parke] to take the benefit of the ayre. He meete him as he returnes, and make way for your suite.   [*Exeunt* STER. IM.

ACT. 2. SCEN. 5.

Enter ACADEMICO, AMORETTO.

Amor. Gallant, I faith.   762

Acad. I see we schollers fish for a liuing in these shallow foardes without a siluer hoock. Why, wold it

---

[1] 'tactive,' MS.   [2] 'in buying,' MS.   [3] 'if,' edits.   [4] 'taken all he hath,' MS.

not gal a man to see a spruse gartered youth, of our
Colledge a while ago, be a broker for a liuing, & an
old Baude for a benefice? This sweet Sir profered me
much kindenesse when hee was of our Colledge, and now
Ile try what winde remaynes in [t]his bladder. God
saue you Sir.   770

Amor. By the masse I feare me I [have scene¹] this
Genus & Species in Cambridge before now : Ile take no
notice of him now : by the faith of a gentleman this is
[a] pretty Ellegy². Of what age is the day fellow?
Syrrha boy, hath the groome saddled my hunting hobby?
can Robin hunter tel where a hare sits.   776

Acad. [Sir³] a poore old friend of yours, [sir] of S.
[John's] Colledge in Cambridge.

Am. Good fayth Sir you must pardon me. I haue
forgotten you.   780

Acad. My name is *Academico* Sir, one that made an
oration for you once on the Queenes day, and a show that
you got some credit by.

Amor. It may be so, it may bee so, but I haue forgotten it: marry yet I remember there was such a fellow
that I was very beneficiall vnto in my time. But howsoeuer Sir, I haue the curtesie of the towne for you. I
am sory you did not take me at my fathers house :
but now I am in exceeding great hast, for I haue vowed
the death of a hare that wee found this morning musing
on her meaze.   791

Acad. Sir I am imboldned, by that great acquaintance that heretofore I had with you, as likewise it hath
pleased you heretofore—

Amor. Looke syrrha, if you see my Hobby come
hetherward as yet.⁴   796

---

¹ 'saw,' edits.   ² 'prety pretye elegie.' MS.   ³ 'See,' edits.
⁴ The last three words omitted in the MS.

Acad. To make me some promises, I am to request your good mediation[1] to the Worshipfull your father, in my behalfe : and I will dedicate to your selfe in the way of thankes, those dayes I haue to liue.   800

Amor. O good sir, if I had knowne your minde before, for my father hath already giuen the induction to a Chaplaine of his owne, to a proper man, I know not of what Vniuersitie he is.

Acad. Signior *Immerito*, they say, hath bidden fayrest for it.   806

Amor. I know not his name, but hee is a graue discreet man I warrant him, indeede hee wants vtterance in some measure.

Acad. Nay, me thinkes he hath very good vtterance, for his grauitie, for hee came hether very graue, but I thinke he will returne light enough, when he is ridde of the heauy element he carries about him.   813

Amor. Faith Sir, you must pardon mee, it is my ordinarie custome to be too studious, my Mistresse hath tolde me of it often, and I finde it to hurt my ordinary discourse : but say sweete Sir, do yee affect the most gentle-man-like game of hunting.   818

Acad. How say you to the crafty gull, hee would faine get mee abroad to make sport with mee in their Hunters termes, which we schollers are not acquainted with : sir I haue loued this kinde of sporte [well], but now I begin to hate it, for it hath beene my luck alwayes to beat the bush, while another kild the Hare.

Amor. Hunters luck, Hunters luck Sir, but there was a fault in your Hounds that did [not] spend well.   826

Acad. Sir, I haue had worse luck alwayes at hunting [of] the Fox.

<hr>

[1] 'meditation,' B.

Am[or]. What sir, do you meane at the vnkennelling, vntapezing¹, or earthing of the Fox?　　　830

Acad. I meane earthing, if you terme it so, for I neuer found yellow earth enough to couer the old Fox your father [in].

Amor. Good faith sir, there is an excellent skill in blowing for the terriers, it is a word that we hunters vse when the Fox is earthed, you must blow one long, two short, the second winde one long two short : now sir in blowing, euery long containeth 7. quauers [one mimim and one quauer, one mimim conteyneth 4 quauers], one short containeth 3. quauers.　　　840

Acad. Sir might I finde any fauour in my sute, I would wind the horne wherein your boone deserts² should bee sounded with so many minims, so many quauers.　　　844

Amor. Sweet sir, I would I could conferre this or any kindnesse vpon you : I wonder the boy comes not away with my Hobby. Now sir, as I was proceeding : when you blow the death of your Fox in the field or couert, then must you sound 3. notes, with 3. windes, and recheat : marke you sir, vpon the same with 3. windes.

Acad. I pray you sir—　　　851

Amor. Now sir, when you come to your stately gate, as you sounded the recheat before, so now you must sound the releefe three times.

Acad. Releefe call you it? it were good euery patron would [wind that horne.]³　　　856

Amor. O sir, but your reliefe is your [cheifest and] sweetest note, that is sir, when your hounds hunt after a game vnknowne, and then you must sound one long

---

¹ 'untapering,' MS.　　² 'Leau deserte,' MS.　　³ 'finde the horne,' edits.

and six short, the second wind, two short and one long, the third wind, one long and two short. 861

Acad. True sir, it is a very good trade now adayes to be a villaine, I am the hound that hunts after a game vnknowne, and [hee] blowes the villaine. 864

Amor. Sir, I will blesse your eares with a very pretty story, my father out of his owne cost and charges keepes an open table for all kinde of dogges.

Acad. And he keepes one more by thee. 868

Amor. He hath your Grey-hound, your Mungrell, your Mastife, your Leurier, your Spaniell, your Kennets, Terriers, Butchers dogs, Bloud-hounds, Dunghill dogges, trindle tailes, prick-card curres, small Ladies puppies, [raches [1]] and Bastards. 873

Acad. What a bawdy knaue hath he to his father, that keepes his *Rachell*, hath [2] his bastards, and lets his [sonne [3]] be plaine Ladies [puppye [4]], to beray a Ladies Chamber. 877

Amor. It was my pleasure two dayes ago, to take a gallant leash of Grey-hounds, and into my fathers Parke I went, accompanied with two or three Noblemen of my neere acquaintance, desiring to show them some of the sport: I causd the Keeper to seuer the rascall Deere, from the Buckes of the first head: now sir, a Bucke the first yeare is a Fawne, the second yeare a pricket, the third yeare a Sorell, the fourth yeare a Soare, the fift a Buck of the first head, the sixt yeare a compleat Buck: as likewise your Hart is the first yeare a Calfe, the second yeare a Brochet, the third yeare a Spade, the fourth yeare a Stagge, the fift yeare a great Stag, the sixt yeare a Hart: as likewise the Roa-bucke is the first

---

[1] 'Caches,' edits.   [2] 'getts,' MS.   [3] 'sonnes,' edits.   [4] 'puppets,' edits.

yeare a Kid, the second yeare a Girle, the third yeare a Hemuse: and these are your speciall beasts for chase, or as wee Huntsmen call[1] it, for venery.

Acad. If chaste be taken for venery, thou art a more speciall beast then any in thy fathers forrest. Sir I am sorry I haue been so troublesome to you.   896

Am. I [knewe[2]] this was the readiest way to chase away the Scholler, by getting him into a subiect he cannot talke of, for his life. Sir I will borrow so much time of you as to finish this my begun storie. Now sir, after much trauell we singled a Buck, I rode that same time vpon a Roane gelding, and stood to intercept [him] from the thicket: the Buck broke gallantly: my great Swift being disaduantaged in his slip was at the first behinde, marry presently [hee] coted and out-stript them, when as the Hart[3] presently discended to the Riuer, and being in the water, proferd, and reproferd, and proferd againe: and at last he vpstarted at the other side of the water which we call [the] soyle of the Hart, and there other huntsmen met him with an adauntreley[4], we followed in hard chase for the space of eight hours, thrise our hounds were at default, and then we cryed a slaine, streight[5] so ho: through good reclaiming my faulty hounds found their game againe, and so went through the wood with gallant noice[6] of musicke, resembling so many Violls Degambo: at last the Hart laid him downe, and [whilst] the Hounds seized vpon him, he groned and wept, and dyed. In good faith it made me weepe too, to think of *Acteons* fortune, which my *Ouid* speakes of. *He reades Ouid.*

> *Militat omnis amans, et habet sua castra Cupido.*

Acad. Sir, can you put me in any hope of obtayning my sute.   922

Amor. In good faith Sir, if I did not loue you as my soule, I would not make you acquainted with the mysteries of my [1] art.   925

Acad. Naye, I will not dye of a discourse yet, if I can choose.

Amor. So sir, when we had rewarded our Dogges with the small guttes and the lights, and the bloud: the Huntsmen hallowed, so ho, [*Venus accoupler* [2]], and so coupled the Dogges, and then .[returning [3]] homeward, another company of Houndes that lay at aduantage, had their couples cast off and we might heare the Huntsmen cry, *horse, decouple, Auant,* but streight we hearde him cry, *le Amond,* and by that I knewe that they had the hare and on foote, and by and by I might see [him] sore and resore, prick and reprick: what is he gone? ha ha ha ha, these schollers are the simplest creatures.   938

ACTUS 2. SCEN. 6.

Enter AMORETTO and his Page.

Page. I wonder what is become of that *Ouid de arte amandi,* my maister he that for the practise of his discourse is wonte to court his hobby abroad and at home, in his chamber makes a sett speech to his greyhound, desiring that most fayre and amiable dog to grace his company in a stately galliard, and if the dog, seeing him practise his [lofty [4]] pointes, as his crospoynt [and his] backcaper, chance to beray the roome, he presently doffes his Cap, most solemnly makes a low-leg to [her] [5] Lady Ship, taking it for the greatest fauour in the world, that shee would vouchsafe to leaue her Ciuet box, or her sweete gloue behind her.   950

---

[1] 'our,' MS.   [2] '*Venue* a coupler,' edits.   [3] 'returned,' edits.
[4] 'lusty,' edits.   [5] 'his,' edits.

Amor. He opens Ouid *and reads it.*[1]

Page. Not a word more Sir, an't please you, your
Hobby will meete you at the lanes end.

Am. What *Iack*[2], faith I cannot but vent vnto thee a
most witty iest of mine.   955

Page. I hope my maister will not breake winde: wilt
please you sir to blesse mine eares with the discourse
of it.

Am. Good faith, the boy begins to haue an elegant
smack of my stile: why then thus it was *Iack*: a scuruie
meere *Cambridge* scholler, I know not how to define
him.   962

Page. Nay maister, let mee define a meere Scholler. I
heard a Courtier once define a meere scholler, to bee *animall
scabiosum*, that is, a liuing creature that is troubled with
the itch: or a meere scholler, is a creature that can strike
fire in the morning at his Tinder-box, put on a pair of
lined slippers, sit rewming till dinner, and then go to his
meate when the Bell rings, one that hath a peculiar gift in
a cough, and a licence to spit: or if you will[3] haue him
defined by negatiues, Ile is one that cannot make a good
legge, one that cannot eat a messe of broth cleanly, one
that cannot ride a horse without spur-galling: one that
cannot salute a woman, and looke on her directly, one that
cannot—   975

Am. Inough *Iacke*, I can stay no longer, I am so
great in child-birth with this iest: Sirrha, this prædicable,
this saucy groome, because when I was in *Cambridge*, and
lay in a Trundlebed vnder my Tutor, I was content in
discreet humilitie, to giue him some place at [my[4]] Table,
and because I inuited the hungrie slaue sometimes to my

---

[1] This line is erroneously printed in Roman type in both editions.
[2] 'Jackey,' MS.   [3] 'would,' MS.   [4] 'the,' edits.

Chamber, to the canuasing of a Turkey Pye, or a piece of Venison, which my Lady Grand-mother sent me, he thought himselfe therefore eternally possest of my loue, and came hither to take acquaintance of me, and thought his old familiaritie did continue, and would beare him out in a matter of weight. I could not tell how to rid my selfe better of the troublesome Burre, then by getting him into the discourse of Hunting, and then tormenting him awhile with our wordes of Arte, the poore Scorpion became speechelesse, and suddenly rauished.   *He reads Ouid.*
simple fellowes, simple fellowes.

Page. Simple indeede they are, for they want your courtly composition of a foole and of a knaue. Good faith sir a most absolute iest, but me thinkes it might haue beene followed a little farther.   996

Am. As how my little knaue.

Page. Why thus Sir, had you inuited him [home] to dinner at your table, and haue put the caruing of a Capon vpon him, you should haue seene him handle the knife so foolishly, then run through a iury of faces, then wagging his head, & shewing his teeth in familiaritie, venter vpon it with the same method that he was wont to vntrusse an apple pie or tyrannise [over] an Egge and Butter; then would I haue [plied[1]] him all dinner time with cleane trenchers, cleane trenchers, and still when he had a good bit of meate, I would haue taken it from him, by giuing him a cleane trencher, and so haue [starv'd[2]] him in kindnesse.   1009

Am. Well said subtle Iack, put me in minde when I returne againe, that I may make my Lady Mother laugh at the Scholler. Ile to my game: for you Iacke, I would haue you imploy your time till my comming[3], in watching what houre[4] of the day my Hawke mutes.   *Exit.*

---

[1] 'applyed,' edits.   [2] 'serv'd,' edits.   [3] 'returne,' MS.   [4] 'the time,' MS.

Page. Is not this an excellent office to be Apothecarie to his worships hawke, to sit [skoring[1]] on the wall, how the Phisicke workes, and is not my maister an absolute villaine, that loues his Hawke, his Hobby, and his Grey-hound, more then any mortall creature: do but dispraise a feather of his hawkes traine, and he writhes his mouth, and sweares, for he can do that onely with a good grace, that you are the most shallow braind fellow that liues : do but say his horse stales with a good presence, and hee's your bond-slaue : when he returnes Ile tell twentie admirable lyes of his hawke, and then I shall be his little rogue, and his white villaine for a whole week after. Well let others complaine, but I thinke there is no felicitie to the scruing of a foole.   1028

ACT. 3. SCEN. 1.

Sir RAD.[2] *Recorder. Page. Sig.* IMMERITO.

S. Rad. Signior *Immerito,* you remember my caution, for the[3] tithes, and my promise for farming my tithes at such a rate.   1031

Im. I, and please your worship Sir.

S. Rad. You must put in security for the performance of it in such sorte as I and maister Recorder shall like[4] of.   1035

Im. I will an't please your worship.

S. Rad. And because I will be sure that I haue con-ferred this kindenesse vpon a sufficient man, I haue desired maister Recorder to take examination of you.   1039

Pag. My maister (it seemes) tak's him for a thiefe, but he hath small reason for it, as for learning it's plaine he neuer stole any, and for the liuing he knowes himselfe how he comes by it, for lett him but eate a measse of fur-

---

[1] 'scouting,' edits.   [2] 'Randoll,' MS.   [3] 'your,' MS.   [4] 'thinke,' MS.

menty this seauen yeare, and yet he shall neuer be able to
recouer himselfe: alas poore sheepe that hath fallen into the
hands of such a fox.   1046

Sir Rad. Good maister Recorder take your place by me,
and make tryall of his gifts, is the clerke there to recorde
his examination, [oh [1]] the Page shall serue the turne.

Pag. Tryal of his gifts, neuer had any gifts a better
trial, why *Immerito* his gifts haue appeared in as many
coloures, as the Rayn-bowe, first to maister *Amoretto* in
colour of the sattine suite he weares: to my Lady in the
similitude of a loose gowne: to my maister, in the likenesse [2]
of a siluer basen, and ewer: to vs Pages in the semblance
of new suites and poyntes. So [that] maister *Amoretto*
playes the gul in a piece of a parsonage: my maister
adornes his cuppoord with a piece of a parsonage, my
mistres vpon good dayes, puts on a piece of a parsonage [3],
and we Pages playe at blowe pointe for a piece of a
parsonage, I thinke heer's tryall inough for one mans
gifts.   1062

Reco. For as much as nature hath done her part in
making you a hansome likely man.

Pag. He is a hansome [4] young man indeed, and hath a
proper gelded parsonage.   1066

Reco. In the next place, some art is requisite for the
perfection of nature: for the tryall whereof, at the request
of my worshipfull friend, I will in some sort propound
questions fitt to be resolued by one of your pro-
fession, say what is a [parson [5]] that was neuer at the
vniuersity?   1072

Im. A [parson [5]] that was neuer in the vniuersity, is a
liuing creature that can eate a tithe pigge.

---

[1] 'or,' MS.   [2] 'similitude,' MS.   [3] 'my misters . . . parsonage'
omitted in the MS.   [4] 'proper,' MS.   [5] 'person,' edits.

I

Rec. Very well answerd, but you should haue added, and must be officious to his patrone: write downe that answer to shew his learning in logick.   1077

Sir Rad. Yea boy write that downe. Very learnedly in good faith, I pray now let me aske you one question that I remember, whether is the Masculine gender or the feminine more worthy?   1081

Im. The Feminine sir.

S. Rad. The right answer, the right answer. In good faith I haue beene of that mind alwayes ; write boy that, to shew hee is a Grammarian.   1085

Pag. No maruell my maister be against the Grammer, for he hath alwayes made false latine in the Genders.

Rec. What Vniuersity are you of?

Im. Of none [sir].   1089

Sir Rad. He tells trueth, to tell trueth is an excellent vertue. Boy make two heads, one for his learning, another for his vertues, and referre this to the head of his vertues, not of his learning.

Pag. What, halfe a messe of good qualities referred to an asse head?   1095

Sir Rad. Nowe maister Recorder, if it please you I will examine him in an author, that will sound him to the depth, a booke of Astronomy otherwise called an Almanacke.   1099

Rec. Very good, Sir *Raderike* [1], it were to be wished that there were no other booke of humanity, then there would not bee such busie state-prying fellowes as are now a dayes, proceede good sir.

Sir Rad. What is the Dominicall letter?

Im. C, sir, and please your worship.   1105

---

[1] ' Randall,' MS.

S. Rad. A very good answer, a very good answer, the very answer of the booke, write downe that, and referre it to his skill in philosophy.

Pag. C, the Dominicall letter: it is true, craft and cunning do so dominere: yet rather C and D, are dominicall letters, that is crafty Dunsery.   1111

S. Rad. How many daies hath September?

Im. [Thirty dayes hath September] Aprill, Iune and Nouember, February hath 28. alone and all the rest hath 30 and one.   1115

S. Rad. Very learnedly in good faith, he hath also a smacke in poetry, write downe that boy, to shew his learning in poetry.
How many miles from Waltham to London?

Im. Twelue Sir.   1120

S. Rad. How many from Newmarket to Grantham?

Im. Ten Sir.

Pag. Without doubt [in his dayes] he hath beene some Carriers horse.

S. Rad. How call you him that is cunning in 1. 2. 3. 4. 5. and the Cipher?   1126

Im. A good Arithmatician.

S. Rad. Write downe that answeare of his, to show his learning [1] in Arithmetick.

Pag. He must nedes be a good Arithmetician that counted money so lately.   1131

S. Rad. When is the new moone?

Im. The last quarter the 5. day, at 2. of the cloke and 38. minuts in the morning.

S. Rad. Write him downe, how cal you him, that is weather-wise?   1136

----

[1] 'cunning,' MS.

Recor. A good Ast[r]onomer.

S. Rad. Sirrha boy, write him downe for a good Astronomer.

Page. *As Colit astra.* 1140

S. Rad. What day of the month lights the Queenes day on?

Im. The 17. of Nouember.

S. Rad. Boy refeere this to his vertues, and write him down a good subiect. 1145

Pag. Faith he were an excellent subiect for 2. or 3. good wits, he would make a fine Asse for an ape to ride vpon.

S. Rad. And these shall suffice for the parts of his learning, now it remaines to try whether you bee a man of good vtterance, that is, whether you can aske for the strayed Heifer with the white face, as also chide the boyes in the belfrie, and bid the Sexton whippe out the dogges: let mee heare your voyce. 1154

Im. If any man or woman.

S. Rad. Thats too high.

Im. If any man or woman.

S. Rad. Thats too lowe.

Im. If any man or woman, can tell any tydings of a Horse with fowre feete, two eares, that did straye about the seuenth howre, three minutes in the forenoone the fift day. 1162

Pag. [He talks [1]] of a horse iust as it were the Ecclipse of the Moone.

S. Rad. Boy wryte him downe for a good vtterance: Maister Recorder, I thinke he hath beene examined sufficiently.

---

[1] 'I tooke,' edits.; 'A talks,' conjectured by Malone.

Rec. I, *Sir Radericke,*[1] tis so, wee haue tride him very throughly.

Pag. I, we haue taken an inuentory of his good parts and prized them accordingly.   1171

S. Rad. Signior *Immerito,* forasmuch as we haue made a double tryall of thee, the one of your learning, the other of your erudition : it is expedient also in the next place to giue you a fewe exhortations, considering [that] the[2] greatest Clarkes are not the wisest men : this is therefore first to exhort you to abstaine from Controuersies. Secondly not to gird at men of worship, such as my selfe, but to vse your [witt[3]] discreetly. Thirdly not to speake when any man or woman coughs : doe so, and in so doing I will perseuer to bee your worshipfull friend and louing patron.   1182

Im. I thanke your worship, you haue beene the deficient cause of my preferment.

Sir Rad. Lead *Immerito* in to my sonne, and let him dispatch him, and remember my tithes to bee reserued, paying twelue pence a yeare. I am going to Moore-fieldes, to speake with an vnthrift I should meete at the middle Temple about a purchase, when you haue done follow vs.

Exeunt IMMERITO *and the Page.*

ACT. 3. SCEN. 2.

SIR RAD.[1] *and Recorder.*

Sir Rad. Harke you Maister Recorder, I haue flesht my prodigall boy notably, notablie in letting him deale for this liuing, that hath done him much, much good I assure you.   1193

---

[1] 'Randall,' MS.   [2] 'this,' B.   [3] 'selfe,' edits.

Rec. You doe well Sir *Raderick*[1], to bestowe your
liuing vpon such an one as will be content to share, and on
Sunday to say nothing, whereas your proud uniuersity
princox thinkes he is a man of such merit the world cannot
sufficiently endow him with preferment, an vnthankfull
viper, an vnthankefull Viper that will sting the man that
reuiued[2] him.   1200

Why ist not strange to see a ragged clarke,
Some [start upp[3]] weauer or some butchers sonne :
That scrubd [of[4]] late within a sleeueles gowne,
When the commencement, like a morice dance,
Hath put a bell or two about his legges,   1205
Created him a sweet cleane gentleman :
How then he gins to follow fashions.
He whose thin sire dwell[s] in a smokye roufe,
Must take Tobacco and must weare a locke.
His thirsty Dad drinkes in a wooden bowle,   1210
But his sweet selfe is seru'd in siluer plate.
His hungry sire will scrape you twenty legges,
For one good Christmas meale on New-yeares day.
But his mawe must be Capon crambd each day,
He must ere long be triple beneficed,   1215
Els with his tongue hee'l thunderbolt the world,
And shake each pesant by his deafe-mans eare.
But had the world no wiser men then I,
Weede pen the prating parates in a cage,
A chayre, a candle and a Tinderbox.   1220
A thacked chamber and a ragged gowne,
Should be their landes and whole possessions,
Knights, Lords, and lawyers[6] should be log'd & dwel
Within those ouer stately heapes of stone.
Which doting syres in old age did erect.   1225

---

[1] 'Randall,' MS.   [3] 'relieued,' MS.   [4] 'stameil,' edits.   [5] 'a,' edits.
                         [6] 'ladies,' MS.

Well it were to be wished that neuer a scholler in England
might haue aboue fortie pound a yeare.

S. Rad. Faith maister Recorder, if it went by wishing,
there should neuer a one of them all haue aboue twentie a
yeare: a good stipend, a good stipend, maister Recorder.
I in the meane time, howsoeuer I hate them all deadly, yet
I am fayne to giue them good words. Oh they are
pestilent fellowes, they speake nothing but bodkins, and
pisse vinegar. Well, do what I can in outward kindnesse
to them, yet they doe nothing but beray[1] my house: as
there was one that made a couple of knauish verses on my
country Chimney now in the time of my soiourning here at
London: and it was thus.   1238

Sir *Raderick*[2] keepes no Chimney Cauelere,
    That takes Tobacco aboue once a yeare.
And an other made a couple of verses on my Daughter that
learnes to play on the viall *de gambo.*

Her vyall *de gambo* is her best content,
    For twixt her legges she holds her instrument. 1244
Very knauish, very knauish, if you looke [intoo't[3]] maister
Recorder. Nay they haue playd many a knauish tricke
beside with me. Well, tis a shame indeede there should be
any such priuilege for proud beggars as Cambridge, and
Oxford are. But let them go, and if euer they light in my
handes, if I do not plague them, let me neuer returne home
againe to see my wifes wayting mayde.   1251

Recor. This scorne of knights is too egregious.
But how should[4] these young coltes proue amblers,
When the old heauy galled iades do trot:
There shall you see a puny boy start vp,   1255
And make a theame against common lawyers:
Then the old vnweldy Camels gin to dance,

---

    [1] 'berime,' MS.   [2] 'Randall,' MS.   [3] 'unto it,' edits.
                [4] 'should' omitted in the MS.

This fiddling boy playing[1] a fit of mirth:
The gray bearde scrubbe, and laugh and cry good, good,
To them againe, boy[2] scurdge the barbarians:　　　1260
But we may giue the loosers leaue to talke,
We haue the coyne, then tel them laugh for mee.
Yet knights and lawyers hope to see the day,
When we may share here there possessions[3],
And make Indentures of their chaffred skins:　　　1265
Dice of their bones to throw in meriment.

Sir Rad. O good fayth maister Recorder, if I could see
that day once.

Rec. Well, remember another day, what I say: schollers
are pryed into of late, and are found to bee busye fellowes,
disturbers of the peace. Ile say no more, gesse at my
meaning, I smel a ratt.　　　1272

Sir Rad. I hope at length England will be wise enough,
I hope so, I faith, then an old knight may haue his wench
in a corner without any Satyres or Epigrams. But the day
is farre spent, Maist. Recorder, & I feare by this time the
vnthrift is arriued at the place appointed in Moore fields,
let vs hasten to him.　　　　　*He lookes on his watch.*

Recor. Indeed this dayes[4] subiect transported vs too late,
I thinke we shall not come much too late.　　　*Exeunt.*

ACT. 3.　SCEN. 3.

Enter AMORETTO, *his page,* IMMERITO *booted.*

Amor. Maister *Immerito* deliuer this letter to the poser
in my fathers name: marry withall some sprinkling, some
sprinkling. *verbum saficnti sat est,* farwell maister *Immerito.*　　　1284

---

[1] 'paying,' B.　　[2] 'boy' omitted in the MS.　　[3] 'share their large
possessions,' MS.　　[4] 'this eager,' MS.

Incr. I thanke your worship most hartely. 1285

Pag. Is it not a shame to see this old dunce learning his Induction at these yeares: but let him go, I loose nothing by him, for Ile be sworne but for the bootye of selling the parsonage I should haue gone in mine old cloathes this Christmas. A dunce I see is a neighbourlike [1] brute beast, a man may liue by him. AMOR. *seemes to make verse.*

Amor. A pox on it, my muse is not so witty as shee was wonte to be; *her nose is like*—not yet [2], plague on these mathematikes, they haue spoyled my brayne in making a verse [3]. 1295

Page. Hang me if he hath any more mathematikes then wil serue to count the clocke, or tell the meridian howre by rumbling of his panch.

Am. Her nose is like—

Page. A coblers shooinghorne. 1300

Am. Her nose is like a beautious maribone.

Pag. Marry a sweete snotty mistres.

Amor. Fayth I do not like it yet: asse as I was to reade a peece of *Aristotle* in greeke yesternight, it hath put mee out of my English vaine quite. 1305

Pag. O monstrous lye [4], let me be a pointtrusser while I liue if he vnderstands any tongue but English.

Amor. Sirrha boy remember me when I come in[to] Paules Churchyard to by a Ronzard, and *Dubartas* in french and Aretine in Italian, and our hardest writers in spanish, they wil sharpen my witts gallantly. I doe rellish these tongues in some sort. Oh now I do remember I

---

[1] 'is a good neighbourly,' MS. [2] The punctuation here is taken from the MS., and was also suggested by Malone. [3] 'veyne in a verse,'. MS.
[4] 'lyar,' MS.

hear[d] a report of a Poet newly come out in hebrew, it is a
pretty harsh tongue, and [doth] rellish a gentleman traueller,
but come letts haste after my father, the fields are fitter
[for][1] heauenly meditations.   [*Exit*[2].]   1316

Page. My maisters, I could wish your presence at an
admirable iest, why presently this great linguist my master
will march through Paules Church-yard. Come to a booke
binders shop, and with a big Italian looke and a spanish
face aske for these bookes in spanish and Italian, then
turning, through his ignorance, the wrong end of the booke
vpward vse action, on[3] this vnknowne tong after[4] this sort,
first looke on the title and wrinckle his browe, next make as
though he red the first page and bites a lip, then with his
nayle score the margent as though there were some notable
conceit, and lastly when he thinkes hee hath gulld the
standers by sufficiently, throwes the booke away in a rage,
swearing that hee could neuer finde bookes of a true printe
since he was last in [Padua[5]], enquire[s] after the next
marte, and so departes. And so must I, for by this time
his contemplation is ariued at his mistres nose end, [and]
he is as [bragg[6]] as if he had taken Ostend : by [t]his time
he begins to spit, and cry boy, carry my cloake : and now
I go to attend on his worship.   1335

ACT. 3.[7] *SCEN. 4.*

Enter INGENIOSO, FUROR, PHANTASMA.

Ing. Come ladds, this wine whetts your resolution in our
designe : it's a needy world with subtill spirits, and there's
a gentlemanlike kinde of begging, that may beseeme Poets
in this age.   1339

[1] 'to,' edits.   [2] 'Exeunt,' edits.   [3] 'over,' MS.   [4] 'on,' MS.
[5] 'Joadna,' edits.   [6] 'glad,' edits.   [7] '2' in A.

Fur. Now by the wing of nimble Mercury,   1340
By my Thalias siluer sounding harpe :
By that cælestiall fier within my brayne,
That giues a liuing genius to my lines :
How ere my dulled[1] intellectuall.
Capres lesse nimbly then it did a fore[2],   1345
Yet will I play a hunt's vp to my muse :
And make her mount from out her sluggish nest[3],
As high as is the highest spheere in heauen :
Awake you paltry trulles of *Helicon*,
Or by this light, Ile Swagger with you streight :   1350
You grandsyre *Phœbus* with your louely eye,
The firmaments eternall vagabond,
The heauens [prompter[4]] that doth peepe and prye,
Into the actes of mortall tennis balls.
Inspire me streight with some rare delicies,   1355
Or Ile dismount thee from thy radiant coach :
And make thee [a] poore Cutchy here on earth.

   Phan. *Currus auriga paterni.*

   Ing. Nay prethee good *Furor*, doe not [roare[5]] in rimes
before thy time : thou hast a very terrible roaring muse,
nothing but squibs and [firewoorks[6]], quiet thy selfe a while,
and heare thy charge.   1362

   Phan. *Huc ades hæc ; animo concipe dicta tuo.*

   Ingeni. Let vs on to our deuise, our plot, our proiect.
That old Sir *Raderick*[7], that new printed *comipendum* of all
in[i]quitye, that hath not ayred his countrey Chimney once
in 3. winters[8] : he that loues to liue in an od corner here at
London, and effect[9] an odde wench in a nooke, one that
loues to liue in a narrow roome, that he may with more
facility in the darke, light vpon his wifes waiting maide, one

---

¹ 'dullard,' MS.   ² 'of yore,' MS.   ³ 'forth her sluggard's nest,' MS.
¹ 'promoter,' edits.   ⁵ 'roaue,' edits.   ⁶ 'fine ierks,' edits.
⁷ 'Randall,' MS.   ⁸ 'yeeres,' MS.   ⁹ 'affect,' MS.

that loues alife a short sermon and a long play, one that
goes to a play, to a whore, to his bedde in [a] Circle, good
for nothing in the world but to sweate night caps, and foule
faire lawne shirtes, feed a few foggy scruing men, and
preferre dunces to liuings. This old Sir *Raderick*[1] (*Furor*) it
shall be thy taske to cudgell with thy thick [thwack[2]]
tearmes, [mary at the first giue him some sugar candy
tearms,] and then if he will not vnty [the] purse stringes, of
his liberality, sting him with tearmes layd in *aqua fortis* and
gunpowder.   1380

Furor.   *In noua fert animus mutatas dicere formas.*
The Seruile current of my slyding verse,
[Gently][3] shal runne into his thick skind eares:
Where it shall dwell like a magnifico,
Command his slymie spright to honour me: 1385
For my high tiptoe strouting poesye.
But if his starrs hath fauour'd him so ill,
As to debarre him by his dunghil thoughts,
Iustly to esteeme my verses [towring[4]] pitch:
If his earth [rooting[5]] snout shal gin to scorne,   1390
My verse that giueth immortality:
Then, *Bella per Emathios.*

   Phan.   *Furor arma ministrat.*

   Furor.   Ile shake his heart vpon my verses poynte,
Rip out his gutts with [riming[6]] poinard: 1395
Quarter his credit with a bloody quill.

   Phan.   [*Scalpellum*] *Calami, Atramentum, charta, libelli,*
Sunt[7] *semper studijs arma parata tuis.*

   Ing.   Inough *Furor*, wee know thou art a nimble swag-
gerer with a goose quill: now for you *Phantasma*, leaue
trussing your pointes, and listen.   1401

---

[1] 'Randall,' MS.   [2] 'thwart,' edits.   [3] 'Gentle,' edits.   [4] 'lowting,'
edits.   [5] 'wroting,' edits.   [6] 'riuing,' edits.   [7] 'Sint,' MS.

Phan. *Omne tulit punctum.*   1402

Ing. Marke you *Amoretto* Sir *Radericks*[1] sonne, to him
shall thy piping poetry and sugar endes of verses be directed,
he is one, that wil draw out his pocket glasse thrise in a
walke, one that dreames in a night of nothing, but muske
and ciuet, and talke[s] of nothing all day long but his
hauke, his hound, and his mistres, one that more admires
the good wrinckle of a boote, [or] the curious crinkling of a
silke stocking, then all the witt in the world : one that loues
no scholler but him whose tyred eares can endure halfe a
day togither, his fliblowne sonnettes of his mistres, and her
louing pretty creatures, her munckey and her puppet : it
shal be thy task (*Phantasma*) to cut this gulles throate with
faire tearmes, and if he hold fast for al thy iuggling rettoricke,
fal at defyance with him, and the poking sticke he weares.

Phan. *Simul extulit ensem.*   1417

Ing. Come braue mips[2], gather vp your spiritts, and let
vs march on like aduenturous knights, and discharge a
hundredth poeticall spiritts vpon them.

Phan. *Est deus in nobis, agitante calescimus illo.*

Exeunt.

ACT. 3. SCEN. 5.

Enter PHILOMUSUS, STUDIOSO.

Stud. Well *Philomusus*, we neuer scaped so faire a
scouring : why yonder are purseuantes out for the french
Doctor, and a lodging bespoken for him and his man in
newgate. It was a terrible feare that made vs cast our
hayre.   1426

Phil. And canst thou sport at our calamityes ?
And countest vs happy to scape prisonment ?

---

[1] 'Randall's,' MS.   [2] 'nimphs,' B.

Why the wide world that blesseth some with wayle,[1]
Is to our chayned thoughts a darkesome gayle: 1430

Stud. Nay prethee friend these wonted tearmes forgo,
He doubles griefe that comments on a wo.

Phil. Why do fond men tearme it impiety,
To send a wearisome sadde grudging Ghost,
Vnto his home, his long, long, lasting home?   1435
Or let them make our life lesse greeuous be,
Or suffer vs to end our misery.

Stud. Oh no the sentinell his watch must keepe,
Vntill his Lord do lycence him to sleepe:

Phil. It's time to sleepe within our hollowe graues,
And rest vs in the darkesome wombe of earth: 1441
Dead things are graued, and bodies are no lesse
Pined and forlorne like Ghostly carcases.

Stud. Not long this tappe of loathed life can runne,
Soone commeth death, and then our woe is done.
Mean time good *Philomusus* be content,   1445
Letts spend our dayes in hopefull merryment.

Phil. Curst be our thoughts when ere they dreame
      of hope:
Band be those happs that henceforth flatter vs,
When mischiefe doggs vs still and still for aye,
From our first byrth vntill our burying day.   1450
In our first gamesome age, our doting sires
Carked and cared to haue vs lettered:
Sent vs to Cambridge where our oyle is spent[2]:
Vs our kinde Colledge from the[3] teate did teare:
And for'st vs walke before we weaned weare,   1455
From that time since [y]wandered haue we still:
In the wide world, vrg'd by our forced will,
Nor euer haue we happy fortune tryed:

---

[1] 'wealth,' MS.   [2] 'yspent,' MS.   [3] 'her,' MS.

Then why should hope with our [rent[1]] state abide?
Nay let vs run vnto the [balefull[2]] caue,   1460
Pight in the hollow ribbs of craggy[3] cliffe,
Where dreary owles do shrike the liue-long night,
Chasing away the byrdes of chearefull light :
Where yawning Ghosts do howle in ghastly wise,
Where that dull hollow ey'd, that staring, syre,   1465
Yclept *Dispaire* hath his sad mansion.
Him let vs finde, and by his counsell we,
Will end our too much yrked misery.[4]

Stud.   To wayle thy happs argues a dastard minde.

Phil.   To heare[5] too long argues an asses kinde.

Stud.[6]   Long since the worst chance of the die was
      cast,   1471

Phil.   But why should that word *worst* so long time
      last?

Stud.   Why doth[7] *thou* now these sleepie[8] plaints com-
      mence?

Phil.   Why should I ere be duld with patience?

Stud.   Wise folke do beare [what][9] strugling cannot
      mend.   1475

Phil.   Good spirits must with thwarting fates contend.

Stud.   Some hope is left our fortunes to redresse,

Phil.   No hope but this, ere[10] to be comfortlesse,

Stud.   Our liues remainder gentler hearts may finde.

Phil.   The gentlest harts to vs will proue vnkind.

---

[1] 'tent,' edits.   [2] 'basefull,' edits.   [3] 'crabby,' MS.   [4] These
two lines form one in the MS., 'And by his counsell end our miserye.'
[5] Corrected to ' beare' in B.   [6] This and the following line are omitted
in the MS.   [7] Corrected to 'dost' in B.   [8] 'thy sleeping,' MS.
[9] 'with,' edits.   [10] 'still,' MS.

ACT. 4. SCEN. 1.

Sir RADERICKE *and* PRODIGO, *at one corner of the Stage. Record*[er] *and* AMORETTO *at the other. Two Pages scouring of Tobacco pipes.*

Sir Rad. M. *Prodigo*, M. *Recorder* hath told you lawe, your land is forfeited: and for me not to take the forfeiture, were to breake the Queenes law, for marke you, its law to take the forfeiture: therfore not to [take[1]] it is to breake the Queenes law, and to breake the Queenes law is not to be a good subiect, and *I* meane to bee a good subiect. Besides, I am a Iustice of the peace, and being Iustice of the peace I must do iustice, that is law, that is to take the forfeiture, especially hauing taken notice of it. Marrie Maister *Prodigo*, here are a few shillings, ouer and besides the bargaine.   1491

Prod. Pox on your shillings, sblood a while agoe, before he had me in the lurch, who but my coozen *Prodigo*, you are welcome my coozen *Prodigo*, take my coozen *Prodigoes* horse, a cup of Wine for my coozen *Prodigo*, good faith you shall sit here good coozen *Prodigo*, a cleane trencher for my coozen *Prodigo*, haue a speciall care of my coozen *Prodigoes* lodging: now maister *Prodigo* with a pox, and a few shillings for a vantage, a plague on your shillings, pox on your shillings, if it were not for the Sergeant which dogges me at my heeles, a plague on your shillings, pox on your shillings, pox on your selfe and your shillings, pox on your worship, if I catch thee at *Ostend*: I dare not staye for the Sergeant.[2]   [*Exit.*

S. Rad. Pag. Good faith Maister *Prodigo* is an excellent fellow, he takes the [Cuban ebullition[3]] so excellently.

Amor. Page. He is a good liberall Gentleman, he hath bestowed an ounce of Tobacco vpon vs, and as long as it

---

[1] 'breake,' edits.   [2] This speech is somewhat shortened in the MS.
[3] '*Gulan ebullitio*,' edits.

lasts, come cut and long-taile, weele spend it as liberally for his sake.[1] 1510

S. Rad. Page. Come fill the Pipe quickly, while my maister is in his melancholic humour, it's iust the melancholy of a Colliers horse.

Amor. Page. If you cough *Iacke* after your Tobacco, for a punishment you shall kisse the Pantofle. 1515

S. Rad. It's a foule ouer-sight, that a man of worship cannot keepe a wench in his house, but there must be muttering and surmising: it was the wisest saying that my father euer vttered, that a wife was the [2] name of necessitie, not of pleasure: for what do men marry for, but to stocke their ground, and to haue one to looke to the linnen, sit at the vpper end of the table, and carue vp a Capon: one that can weare a hood like a Hawke, and couer her foule face with a Fanne: but there's no pleasure alwayes to be tyed to a piece of Mutton, sometimes a messe of stewd broth will do well, and an vnlac'd Rabbet is best of all: well for mine owne part, I haue no great cause to complaine, for I am well prouided of three bounsing wenches, that are mine owne fee-simple: one of them I am presently to visit, if I can rid my selfe cleanly of this company [without berayeing]. Let me see how the day goes: (*hee puls his Watch out.*) precious coales, the time is at hand, I must meditate on an excuse to be gone. 1533

Record. The [3] which I say, is grounded on the Statute I spake of before, enacted in the raigne of *Henry* the 6.

Amor. It is a plaine case, whereon I mooted in our Temple, and that was this: put case there be three bretheren, *Iohn a Nokes, Iohn a Nash,* and *Iohn a Stile: Iohn a Nokes* the elder, *Iohn a Nash* the younger, *Iohn a Stile* the youngest of all, *Iohn a Nash* the yonger dyeth

---

[1] 'their sakes,' MS. [2] 'a,' MS. [3] 'That,' B.

K

without issue of his body lawfully begotten: whether shall his lands ascend to *Iohn a Noakes* the elder, or discend to *Iohn a Stile* the youngest of all? The answer is: The lands do collaterally descend, not ascend.   1544

Recor. Very true, and for a proofe hereof I will shew you a place in *Littleton*, which is verye pregnant in this point.

ACTUS 4. SCENA 2.

Enter INGENIOSO, FUROR, PHANTASMA.

Ing. Ile pawne my wittes, that is, my reuenues, my land, my money, and whatsoeuer I haue, for I haue nothing but my wit, that they are at hand: why any sensible snout may winde [out] Maister *Amoretto* and his Pomander, Maister *Recorder* and his two neates feete that weare no sockes, Sir *Radericke*[1] by his rammish complexion. *Olet Gorgoinus hyrcum, S't. Lupus in fabula.* *Furor* fire the Touch-box of your[2] witte: *Phantasma*, let your in-uention play tricks like an Ape: begin thou *Furor*, and open like a phlapmouthed hound: follow thou *Phantasma* like a Ladies Puppie: and as for me, let me alone, Ile come after like a [good] Water-dogge that will shake them off, when I haue no vse of them. My maisters, the watch-word is giuen. *Furor* discharge.   1561

Furor to S. Rad. The great proiector of the Thunder-bolts,
He that is wont to pisse whole cloudes of raine,
Into the earth vast gaping vrinall,
Which that one ey'd subsicer of the skie,   1565
Don Phœbus empties by caliditie:
He and his Townesmen *Planets* [bring[3]] to thee,
Most fatty lumpes of earths [felicitie[4]].

----

[1] 'Randall,' MS.   [2] 'thy cannon—' MS.   [3] 'brings,' edits.
[4] 'facilitie,' edits.

S. Rad. Why will this fellowes English breake the
Queenes peace, I will not seeme to regard him. 1570

Phan. to Am. Mecænas atauis edite regibus,
O et præsidium, et dulce decus meum,
Dij faciant votis vela secunda tuis.

Inge. God saue you good maister *Recorder*, and good
fortunes follow your deserts. I thinke I haue curst him
sufficiently in few words. 1576

S. Rad. What haue we here, three begging Souldiers,
come you from *Ostend*, or from *Ireland*?

Pag. Cuium pecus, an Mælibei? I haue vented all the
Latin one man had. 1580

Phan. Quid dicam amplius? domini similis os.

Amor. pag. Let him alone I pray thee, to him againe,
tickle him there.

Phan. Quam dispari domino dominaris? 1584

Rec. Nay that's plaine in *Littleton*, for if that fee-simple
and the fee taile be put together, it is called hotch potch :
now this word hotch potch in English is a Pudding, for in
such a pudding is not commonly one thing onely, but one
thing with another. 1589

Amor. I thinke I do remember this also at a mooting
in our Temple : so then this hotch potch seemes a terme of
similitude.

Furor to S. Rad. Great *Capricornus*, of thy[1] head
take keepe,
Good *Virgo* watch, while that thy worship sleepe,
And when thy swelling [bladder] vents amaine, 1595
Then *Pisces* be thy sporting Chamberlaine.

S. Rad. I thinke the deuill hath sent some of his family
to torment me.

[1] 'the,' B.

K 2

Amor. There is taile generall and taile speciall, and *Littleton* is very copious in that theame : for taile generall is, when lands are giuen to a man, and his heyres of his body begotten : Taile speciall, is when lands are giuen to a man, and to his wife, and to the heires of their two bodyes lawfully begotten, and that is called Taile speciall.   1605

[*Rec.*[1]] Very well, and for his oath I will giue a distinction: there is a materiall oath, and a formall oath : the formall oath may be broken, the materiall may not be broken : for marke you sir, the law is to take place before the conscience, and therfore you may, vsing me your counseller, cast him in the suit: there wants nothing to the full meaning of this place,   1612

     Phan. Nihil hic nisi Carmina desunt.

Ing. An excellent obseruation in good faith, see how the old Fox teacheth the yong Cub to wurry a sheepe, or rather sits himselfe like an old Goose, hatching the addle braine of maister *Amoretto :* there is no foole to the Sattin foole, the Veluet foole, the perfumde foole, and therefore the witty Taylors of this age, put them vnder colour of kindnesse into a paire of cloath-bags, [breeches and so the fooles are taken away in a cloak-bagg] where a voyder will not serue the turne : and there is no knaue to the barbarous knaue, the [mooting[2]] knaue, the pleading knaue : what ho maister *Recorder?* Maister *Nouerint vniuersi per presentes,* not a word he, vnlesse he feele it in his fist.   1625

     Phan. Mitto tibi metulas, cancros imitare legendo.

     S. Rad. to Furor. Fellow what art thou that art so bold ?

     Fur. I am the bastard of great *Mercurie,*
Got on *Thalia* when she was a sleepe :

---

     [1] 'S. Rad.,' edits.   [2] 'moulting,' edits.

My Gawdie Grandsire great *Apollo* high,   1630
Borne was I hearc, but that[1] my luck was ill,
To all the land vpon the forked hill.

Phant.   *O crudelis Alexi nil mea carmina curas?*
Nil nostri miscrere mori me deinque coges[2]*?*

S. Rad. Pag.   If you vse them thus, my maister is a
Iustice of peace, and will send you all to the gallowes.

Phant.   *Hei mihi quod domino non licet ire tuo.*

Ing.   Good maister *Recorder*, let me retaine you this
terme for my cause, for my cause good maister *Recorder*.

Recor.   I am retained already on[3] the contrary part, I
haue taken my fee, be gon, be gon.   1641

Ing.   It's his meaning I should come off: why here is
the true stile[4] of a villaine, the true faith of a Lawyer : it is
vsuall with them to be bribed on the one side, and then to
take a fee of the other : to plead weakely, and to be bribed
and rebribed on the one side, then to be feed and refeed of
the other, till at length, *per varios casus,* by putting the case
so often, they make their client so lanke, that they may case
them[5] vp in a combe case, and pack them home from the
tearme, as though he had trauelled to London to sell his
horse onely, and hauing lost their flecces, liue afterward
like poore shorne sheepe.

Furor.   The Gods aboue that know great *Furors* fame,
And do adore grand poet *Furors* name :
Granted long since at heauens high parliament,   1655
That who so *Furor* shal immortalize,
No yawning goblins shall frequent his graue,
Nor any bold presumptuous curr shall dare
To lifte his legge against his sacred dust.
Where cre I [leaue[6]] my rymes, thence vermin fly   1660

---

[1] 'all,' MS.   [2] 'cogis,' MS.   [3] 'by,' MS.   [4] 'slight,' MS.
[5] 'might case him,' MS.   [6] 'haue,' edits.

All, sauing that foule-fac'd vermin pouerty.
This sucks the eggs of my inuention:
Euacuates my witts full pigeon house.
Now may it please thy generous dignity,
To take this vermin napping as he lyes, 1665
In the true trappe of liberallity:
Ile cause the Pleiades to giue thee thanks,
Ile write thy name within the sixteenth spheare:
Ile make the Antarticke pole to kisse thy toa,
And *Cinthia* to do homage to thy tayle. 1670

Sir Rad. Pretious coles, thou a man of worship and
Iustice too? It's euen so, he is ether a madde man or a
coniurer: it were well if his words were examined, to see if
they be the Queenes [frendes] or no.

Phant. *Nunc si nos audis vt qui es diuinus Apollo,*
Dic mihi, qui nummos non habet vnde petat? 1676

Amor. I am stil haunted with these needy [Lattinists;
fellow,¹] the best counsell I can giue, is to be gone.

Phan. *Quod peto da Caie, non peto consilium.*

Am. Fellow looke to your braines; you are mad; you
are mad. 1681

Phan. *Semel insaniuimus omnes.*

Am. Maister Recorder, is it not a shame that a gallant
cannot walke the streete for [these] needy fellowes, and
that, after there is a statute come out against begging?

He strikes his brest.

Phant. *Pectora percussit, pectus quoque robora fiunt.*

Recor. I warrant you, they are some needy *graduates*:
the Vniuersity breakes winde twise a yeare, and lets flie
such as these are. 1689

Ing. So ho maister Recorder, you that are one of the

¹ 'Lattinist fellowes,' edits.

Diuels fellow commoners, one that sizeth [in] the Deuils
butteries, sinnes and periuries very lauishly : one that art
so deare to *Lucifer*, that he neuer puts you out of commons
for non paiment : you that liue like a summer vpon the
sinnes of the people : you whose vocation serues to enlarge
the territories of Hell, that (but for you) had beene no bigger
then a paire of Stockes or a Pillorie : you that hate a
scholler, because he descries your Asses eares : you that are
a plague[1] stuffed Cloake-bagge of all iniquitie, which the
grand Scruing-man of Hell will one day trusse vp behind
him, and carry to his smokie Warde-robe.   1701

Recor. What frantick fellow art thou, that art possest
with the spirit of malediction ?

Furor. Vile muddy clod of base vnhallowed clay,
Thou slimie sprighted vnkinde Saracen :   1705
When thou wert borne dame *Nature* cast her Calfe,
Forrage and time [hath[2]] made thee a great Oxe,
And now thy grinding iawes deuoure quite,
The fodder due to vs of heauenly spright.

*Phant.   Nefasto te posuit die quicunque primum et sacri-
lega manu*   1710
Produxit arbos in nepotum perniciem obopropriumque pagi[3].

Ingeni. I pray you *Monseiur Ploidon*, of what Vniuersitie
was the first Lawyer of, none forsooth, for your Lawe is
ruled by reason, and not by Arte : great reason indeed that
a Ploydenist should bee mounted on a trapt Palfrey, with
a round Veluet dish on his head, to keepe warme the broth
of his witte, and a long Gowne, that makes him looke like
a *Cedant arma togæ*, whilest the poore *Aristotelians* walke
in a shorte cloake and a close *Venetian* hoase, hard by the
Oyster-wife : and the silly Poet goes muffled in his Cloake to
escape the Counter.   And you Maister *Amoretto*, that art
the chiefe Carpenter of Sonets, a priuileged Vicar for the

---

¹ 'plaine,' MS.   ² 'had,' edits.   ³ 'pugi,' edits.

lawlesse marriage of Inke and Paper, you that are good for nothing but to commend in a sette speach, [the colour and quantitie[1]] of your Mistresses stoole, and sweare it is most sweete Ciuet: it's fine when that Puppet-player *Fortune*, must put such a Birchen-lane post in so good a suite, [and suite] such an Asse in so goode fortune.

Amor. Father shall I draw?   1729

S. Rad. No sonne, keepe thy peace, and hold the peace.

Inge. Nay do not draw, least you chance to bepisse your credit.

Furor. *Flectere si nequeo superos, Cheronta mouebo.*
Fearefull *Megæra* with her snakie twine,   1735
Was cursed dam vnto thy damned selfe:
And *Hircan tigers* in the desert Rockes,
Did foster vp thy loathed hatefull life,
Base *Ignorance* the[2] wicked cradle rockt,
Vile *Barbarisme* was wont to dandle thee: 1740
Some wicked hell-hound tutored thy youth,
And all the grisly sprights of griping hell,
With mumming [lookes have[3]] dogd thee since thy birth:
See how the spirits do houer ore thy head,
As thick as gnattes in summer euening tide,   1745
Balefull *Alecto*, preethe stay a while,
Till with my verses I haue rackt his soule:
And when thy soule departs a Cock [may't[4]] be,
No blanke at all in hells great Lotterie.
Shame [sit and howle[5]] vpon thy loathed graue,   1750
And howling vomit vp in filthy guise,
The hidden stories of thy villanies.

S. Rad. The Deuill my maisters, the deuill in the likenesse of a Poet, away my maisters, away.   [*Exit.*

Phan.   *Arma virumque cano,*   1755
         Quem fugis ah demens?

Amor.   Base dog, it is not the custome in Italy to draw
vpon euery idle cur that barkes, and did it stand with
my reputation: oh, well go too, thanke my Father for
your liues.   1760

Ing.   Fond gul, whom I would vndertake to bastinado
quickly, though there were a musket planted in thy mouth,
are not you the yong drouer of liuings *Academico* told me
of, that ha[u]nts steeple faires. Base worme must thou
needes discharge thy craboun [1] to batter downe the walles
of learning.   1766

Amor.   I thinke I haue committed some great sinne
against my Mistris, that I am thus tormented with notable
villaines: bold pesants I scorne [them], I scorne them.

Furor to Recor.   Nay pray thee good sweet diuell do not
        thou part,   1770
I like an honest deuill that will shew
Himselfe in a true hellish smoky hew:
How like thy snowt is to great Lucifers!
Such tallents had he, such a glaring [2] eye,
And such a cunning slight in villanie.   1775

Recor.   Oh the impudencie of this age, and if I take you
in my quarters.

Furor.   Base slaue ile hang thee on a crossed rime,
And quarter [—]

Ing.   He is gone, *Furor*, stay thy fury.   1780

S. Rad. Pag.   I pray you gentlemen giue 3. groats for
a shilling.

Amo. Pag.   What wil you giue me for a good old sute
of apparell?

Phan.   *Habet et musca splenem, et formicæ sua bilis inest.*

---

[1] 'crabbyanne,' MS.   [2] 'gleering,' B.

Ing. Gramercie good lads: this is our share in hap-
pinesse, to torment the happy: lets walke a long and laugh
at the iest, its no staying here long, least *Sir Radericks*[1]
army of baylifes and clownes be sent to apprehend vs.

Phan. Procul hinc, procul ite prophani.   1790
Ile lash [Apolles [2]] selfe with ierking hand,
Vnlesse he pawne his wit to buy me land:

ACT. 4. SCEN. 3.

BURBAGE[3]. KEMPE.

Bur. Now *Will Kempe*, if we can intertaine these
schollers at a low rate, it wil be well, they haue often-
times a good conceite in a part.   1795

Kempe. Its true indeede, honest *Dick*, but the slaues are
somewhat proud, and besides, it is a good sport in a
part, to see them neuer speake in their walke, but at the
end of the stage, iust as though in walking with a fellow
we should neuer speake but at a stile, a gate, or a ditch,
where a man can go no further. I was once at a Comedie
in Cambridge, and there I saw a parasite make faces and
mouths of all sorts on this fashion.

Bur. A little teaching will mend these faults, and it may
bee besides they will be able to pen a part.   1805

Kemp. Few of the vniuersity [men] pen plaies well, they
smell too much of that writer *Ouid*, and that writer *Meta-
morphosis*, and talke too much of *Proserpina* & *Iuppiter*.
Why heres our fellow *Shakespeare* puts them all downe, I
and *Ben Ionson* too. O that *Ben Ionson* is a pestilent fellow,
he brought vp *Horace* giuing the Poets a pill, but our fellow
Shakespeare hath giuen him a purge that made him beray
his credit: 1813

---

[1] 'Randall's, MS.   [2] 'Apollon,' edits.   [3] 'Burbidge,' MS.

Bur. Its a shrewd fellow indeed : I wonder these schollers stay so long, they appointed to be here presently that we might try them : oh here they come.

Stud. Take heart, these lets our clouded thoughts refine,

The sun shines brightest when it gins decline.

Bur. M. *Phil*, and M. *Stud.* God saue you.

Kemp. M. *Phil.* and M. *Otioso*[1] well met.   1820

Phil. The same to you good M. *Burbage*. What M. *Kempe* how doth the Emperour of Germany ?

Stud. God saue you M. *Kempe:* welcome M. *Kempe* from dancing the morrice ouer the Alpes,   1824

Kemp. Well you merry knaues you may come to the honor of it one day, is it not better to make a foole of the world as I haue done, then to be fooled of the world, as you schollers are ? But be merry my lads, you haue happened vpon the most excellent vocation in the world for money : they come North and South to bring it to our playhouse, and for honours, who of more report, then *Dick Burbage* & *Will: Kempe*, he is not counted a Gentleman, that knowes not *Dick Burbage* & *Wil Kemp*, there's not a country wench tha[t][2] can dance Sellengers Round but can talke of *Dick Burbage* and *Will Kempe*.   1835

Phil. Indeed M. *Kempe* you are very famous, but that is as well for [your] workes in print as your part in [que[3]].

Kempe. You are at Cambridge still with [size que[4]] and be lusty humorous poets, you must vntrusse, I [made[5],] this my last circuit, purposely because I would be iudge of your actions.   1841

Bur. M. *Stud.* I pray you take some part in this booke and act it, that I may see what will fit you best, I thinke

---

[1] 'Studioso,' MS.   [2] 'than,' edits.   [3] 'kne,' edits., for 'kue.'
            [4] 'sice kne,' edits.   [5] 'road,' edits.

your voice would serue for *Hieronimo*, obseruc how I act it
and then imitate mee.   1845

Stud. Who call[s] *Hieronimo* from his naked bed?
And, &c.

Bur. You will do well after a while.

Kemp. Now for you, [Mr. Philo] me thinkes you should
belong to my tuition, and your face me thinkes would be
good for a foolish Mayre or a foolish iustice of peace:
marke me.——Forasmuch as there be two states of a
common wealth, the one of peace, the other of tranquility:
two states of warre, the one of discord, the other of dissen-
tion: two states of an incorporation, the one of the
Aldermen, the other of the Brethren: two states of magis-
trates, the one of gouerning, the other of bearing rule, now,
as I said euen now, for a good thing, thing cannot be said
too often: Vertue is the shooinghorne of iustice, that
is, vertue is the shooinghorne of doing well, that is,
vertue is the shooinghorne of doing iustly, it behooueth
mee and is my part to commend this shooinghorne vnto
you. I hope this word shooinghorne doth not offend any
of you my worshipfull brethren, for you beeing the worshipfull headsmen of the towne, know well what the horne
meaneth. Now therefore I am determined not onely to teach
but also to instruct, not onely the ignorant, but also the
simple, not onely what is their duty towards their betters,
but also what is their dutye towards their superiours: come
let mee see how[1] you can doe, sit downe in the chaire. 1870

Phil. Forasmuch as there be. &c.

Kemp. Thou wilt do well in time, if thou wilt be ruled by
thy betters, that is by my selfe, and such graue Aldermen of
the playhouse as I am.

Bur. I like your face, and the proportion of your body

<hr>

[1] 'what,' MS.

for *Richard* the 3. I pray M. *Phil.* let me see you act a
little of it.   1877

   Phil.   Now is the winter of our discontent,
Made glorious summer by the sonne of Yorke,

   Bur.   Very well I assure you, well M. *Phil.* and M. *Stud.*
wee see what ability you are of: I pray walke with vs to
our fellows, and weele agree presently.

   Phil.   We will follow you straight M. *Burbage.*

   Kempe.   Its good manners to follow vs, Maister *Phil.* and
Maister *Otioso*[1].   1885

   Phil.   And must the basest trade yeeld vs reliefe?
Must we be practis'd to those leaden spouts,
That nought [doe[2]] vent but what they do receiue?
Some fatall fire hath scorcht our fortunes wing,
And still we fall, as we do vpward spring: 1890
As we striue vpward to the vaulted skie,
We fall and feele our hatefull destiny.

   Stud.   Wonder it is sweet friend thy pleading breath,
So like the sweet blast of the southwest wind,
Melts not those rockes of yce, those mounts of woe,
Congeald in frozen hearts of men below.   1896

   Phil.   Wonder as well thou maist why mongst the waues,
Mongst the tempestuous [surges of the[3]] sea,
The [waiting[4]] Marchant can no pitty craue.
What cares the wind and weather for their paines?   1900
One strikes[5] the sayle, another turnes the same,
He [slacks[6]] the maine, an other takes the Ore,
An other laboureth and taketh paine,
To pumpe the sea into the sea againe.
Still they take paines, still the loud windes do blowe,
Till the ships prouder mast be layd belowe: 1906

---

   [1] 'Studioso,' MS.   [2] 'downe,' edits.   [3] 'waves on raging,' edits.
   [4] 'walting,' edits.   [5] 'strikss,' A.   [6] 'shakes,' edits.

Stu. Fond world that nere thinkes on that aged man,
That *Ariostocs* old swift paced man,
Whose name is Tyme, who neuer lins to run,
Loaden with bundles of decayed names,   1910
The which in Lethes lake he doth intombe,
Saue onely those which swanlike schollers take,   .
And doe deliuer from that greedy lake.
Inglorious may they liue, inglorious die,
That suffer learning liue in misery.   1915

Phil. What caren they, what fame[1] their ashes haue,
When once thei'r coopt vp in silent graue?

Stud. If for faire fame they hope not when they dye,
Yet let them feare graues stayning Infamy.

Phil. Their spendthrift heires will [all] those firebrands
     quench   1920
Swaggering full moistly on a tauernes bench.

Stud. No shamed sire for all his glosing heire,
Must long be talkt of in the empty ayre.

Stud. Beleeue me thou that art my second selfe,
My vexed soule is not disquieted,   1925
For that I misse [th]is gaudy painted state,
Whereat my fortunes fairely aim'd of late.
For what am I, the meanest of many mo,
That earning profit are repaide with wo?
But this it is that doth my soule torment,   1930
To thinke so many actiueable wits,
That might contend with proudest birds of *Po*,
Sits now immur'd within their priuate cells,
Drinking a long lank watching candles smoake,
Spending the marrow of their flowring age,   1935
In fruitelesse poring on some worme eate leafe :
When their deserts shall seeme of due to claime,
A cheerfull crop of fruitfull swelling sheafe,

<hr>

[1] 'forme,' MS.

Cockle their haruest is, and weeds their graine [1],
Contempt their portion their possession paine : 1940

Stud. Schollers must frame to liue at a low sayle,

Phil. Ill sayling where there blowes no happy gale.

Stud. Our ship is ruin'd, all her [2] tackling rent.

Phil. And all her gaudy furniture is spent.

Stud. Teares be the waues whereon ·her ruines bide.

Phil. And sighes the windes that wastes her broken
side. 1946

Stud. Mischiefe the Pilot is the ship to steare.

Phil. And Wo the passenger this ship doth beare.

Stud. Come *Philomusus*, let vs breake this chat,

Phil. And breake my heart, oh would I could breake
that. 1950

Stud. Lets learne to act that Tragick part we haue.

Phil. Would I were silent actor in my graue.

ACTUS 5. SCENA 1.

PHIL. *and* STUD. *become Fidlers with their consort.*

Phil. And tune fellow Fiddlers, *Studioso* & I are
ready. [*They tune.*

Stud. (*going aside sayeth.*) Fayre fell [3] good *Orpheus*, that
would rather be
King of a mole hill, then a Keysars slaue : 1955
Better it is mongst fidlers to be chiefe,
Then at [a] plaiers trencher beg reliefe.
But ist not strange [these [4]] mimick apes should prize
Vnhappy Schollers at a hireling rate.

---

[1] 'gaine,' MS.   [2] 'and our,' MS.   [3] 'fall,' MS.   [4] 'this,' edits.

Vile world, that lifts them vp to hye degree,   1960
And treades vs downe in groueling misery.
England affordes those glorious vagabonds,
That carried earst their fardels on their backes,
Coursers to ride on through the gazing streetes,
Sooping it in their glaring Satten sutes,   1965
And Pages to attend their maisterships:
With mouthing words that better wits haue framed,
They purchase lands, and now Esquiers are [namde¹].

Phil. What ere they seeme being euen at the best,
They are but sporting fortunes scornfull [iest²].   1970

Stud. So merry fortune is wont from ragges to take,
[A³] ragged grome, and him [a³] gallant make.

Phil. The world and fortune hath playd on vs too long.

Stud. Now to the world we fiddle must a song.

Phil. Our life is a playne song with cunning pend,
Whose highest pitch in lowest base doth end.   1976
But see our fellowes vnto play are bent:
If not our mindes, letts tune our instruments⁴.

Stud. Letts in a priuate song our cunning try,
Before we sing to stranger company.   1980

PHIL. *sings.*   *The⁵ tune.*

How can he sing whose voyce is hoarse with care?
How can he play whose heart stringes broken are?
How can he keepe his rest that nere found rest?
How can he keepe his time whome time nere blest?
Onely he can in sorrow beare a parte,   1985
With vntaught hand, and with vntuned hart.
Fond arts farewell, that swallowed haue my youth.
Adew vayne muses, that haue wrought my ruth.

---

¹ 'made,' edits.   ² 'jests,' edits.   ³ 'some—some,' edits.   ⁴ 'instrument,' B.   ⁵ 'They,' B.

Repent fond syre that traynd'st thy happlesse sonne,
In learnings loare since bounteous almes are done.   1990
Cease, cease harsh tongue, vntuned musicke rest :
Intombe thy sorrowes in thy hollow breast.

Stud. Thankes *Phil.* for thy pleasant song :
Oh had this world a tutch of iuster griefe,
Hard rockes would weepe for want of our releife.   1995

Phil. The cold of wo hath quite vntun'd my voyce,
And made it too too harsh for listining eare :
Time was in time of my young fortunes spring,
I was a gamesome boy and learned to sing.

But say fellow musitians, you know best whether we go
at what dore must we imperiously beg.   2001

Iack. fid. Here dwells Sir *Raderick*[1] and his sonne : it
may be now at this good time of Newyeare he will be
liberall, let vs stand neere and drawe.

Phil. Draw callest thou it, indeed it is the most desperate
kinde of seruice that euer I aduentured on.   2006

ACT. 5.   SCENA 2.

Enter the two Pages.

Sir Rad. pa. My maister bidds me tell you that he is
but newly fallen a sleepe, and you [forsooth] base slaues
must come and disquiet him : what neuer a basket of
Capons? masse, and if he comes, heele commit you all.

Amor. Pag. Sirra *Iack,* shall you and I play Sir
Raderick[1] and *Amoretto,* and reward these fiddlers. Ile
[play] my maister *Amoretto,* and giue them as much as he
vseth.   2014

Sir Rad. [page]. And I my old maister Sir *Raderick*[1] :
fiddlers play : Ile reward you, fayth I will.

[1] 'Randall,' MS.

L

Amor. pag.   Good fayth this pleaseth my sweete mistres
admirably : cannot you play twytty twatty foole, or to be at
her, to be at her.   2019

Rad. pag.   Haue you neuer a song of maister *Dowlands*
making?

Am. pag.   Or *Hos ego. versiculos feci &c.*   A pox on it,
my maister *Am.* vseth it very often.   I haue forgotten the
verse.   2024

Rad. pag.   [Sirrha Amoretto[1]] : here are a couple of
fellowes brought before me, and I know not how to decide
the cause, looke in my Christmas booke [which of them[2]]
brought me a present.

Am. pag.   On New-yeares day goodman Foole brought
you a present, but goodman Clowne brought you none.

Rad. pag.   Then the right is on goodman fooles side.

Am. pag.   My mistres is so sweete, that al the Phisitions
in the towne cannot make her stinck, she neuer goes to the
stoole, oh she is a most sweete little munkey.   Please your
worship good father yonder are some would speake with
you.   2036

Rad. pag.   What haue they brought me any thing, if they
haue not, say I take Phisick.

Forasmuch fiddlers, as I am of the peace, I must needs
loue all weapons and instruments, that are for the peace,
among which I account your fiddles, because they can
neither bite nor scratch, marry now finding your fiddles to
iarre, and knowing that iarring is a cause of breaking the
peace, I am by the vertue of my office and place to commit
your quarelling fiddles to close prisonment in their cases.

They call within.

[What][3] ho Richard, Iack.   2046

Am. Page.   The foole within, marres our play without.

[1] 'Sir Theon,' edits.   [2] 'who,' edits.   [3] 'sha,' edits.

Fiddlers set it on my head, I vse to size my musicke, or go on the score for it, Ile pay it at the quarters end.

Rad. Page. Farewell good *Pan*, sweete [*Ismenias*[1]] *adieu*, *Don Orpheus* a thousand times farewell.　　　　2051

Iack Fid. You swore you would pay vs for our musick.

Rad. page. For that Ile giue Maister *Recorders* law, and that is this, there is a double oath, a formall oath, and a materiall oath: a materiall oath cannot be broken, the formall oath may be broken, I swore formally: farewell Fidlers.　　　　2057

Phil.　Farewell good wags, whose wits praise worth I
deeme,
Though somewhat waggish, so we all haue beene.

Stud. Faith fellow Fidlers, heres no siluer found in this place, no not so much as the vsuall Christmas entertainment of Musitians, a black Iack of Beare, and a Christmas Pye.　　　　*They walke aside from their fellowes.*

Phil.　Where ere we in the wide world playing be,
Misfortune beares a part[2], and marres our melody,
Impossible to please with Musickes straine,　　　2066
Our hearts strings [broke will nere be[3]] tun'd againe.

Stud. Then let vs leaue this baser fidling trade,
For though our purse should mend, our credit fades.

Phil.　Full glad I am to see thy mindes free course,
Declining from this trencher waiting trade.
Well may I now disclose in plainer guise,
What earst I meant to worke in secret wise:
My busie conscience checkt my guilty soule,
For seeking maintenance by base vassallage,　　　2075

---

[1] ‘*Irenias*,’ edits.　　　[2] ‘misfortune howles,’ MS.　　　[3] ‘broken are nere to be,’ edits.

And then suggested to my searching[1] thought,
A shepheards poore secure contented life,
On which since then I doted euery houre,
And meant this same houre[2] in sadder plight,
To haue stolne from thee in secrecie[3] of night.   2080

[*Stud.*[4]] Deare friend thou seem'st to wrong my soule[5]
  too much,
Thinking that *Studioso* would account,
That fortune sowre, which thou accomptest sweete,
Nor any life to me can sweeter be,
Then happy swaines in plaine of *Arcady*.   2085

Phil. Why then letts both go spend our little store,
In the prouision of due furniture :
A shepards hooke, a tarbox and a scrippe.
And hast vnto those sheepe adorned hills,
Where if not blesse our fortunes we may blesse our
  wills.   2c90

Stud.[6] True mirth we may enioy in thacked stall,
Nor hoping higher rise, nor fearing lower fall.

Phil.[7] Weele therefore discharge these fidlers. Fellow
musitions, wee are sory that it hath beene your ill happe to
haue had vs in your company, that are nothing but scritch-
owles, and night Rauens, able to marre the purest melody :
and besids, our company is so ominous, that where we are,
thence liberality is packing, our resolution is therefore to ·
wish you well, and to bidde you farewell.
          [8]Come *Stud*: let vs hast away,   2100
          Returning neare to this accursed place[9].

---

[1] 'secret,' MS.   [2] 'the same how ere,' MS.   [3] 'in secret time,' MS.
[4] Inserted correctly in B and in MS.   [5] 'love, MS.   [6] Part of
Philomusus' speech in the MS.   [7] 'Stud.,' MS.   [8] 'Philo,' MS.
[9] 'this unhappy baye,' MS.

ACTUS 5. SCENA 3.

Enter INGENIOSO, ACADEMICO.

Inge. Faith *Academico*, it's the feare of that fellow, I meane the signe of the seargeants head, that makes me to be so hasty[1] to be gone: to be briefe *Academico*, writts are out for me, to apprehend me for my playes, and now I am bound for the Ile of doggs. *Furor* and *Phantasma* comes after, remoouing the campe as fast as they can: farewell, *mea si quid vota valebunt.*   2108

Acad. Fayth *Ingenioso*: I thinke the Vniuersity is a melancholik life, for there a good fellow cannot sit two howres in his chamber, but he shall be troubled with the bill of a [Draper[2]] or a Vintner: but the point is, I know not how to better my selfe, and so I am fayne to take it.

ACT. 5. SCEN. 4.

PHIL. STUD. FUROR, PHANT.

Phil. Who haue we there, *Ingenioso*, and *Academico*?

Stud. The verye same, who are those, *Furor* and *Phantasma*?   FUROR *takes a louse off his sleeue.*

Furor. And art thou there six footed Mercury?

Phan. (with his hand in his bosome.)   Are rymes become such creepers now a dayes?
Presumptuous louse, that doth good manners lack,
Daring to creepe vpon Poet *Furors* back:
Multum[3] *refert quibuscum vixeris.*   2120
Non videmus Manticæ quod in tergo est.

---

[1] 'hastely,' MS.   [2] Drawer,' edits.   [3] 'Multi,' MS.

Phil. What *Furor* and *Phan.* too, our old colledge fellowes, let vs incounter them all. *Ing:* *Acad. Furor. Phantasma.* God saue you all.

Stud. What *Ingen. Acad. Furor. Phantasma:* howe do you braue lads.   2026

Ing. What our deere friends *Phil.* and *Stud.?*

Acad. What our old friends *Phil.* and *Stud.?*

Fur. What my supernaturall friends?

[*Phant.* What my good phantasticall frends?]

Ing. What newes with you in this quarter of the Citty?

Phil. We haue run through many trades, yet thriue by
    none
Poore in content, and onely rich in moane,
A shephards life thou knowst I wont to admire,
Turning a Cambridge apple by the fire.   2135
To liue in humble dale we now are bent,
Spending our dayes in fearelesse merriment.

Stud. Weel teach each tree euen of the hardest[1] kind,
To keepe our woefull name within their rinde:
Weel watch our flock, and yet weele sleepe withall.
Weele tune our sorrowes to the waters fall,   2141
The woods and rockes with our shrill songs weele blesse,
Let them proue kind since men proue pittilesse.
But say whether are you and your company iogging: it
seemes by your apparell you are about to wander.   2145

Ing. Faith we are fully bent to be Lords of misrule in
the worlds wide [hall[2]]; our voyage is to the Ile of Dogges,
there where the blattant[3] beast doth rule and raigne Renting
the credit of whom it please[4].
Where serpents tongs the pen men are to write,   2150
Where cats[5] do waule by day, dogges [barke] by night:

---

[1] 'knottiest,' MS.   [2] 'heath,' edits.   [3] 'barcking,' MS.   [4] 'whom
ere he please,' MS.   [5] 'goates,' MS.

There shall engoared venom be my inke,
My pen a sharper quill of porcupine,
My stayned paper, this sin loaden earth:
There will I write in lines shall neuer die,   2155
Our feared Lordings crying villany.

Phil. A gentle wit thou hadst, nor is it blame,
To turne so tart for time hath wronged the same,

Stu. And well thou dost from this fond earth to flit,
Where most mens pens are hired parasites.   2160

Aca. Go happily, I wish thee store of gal,
Sharpely to wound the guilty world withall:

Phil. But say, what shall become of *Furor* and *Phan-*
tasma?

Ing. These my companions still with mee must wend,

Aca. Fury and Fansie on good wits attend.   2165

Fur. When I arriue within the ile of Doggs,
Don Phœbus I will make thee kisse the pumpe.
Thy one eye pries in euery Drapers stall,
Yet neuer thinkes on poet *Furors* neede:
Furor is lowsie, great *Furor* lowsie is,   2170
Ile make thee run this lowsie case I wis.
And thou my [sluttish[1]] landresse Cinthia,
Nere thinkes on *Furors* linnen, *Furors* shirt:
Thou and thy squirting boy *Endimion*,
Lies slauering still vpon a lawlesse couch.   2175
Furor will haue thee carted through the dirt,
That makest great poet *Furor* want his shirt.

Inge. Is not here a [true[2]] dogge that dare barke so
boldly at the Mooone[3].

Phil. Exclayming want and needy care and carke,
Would make the mildest spright to bite and barke.

Phan. *Canes timidi vehementius latrant.* There are certaine burrs in the Ile of doggs called in our English tongue, men of worship, certaine briars as the *Indians* call them, as we say certayne lawyers, certayne great lumps of earth, as the *Ar[a]bians* call them, certayne grosers as wee tearme them, *quos ego sed motos præstat componere fluctus.*

Inge. We three vnto the[1] snarling Iland hast,
And there our vexed breath in snarling wast.   2189

Phil. We will be gone vnto the downes of Kent,
Sure footing we shall find in humble dale:
Our fleecy flocke weel learne to watch and warde,
In Iulyes heate and cold of Ianuary:
Weel chant our woes vpon an oaten reede,
Whiles bleating flock vpon their supper feede: 2195

Stud. So shall we shun the company of men,
That growes more hatefull as the world growes old,
Weel teach the murmering brookes in tears to flow:
And steepy rocke to wayle our passed wo.

Acad. Adew you gentle spirits, long adew: 2200
Your witts I loue and your ill fortunes rue:
Ile hast me to my Cambridge cell againe,
My fortunes cannot wax but they may waine.

Inge. Adew good sheppards, happy may you liue,
And if heereafter in some secret shade,   2205
You shall recount poore schollers miseries,
Vouchsafe to mention with [teare[2]] swelling eyes,
Ingeniosoes thwarting destinyes,
And thou still happy *Academico*,
That still maist rest vpon the muses bed,   2210
Inioying there a quiet slumbering,
When thou repay[r]est vnto thy Grantaes streame,
Wonder at thine owne blisse, pitty our case,

That still [doe[1]] tread ill fortunes endless maze.
Wish them that are preferments Almoners,   2215
To cherish gentle wits in their greene bud:
For had not Cambridge bin to me vnkinde,
I had not turn'd to gall a milkye minde.

Phil. I wish thee of good hap a plentious store,
Thy wit deserues no lesse, my loue can wish no more.
Farewell, farewell good *Academico.*   2221
Neuer maist thou tast of our forepassed woe.
Wee wish thy fortunes may attaine their due:
Furor and you *Phantasma* both adue.

Acad. Farewell, farewell, farewell, o long farewell,
The rest my tongue conceales, let sorrow tell,   2226

Phan. *Et longum vale, inquit Iola.*

Furor. Farewell my masters, *Furor*'s a masty dogge,
Nor can with a smooth glozing farewell cog.
Nought can great *Furor* do, but barke and howle,
And snarle and grin, and [lowre, and lugge[2]] the world,
Like a great swine by his long leane eard[3] lugges.
Farewell musty, dusty, rusty, fusty London,
Thou art not worthy of great *Furors* wit,
That cheatest vertue of her due desert,   2235
And sufferest great *Apolloes* sonne to want.

Inge. Nay stay a while and helpe me to content:
So many gentle witts attention,
Who [kenne[4]] the lawes of euery comick stage,
And [wonder[5]] that our scene ends discontent.   2240
Ye ayrie witts subtill,
Since that few schollers fortunes are content,
Wonder not if our scene ends[6] discontent.
When that our[7] fortunes reach their due[8] content,
Then shall our scene end in her[9] merriment.   2245

---

[1] 'doth,' edits.   [2] 'carle, and towze,' edits.   [3] 'leverd,' MS.   [4] 'kennes,' edits.   [5] 'wonders,' edits.   [6] 'end,' B.   [7] B. 'your,' A. and MS.   [8] 'owne.' MS.   [9] 'here in,' B.

Phil. Perhaps some happy wit with feeling hand,
Hereafter may recorde the pastorall
Of the two schollers of[1] *Pernassus* hill,
And then our scene may end and haue content.

Inge. Meane time if there be any spightfull Ghost,
That smiles to see poore schollers misery[2]   2251
Cold is his charity, his wit too dull,
We scorne his censure, he is a ieering gull.
But whatsoere refined sprights there be,
That deepely grone at our Calamity: 2255
Whose breath is turned to sighes, whose eyes are wet,
To see bright arts bent to their latest set:
Whence[3] neuer they againe their heads shall reere,
To blesse our art disgracing hemisphere.

Ing.   Let them.
Fur.   Let them.   }   All giue vs a
Phan.   Let them.   *plaudite.*
Acad.   And none but them.
Phil.   And none but them.
Stud.   And none but them.

---

[1] 'to,' MS.   [2] 'miseries,' B and MS.   [3] 'where,' MS.

FINIS.

NOTES.

Page 5. l. 131. *Jack Seton.* John Seton, a Fellow of St. John's College, Chaplain to Bishop Gardiner, and Canon of Winchester, but one who was deprived of his preferments as a recusant on the accession of Queen Elizabeth, wrote a treatise on Logic, on Aristotelian lines, which was for some years the recognised text-book at Cambridge. While the treatise of Ramus, the anti-Aristotelian (whose system was eagerly adopted by Calvinistic Protestants, partly because its author was a Calvinist), was the favourite book with the New School, the men of the Old School adhered to Seton.

'Thomas Dranta,' in prefixing encomiastic verses to an edition of Seton by P. Carter in 1577, is careful at the same time to give special praise to Ramus as the popular teacher at that time.

5. 137. *Pacius.* Julius Pacius (born at Vicenza in 1550, died in 1635) wrote a treatise on Logic 'in usum Scholae Sedanensis.'

5. 138. *Carterus.* Peter Carter, Fellow of St. John's College (living in 1577), wrote annotations on the *Dialectica* of his brother collegian Seton, which were often printed with it ; but to understand the allusion in the text to his vindication of Pacius would probably require such an acquaintance with their respective treatises as *ne vaut pas la chandelle*, at least to the present Editor.

8. 212-3. John Marston published one of his volumes of *Satyres* in 1598 under the name of W. Kinsayder. Thomas Lodge's *Fig for Momus* was published in 1595 ; Thomas Bastard's *Chrestoleros : seven bookes of Epigrams* in 1598 ; and Richard Lichfield's *Trimming of Thomas Nashe* in 1597.

8. 223 ; 30. 141. Posts were used as hoardings for the exhibition of placards of all kinds, play-bills, &c., in the Elizabethan time as in the nineteenth century.

9. 244 ; 11. 325. *Ramus.* Peter Ramus first published his system of logic in 1543. See the note to Seton, *supra*. Ramus was murdered in the massacre on St. Bartholomew's day, 1572.

10. 299. *Muretus.* The reference is to the well-known commentaries of Marc. Ant. Fr. Muretus on the Rhetoric of Aristotle. Muretus died in 1585.

10. 299, 300. *Bembus, Ascham.* The *Epistolae* of Peter Bembus, a cardinal, and secretary (with Sadoletus) to Pope Leo X, who died in 1547, are the 'prettie notes' which he is said to chirp, together with the like 'notes' of Roger Ascham, the Latin secretary to three sovereigns, Edward VI, Mary, and Elizabeth, and Greek tutor to the last.

Sadolet. Jac. Sadoletus, a cardinal, who died in 1547, wrote a treatise *De laudibus philosophiae*, which was highly praised by Bembus.

Haddon. Walter Haddon, Professor of Law at Cambridge, who died in 1572, wrote *Orationes* which were greatly esteemed for their style.

12. 366. Giles Wiggington, of Trinity College, was several times prosecuted and imprisoned for non-conformity, and was accused of being engaged with John Penry (the 'Mr. Martin' of l. 355) in writing the *Martin Marprelate* tracts.

18. 549. *Potato rootes.* See *Merry Wives of Windsor*, v. 5.

18. 562; 19. 572. *Javel.* Chrysost. Javel, a Dominican, who died about or after 1540, wrote a *Compendium Logicae* and several commentaries on Aristotle.

Peter Tartoret, or Tataret, was a lecturer at Paris on Aristotle at the end of the fifteenth century, and his commentaries were several times printed.

Tollet. Francis Tolet, a cardinal, born at Cordova in 1532, died in 1596. He wrote *Introductio ad Logicam*.

21. As the reference to 'Hobson' in l. 638 is to a real person, the well-known Cambridge carrier, so no doubt 'hoste Johns of the Crowne' and 'Newman the cobler' were real Cambridge characters equally well known in their time. The carrier 'Leonarde' of p. 26 and 'Simson the Tapster' of p. 42 could also, we may believe, have answered to their names.

22. 691. *Put on the smock on Mundaye.* A country dance tune. It is printed in Chappell's *Popular Music of the Olden Time*, i. 193. It appears from that valuable and interesting work that it was a tune of great popularity, and that for upwards of two hundred years it was the tune to which dying lamentations of criminals were usually chanted.

25. 6. *lambskins weare*; the lambskin hood of the Bachelor of Arts.

25. 8, 9. Plucked at Cambridge, the poor poet had to betake himself to Germany. Were some German degrees supposed then to be as easily attainable as sometimes and in some places in more recent years, only not '*in absentia*'?

29. 113. *Fortune my foe.* This ballad is alluded to by Shakespeare, *Merry Wives of Windsor*, ii. 3. The air is printed in Chappell's *Popular Music of the Olden Time*, i. 162.

30. 142. *Dick Pinner.* No such name of a publisher occurs in the Stationers' Hall Registers in the time of Queen Elizabeth or James I, as I am informed by the Editor of the Registers, Professor Arber. May Pinner have been only some well-known vendor at Cambridge of popular ballads and booklets?

31. 188. *Three blinde beggars.* This ballad is not mentioned in Chappell's *Popular Music.* There is one called *The Blind Beggar's Daughter*, otherwise *The Cripple*, of which Mr. Chappell gives the history and the music at pp. 158-9 of his first volume.

38. 425. *Balletmaker deceaste.* Probably William Elderton, the 'drunken rhymer' satirized by Bishop Hall, the date of whose death, however, is not known.

42. 543. *Ita est.* The words used sometimes as the commencing words of the condition of a bond; hence used in the text for the bond itself.

49. 757. *Pedantius*, one of the principal characters in the Latin comedy so entitled, which was acted at Trinity College before 1591, but was not printed until 1631, and of which the authorship is assigned to Matth. or Anth. Wingfield.

51. 825. *Captaine couragious*, &c. This is the first line in the earliest version of the famous ballad of *Mary Ambree*, as given in Bp. Percy's Folio MS. The common version begins—' When capteins courageous whom death could not daunt.'

Elderton, who is mentioned in the next line in the text, was certainly dead before this ballad was written.

56. 981. *Epigram made by a Cambridge man, one weaver fellow.* This is no doubt an allusion to an epigram 'in obitum sepulcrum (*sic*) Gullionis' in John Weaver's *Epigrammes* (ii. 21) 12°. Lond. 1599. It begins 'Here lies fat Gullio,' and describes him as one who had been hanged at Tyburn in 1598. That Weaver was a Cambridge man appears from references to 'Granta' in commendatory verses prefixed to his Epigrams. In Hall's *Satires* also there are lines (iii. 6) in ridicule of a 'thirstie Gullion' beginning 'When Gullion dy'd (who knowes not Gullion?)'

61. 1132. *lorde Coulton.* I cannot explain this allusion. May Coulton have been some keeper of a debtors' prison, who was jocularly styled 'lord'?

61. 1144. The gibberish put as a pretended quotation from Ronsard in the mouth of the pretentious braggart appears to represent a proverbial saying—

> *Qui péore se fa*
> *Il loup la mangera.*

A prose version of the proverb is *Qui se fait brebis le loup le mange.*

73. 1534. *sonnets at there pales*, scil., at their milking-pails. 'Sung to the wheele and sung unto the payle,' says Bp. Hall of Elderton's ballads, *Sat.* iv. 6.

83. 188-9. These lines (from Tibullus, i. 4) are the motto on the title-page of both editions (1600 and 1610) of Bodenham's *Bel-vedere*; and on that of the first edition there was the engraved device of the sun shining on a laurel, which is unfairly ridiculed in lines 195-7.

98. The idea of this dialogue in question and answer with Echo is probably taken from a like dialogue in Book II of Sir P. Sidney's *Arcadia*. The quotation of 'Jove's breakfast' at p. 100, l. 653 is probably from the same work.

119. 1256. Probably the reference to a 'theme against common lawyers' is to some then well-known academical exercise at Cambridge, in which the form of learned disputation had been used as a vehicle for disguised satire.

GLOSSARIAL INDEX OF WORDS.

Alate, lately, 67. 1347.

All-to-be = all-to ; altogether, very much, 37. 371.

Anchors, anchorites, 74. 1563. 'An anchor's cheer in prison,' *Hamlet*, iii. 2.

Ayning-time, yeaning-time, 48. 738.

Bastard, brown, a thick Spanish wine, 7. 203. 'Score a pint of bastard in the Half Moon,' 1 *Hen. IV*, iv. 2.

Bear coals, to, to submit to mean offices, to do dirty work, 73. 1553. 'We'll not carry coals,' *Romeo and Juliet*. 1. i. 'The men would carry coals,' *Henry V*, iii. 2.

Bearwood, a bearward? *or* a wood-carrier? 70. 1445.

Beray *or* bewray, to, to soil, defile, 64. 1261 ; 66. 1320; 70. 1435; 107. 876; 109. 946; 119. 1235; 129. 1530; 138. 1812.

Bezoling ; drinking to excess, guzzling, 10. 203.

Blow-point, 'a childish game' [Nares' *Gloss*. q. v.], 113. 1060.

Boss, a hassock *or* foot-stool, 49. 765.

Brewis, bread soaked in pot-liquor, and made savoury, 33. 254.

Burr, one who sticks fast to you, of whom you cannot get rid, 111. 988 ; 152. 2183.

Cast-boy, cast-off, dismissed, boy ; one without employment, 32. 204.

Chuffs, miserly churls, 84. 232.

Clarigols, constables. Apparently a humorous application of the word used for an 'instrument of one string,' their instrument of one string

being a whip, 65. 1269; 73. 1544. 'Clari-cords' in John Weever's *Epigrammes*, Epig. i. 16.

Clothwritt, a clothwright, applied in contempt to a draper, 42. 536.

Cockpence, holy pence (*q. d.* 'God's pence'), ecclesiastical dues and offerings, 19. 594.

Cog, to, to cheat, 153. 2229.

Counter, prisons in London so called, 49. 776.

Coursie, a race, 36. 353.

Craboun, a carbine, 137. 1765.

Cross and pile. The same as the modern game of *Heads and tails*, the coinage having then a cross on one side, 49. 766.

Cut and long-tail, a term used for all kinds of dogs ; 'come cut and long-tail,' come who will, 129. 1509.

Cutchy, qu. *coachee*, a mean coach-driver? 123. 1357.

Cypress, crape, 41. 512.

Dandiprat, used in contempt as equivalent to *little brat* or *little conceited fool*, 49. 767.

Dopping, dipping, 25. 2.

Dottrell, dotterel, a species of plover, said to be easily caught; hence, a silly fellow, easily deceived, 32. 226.

Drafty, worthless ; 'drafty ballatts,' 83. 195.

Dromeder : 'an ould sober Dromeder.' Can this be put for *dromedary*, a patient, toiling beast of burden ? If not, I am at a loss for explanation. 8. 217.

Eld, old age, 2. 22.

Qu *or* que, a farthing; a farthing's-worth, 39. 434; 139. 1838.

Que, cue, the prompter's catch-word, 139. 1837.

Ram Alley. A notorious passage leading from Fleet Street to the Temple, 86. 278.

Rood Day, Holy Rood Day, 14 Sept. 48. 739.

Round, to, to whisper, 27. 45.

Royster doyster, in a ruffianly turbulent manner, 86. 276.

Rubbers, contested decisive games; trials of skill, 37. 396; 38. 402. Probably in this second line '*ruled*' is a mistake in the MS. for '*rubbed*.'

Sacket, *qu.* a contracted form of sack-posset ? 38. 419.

Saint = *cent*, a game with cards, in which 100 was the winning number, 77. 13.

Seely, simple, 69. 1420.

Sen, say, 48. 730.

Size, to, to take college commons, to battell, 135. 1691; ' to size my musick,' to take it like college commons on credit for the term, 147. 2048.

Size que, farthing allowances of food and drink; used at p. 139, 1838, for the commons of poor scholars, called sizers at Cambridge. Used as late as 1670 in Eachard's *Contempt of the Clergy*, p. 31.

Skinkers, tapsters, 6. 157.

Skipjack, an upstart, a conceited puppy, 39. 464; 42. 535.

Snuff, in, in anger or contempt, 6. 174. [To snuff at = to make a contemptuous snuffing sound.]

Sooping, sweeping, 85. 262; 144. 1965.

Stale, a trick, decoy, 67. 1347.

Standish, an inkstand, 19. 593.

Stanging, stinging, 78. 33.

Stigmatic, a; one who is branded and marked as a criminal; used in the text apparently with reference to one marked with a University degree or distinction, 8. 217; 92. 437.

Stocado, stockado, a rapier-thrust, 53. 887; 87. 315.

Subcicer, a sub-sizar (used as of a very poor scholar, who performed all menial offices), 130. 1565.

Subligation, used as a mispronunciation of 'supplication,' 64. 1249.

Sumner, a summoner or apparitor, 135. 1694.

Surquerie, apparently intended for *suquerie*, sugariness, 16. 486.

Swadds, coarse rough bumpkins, 81. 138.

Tallents *for* talons, 137. 1774.

Teen, grief, 91. 407; 96 *note*.

Thacked, thatched, 29. 134; 118. 1221; 148. 2091.

Thick thwack, fast and furious, 124. 1376. ' If Jove speak English in a thund'ring cloud, Thwick thwack and riff raff, roars he out aloud,' Hall's *Satires*, i. 6.

Trouan, truant, 74. 1572.

Untapezing, uncovering, coming out of concealment, 106. 830.

Voider, a tray or basket for removing dishes, &c., 23. 705; 132. 1621.

Vouchsake = vouchsafe, 36. 339; 54. 945.

Whott, hot, 73. 1239.

Wilningly, whether we will or no, of necessity, 44. 618.

Wonn, will; 'when you wonn,' when you will, 48. 747.

Yonts, joints, 3. 62.

THE END.

Clarendon Press, Oxford

A SELECTION OF

BOOKS

PUBLISHED FOR THE UNIVERSITY BY

HENRY FROWDE,

AT THE OXFORD UNIVERSITY PRESS WAREHOUSE,

AMEN CORNER, LONDON.

ALSO TO BE HAD AT THE

CLARENDON PRESS DEPOSITORY, OXFORD.

[*Every book is bound in cloth, unless otherwise described.*]

LEXICONS, GRAMMARS, ORIENTAL WORKS, &c.

ANGLO-SAXON.—*An Anglo-Saxon Dictionary*, based on the MS. Collections of the late Joseph Bosworth, D.D., Professor of Anglo-Saxon, Oxford. Edited and enlarged by Prof. T. N. Toller, M.A. (To be completed in four parts.) Parts I and II. A—HWISTLIAN. 4to. 15*s.* each.

CHINESE.—*A Handbook of the Chinese Language.* By James Summers. 1863. 8vo. half bound, 1*l.* 8*s.*

—— *A Record of Buddhistic Kingdoms*, by the Chinese Monk Fâ-HIEN. Translated and annotated by James Legge, M.A., LL.D. Crown 4to. cloth back, 10*s.* 6*d.*

ENGLISH.—*A New English Dictionary, on Historical Principles:* founded mainly on the materials collected by the Philological Society. Edited by James A. H. Murray, LL.D., with the assistance of many Scholars and men of Science. Part I. A—ANT. Part II. ANT—BATTEN. Imperial 4to. 12*s.* 6*d.* each.

—— *An Etymological Dictionary of the English Language.* By W. W. Skeat, M.A. *Second Edition.* 1884. 4to. 2*l.* 4*s.*

——Supplement to the First Edition of the above. 4to. 2*s.* 6*d.*

—— *A Concise Etymological Dictionary of the English Language.* By W. W. Skeat. M.A. *Second Edition.* 1885. Crown 8vo. 5*s.* 6*d.*

GREEK.—*A Greek-English Lexicon*, by Henry George Liddell, D.D., and Robert Scott, D.D. Seventh Edition, Revised and Augmented throughout. 1883. 4to. 1*l.* 16*s.*

—— *A Greek-English Lexicon*, abridged from Liddell and Scott's 4to. edition, chiefly for the use of Schools. Twenty-first Edition. 1884. Square 12mo. 7*s.* 6*d.*

—— *A copious Greek-English Vocabulary*, compiled from the best authorities. 1850. 24mo. 3*s.*

—— *A Practical Introduction to Greek Accentuation*, by H. W. Chandler, M.A. Second Edition. 1881. 8vo. 10*s.* 6*d.*

[9] B

HEBREW.—*The Book of Hebrew Roots*, by Abu 'l-Walid
Marwân ibn Janâh, otherwise called Rabbî Yônâh. Now first edited, with an
Appendix, by Ad. Neubauer. 1875. 4to. *2l. 7s. 6d.*

—— *A Treatise on the use of the Tenses in Hebrew.* By
S. R. Driver, D.D. Second Edition. 1881. Extra fcap. 8vo. *7s. 6d.*

—— *Hebrew Accentuation of Psalms, Proverbs, and Job.*
By William Wickes, D.D. 1881. Demy 8vo. stiff covers, *5s.*

ICELANDIC.—*An Icelandic-English Dictionary*, based on the
MS. collections of the late Richard Cleasby. Enlarged and completed by
G. Vigfússon. M.A. With an Introduction, and Life of Richard Cleasby, by
G. Webbe Dasent, D.C.L. 1874. 4to. *3l. 7s.*

—— *A List of English Words the Etymology of which is
illustrated by comparison with Icelandic.* Prepared in the form of an
APPENDIX to the above. By W. W. Skeat, M.A. 1876. stitched, *2s.*

—— *An Icelandic Primer*, with Grammar, Notes, and
Glossary. By Henry Sweet, M.A. Extra fcap. 8vo. *3s. 6d.*

—— *An Icelandic Prose Reader*, with Notes. Grammar and
Glossary. by Dr. Gudbrand Vigfússon and F. York Powell, M.A. 1879.
Extra fcap. 8vo. *10s. 6d.*

LATIN.—*A Latin Dictionary*, founded on Andrews' edition
of Freund's Latin Dictionary, revised, enlarged, and in great part rewritten
by Charlton T. Lewis, Ph.D., and Charles Short, LL.D. 1879. 4to. *1l. 5s.*

MELANESIAN.—*The Melanesian Languages.* By R. H.
Codrington, D.D., of the Melanesian Mission. 8vo. *18s.*

SANSKRIT.—*A Practical Grammar of the Sanskrit Language,*
arranged with reference to the Classical Languages of Europe. for the use of
English Students, by Sir M. Monier-Williams, M.A. Fourth Edition. 8vo. *15s.*

—— *A Sanskrit-English Dictionary*, Etymologically and
Philologically arranged, with special reference to Greek, Latin, German, Anglo-
Saxon, English, and other cognate Indo-European Languages. By Sir M.
Monier-Williams, M.A. 1872. 4to. *4l. 14s. 6d.*

—— *Nalopákhyánam.* Story of Nala. an Episode of the
Mahá-Bhárata: the Sanskrit text, with a copious Vocabulary. and an improved
version of Dean Milman's Translation, by Sir M. Monier-Williams, M.A.
Second Edition, Revised and Improved. 1879. 8vo. *15s.*

—— *Sakuntalá.* A Sanskrit Drama. in Seven Acts. Edited
by Sir M. Monier-Williams, M.A. Second Edition, 1876. 8vo. *21s.*

SYRIAC.—*Thesaurus Syriacus :* collegerunt Quatremère, Bern-
stein, Lorsbach, Arnoldi. Agrell, Field, Roediger: edidit R. Payne Smith,
S.T.P. Fasc. I-VI. 1868-83 sm. fol. each, *1l. 1s.* Fasc. VII. *1l. 11s. 6d.*
Vol. I, containing Fasc. I-V, sm. fol. *5l. 5s.*

—— *The Book of Kalîlah and Dimnah.* Translated from Arabic
into Syriac. Edited by W. Wright, LL.D. 1884. 8vo. *21s.*

GREEK CLASSICS, &c.

Aristophanes: A Complete Concordance to the Comedies and Fragments. By Henry Dunbar, M.D. 4to. 1*l.* 1*s.*

Aristotle: The Politics, translated into English, with Introduction, Marginal Analysis, Notes, and Indices, by B. Jowett, M.A. Medium 8vo. 2 vols. 21*s.*

Catalogus Codicum Graccorum Sinaiticorum. Scripsit V. Gardthausen Lipsiensis. With six pages of Facsimiles. 8vo. *linen,* 25*s.*

Heracliti Ephesii Reliquiae. Recensuit I. Bywater, M.A. Appendicis loco additae sunt Diogenis Laertii Vita Heracliti, Particulae Hippocratei De Diaeta Libri Primi, Epistolae Heracliteae. 1877. 8vo. 6*s.*

Herculanensium Voluminum Partes II. 1824. 8vo. 10*s.*

Fragmenta Herculanensia. A Descriptive Catalogue of the Oxford copies of the Herculanean Rolls, together with the texts of several papyri, accompanied by facsimiles. Edited by Walter Scott, M.A., Fellow of Merton College, Oxford. Royal 8vo. *cloth,* 21*s.*

Homer: A Complete Concordance to the Odyssey and Hymns of Homer; to which is added a Concordance to the Parallel Passages in the Iliad, Odyssey, and Hymns. By Henry Dunbar, M.D. 1880. 4to. 1*l.* 1*s.*

—— *Scholia Graeca in Iliadem.* Edited by Professor W. Dindorf, after a new collation of the Venetian MSS. by D. B. Monro, M.A., Provost of Oriel College. 4 vols. 8vo. 2*l.* 10*s.* Vols. V and VI. *In the Press.*

—— *Scholia Graeca in Odysseam.* Edidit Guil. Dindorfius. Tomi II. 1855. 8vo. 15*s.* 6*d.*

Plato: Apology, with a revised Text and English Notes, and a Digest of Platonic Idioms, by James Riddell, M.A. 1878. 8vo. 8*s.* 6*d.*

—— *Philebus,* with a revised Text and English Notes, by Edward Poste, M.A. 1860. 8vo. 7*s.* 6*d.*

—— *Sophistes and Politicus,* with a revised Text and English Notes, by L. Campbell, M.A. 1867. 8vo. 18*s.*

—— *Theaetetus,* with a revised Text and English Notes, by L. Campbell, M.A. Second Edition. 8vo. 10*s.* 6*d.*

—— *The Dialogues,* translated into English, with Analyses and Introductions, by B. Jowett, M.A. A new Edition in 5 volumes, medium 8vo. 1875. 3*l.* 10*s.*

—— *The Republic,* translated into English, with an Analysis and Introduction, by B. Jowett, M.A. Medium 8vo. 12*s.* 6*d.*

Thucydides: Translated into English, with Introduction, Marginal Analysis, Notes, and Indices. By B. Jowett, M.A. 2 vols. 1881. Medium 8vo. 1*l.* 12*s.*

THE HOLY SCRIPTURES, &c.

STUDIA BIBLICA.—Essays in Biblical Archæology and Criticism, and kindred subjects. By Members of the University of Oxford. 8vo. 10s. 6d.

ENGLISH.—*The Holy Bible in the earliest English Versions,* made from the Latin Vulgate by John Wycliffe and his followers: edited by the Rev. J. Forshall and Sir F. Madden. 4 vols. 1850. Royal 4to. 3l. 3s.

[Also reprinted from the above, with Introduction and Glossary by W. W. Skeat, M.A.

—— *The Books of Job, Psalms, Proverbs, Ecclesiastes, and the Song of Solomon:* according to the Wycliffite Version made by Nicholas de Hereford, about A.D. 1381, and Revised by John Purvey, about A.D. 1388. Extra fcap. 8vo. 3s. 6d.

—— *The New Testament in English,* according to the Version by John Wycliffe, about A.D. 1380, and Revised by John Purvey, about A.D. 1388. Extra fcap. 8vo. 6s.]

—— *The Holy Bible:* an exact reprint, page for page, of the Authorised Version published in the year 1611. Demy 4to. half bound, 1l. 1s.

—— *The Psalter, or Psalms of David, and certain Canticles,* with a Translation and Exposition in English, by Richard Rolle of Hampole. Edited by H. R. Bramley, M.A., Fellow of S. M. Magdalen College, Oxford. With an Introduction and Glossary. Demy 8vo. 1l. 1s.

—— *Lectures on Ecclesiastes.* Delivered in Westminster Abbey by the Very Rev. George Granville Bradley, D.D., Dean of Westminster. Crown 8vo. 4s. 6d.

GOTHIC.—*The Gospel of St. Mark in Gothic,* according to the translation made by Wulfila in the Fourth Century. Edited with a Grammatical Introduction and Glossarial Index by W. W. Skeat, M.A. Extra fcap. 8vo. 4s.

GREEK.—*Vetus Testamentum* ex Versione Septuaginta Interpretum secundum exemplar Vaticanum Romae editum. Accedit potior varietas Codicis Alexandrini. Tomi III. Editio Altera. 18mo. 18s.

—— *Origenis Hexaplorum* quae supersunt; sive, Veterum Interpretum Graecorum in totum Vetus Testamentum Fragmenta. Edidit Fridericus Field, A.M. 2 vols. 1875. 4to. 5l. 5s.

—— *The Book of Wisdom:* the Greek Text, the Latin Vulgate, and the Authorised English Version; with an Introduction, Critical Apparatus, and a Commentary. By William J. Deane, M.A. Small 4to. 12s. 6d.

—— *Novum Testamentum Graece.* Antiquissimorum Codicum Textus in ordine parallelo dispositi. Accedit collatio Codicis Sinaitici. Edidit E. H. Hansell, S.T.B. Tomi III. 1864. 8vo. half morocco. Price reduced to 24s.

GREEK.—*Novum Testamentum Graece.* Accedunt parallela
S. Scripturae loca, etc. Edidit Carolus Lloyd, S.T.P.R. 18mo. 3*s*.
On writing paper, with wide margin, 10*s*.

—— *Novum Testamentum Graece* juxta Exemplar Millianum.
18mo. 2*s*. 6*d*. On writing paper, with wide margin, 9*s*.

—— *Evangelia Sacra Graece.* Fcap. 8vo. limp, 1*s*. 6*d*.

—— *The Greek Testament,* with the Readings adopted by
the Revisers of the Authorised Version:—

    (1) Pica type, with Marginal References. Demy 8vo. 10*s*. 6*d*.

    (2) Long Primer type. Fcap. 8vo. 4*s*. 6*d*.

    (3) The same, on writing paper, with wide margin, 15*s*.

—— *The Parallel New Testament,* Greek and English; being
the Authorised Version, 1611; the Revised Version, 1881; and the Greek
Text followed in the Revised Version. 8vo. 12*s*. 6*d*.
The Revised Version is the joint property of the Universities of Oxford and Cambridge.

—— *Canon Muratorianus:* the earliest Catalogue of the
Books of the New Testament. Edited with Notes and a Facsimile of the
MS. in the Ambrosian Library at Milan, by S. P. Tregelles, LL.D. 1867.
4to. 10*s*. 6*d*.

—— *Outlines of Textual Criticism applied to the New Testament.* By C. E. Hammond, M.A. Fourth Edition. Extra fcap. 8vo. 3*s*. 6*d*.

HEBREW, etc.—*The Psalms in Hebrew without points.* 1879.
Crown 8vo. 3*s*. 6*d*.

—— *A Commentary on the Book of Proverbs.* Attributed
to Abraham Ibn Ezra. Edited from a MS. in the Bodleian Library by
S. R. Driver, M.A. Crown 8vo. paper covers, 3*s*. 6*d*.

—— *The Book of Tobit.* A Chaldee Text, from a unique
MS. in the Bodleian Library; with other Rabbinical Texts, English Translations, and the Itala. Edited by Ad. Neubauer, M.A. 1878. Crown 8vo. 6*s*.

—— *Horae Hebraicae et Talmudicae,* a J. Lightfoot. A new
Edition, by R. Gandell, M.A. 4 vols. 1859. 8vo. 1*l*. 1*s*.

LATIN.—*Libri Psalmorum* Versio antiqua Latina, cum Para-
phrasi Anglo-Saxonica. Edidit B. Thorpe, F.A.S. 1835. 8vo. 10*s*. 6*d*.

—— *Old-Latin Biblical Texts: No. I.* The Gospel according
to St. Matthew from the St. Germain MS. (g₁). Edited with Introduction
and Appendices by John Wordsworth, D.D. Small 4to., stiff covers, 6*s*.

—— *Old-Latin Biblical Texts: No. II.* Portions of the Gospels
according to St. Mark and St. Matthew, from the Bobbio MS. (k), &c.
Edited by John Wordsworth, D.D., W. Sanday, M.A., D.D., and H. J. White,
M.A. Small 4to., stiff covers, 21*s*.

OLD-FRENCH.—*Libri Psalmorum* Versio antiqua Gallica e
Cod. MS. in Bibl. Bodleiana adservato, una cum Versione Metrica aliisque
Monumentis pervetustis. Nunc primum descripsit et edidit Franciscus Michel,
Phil. Doc. 1860. 8vo. 10*s*. 6*d*.

FATHERS OF THE CHURCH, &c.

St. Athanasius: Historical Writings, according to the Benedictine Text. With an Introduction by William Bright, D.D. 1881. Crown 8vo. 10s. 6d.

—— *Orations against the Arians.* With an Account of his Life by William Bright, D.D. 1873. Crown 8vo. 9s.

St. Augustine: Select Anti-Pelagian Treatises, and the Acts of the Second Council of Orange. With an Introduction by William Bright, D.D. Crown 8vo. 9s.

Canons of the First Four General Councils of Nicaea, Constantinople, Ephesus, and Chalcedon. 1877. Crown 8vo. 2s. 6d.

—— *Notes on the Canons of the First Four General Councils.* By William Bright, D.D. 1882. Crown 8vo. 5s. 6d.

Cyrilli Archiepiscopi Alexandrini in XII Prophetas. Edidit P. E. Pusey, A.M. Tomi II. 1868. 8vo. cloth, 2l. 2s.

—— *in D. Joannis Evangelium.* Accedunt Fragmenta varia necnon Tractatus ad Tiberium Diaconum duo. Edidit post Aubertum P. E. Pusey, A.M. Tomi III. 1872. 8vo. 2l. 5s.

—— *Commentarii in Lucae Evangelium* quae supersunt Syriace. E MSS. apud Mus. Britan. edidit R. Payne Smith, A.M. 1858. 4to. 1l. 2s.

—— Translated by R. Payne Smith, M.A. 2 vols. 1859. 8vo. 14s.

Ephraemi Syri, Rabulae Episcopi Edesseni, Balaei, aliorumque Opera Selecta. E Codd. Syriacis MSS. in Museo Britannico et Bibliotheca Bodleiana asservatis primus edidit J. J. Overbeck. 1865. 8vo. 1l. 1s.

Eusebius' Ecclesiastical History, according to the text of Burton, with an Introduction by William Bright, D.D. 1881. Crown 8vo. 8s. 6d.*

Irenaeus: The Third Book of St. Irenaeus, Bishop of Lyons, against Heresies. With short Notes and a Glossary by H. Deane, B.D. 1874. Crown 8vo. 5s. 6d.

Patrum Apostolicorum, S. Clementis Romani, S. Ignatii, S. Polycarpi, quae supersunt. Edidit Guil. Jacobson, S.T.P.R. Tomi II. Fourth Edition, 1863. 8vo. 1l. 1s.

Socrates' Ecclesiastical History, according to the Text of Hussey, with an Introduction by William Bright, D.D. 1878. Crown 8vo. 7s. 6d.

ECCLESIASTICAL HISTORY, BIOGRAPHY, &c.

Ancient Liturgy of the Church of England, according to the uses of Sarum, York, Hereford, and Bangor, and the Roman Liturgy arranged in parallel columns, with preface and notes. By William Maskell, M.A. Third Edition. 1882. 8vo. 15*s.*

Baedae Historia Ecclesiastica. Edited, with English Notes, by G. H. Moberly, M.A. 1881. Crown 8vo. 10*s. 6d.*

Bright (W.). Chapters of Early English Church History. 1878. 8vo. 12*s.*

Burnet's History of the Reformation of the Church of England. A new Edition. Carefully revised, and the Records collated with the originals, by N. Pocock, M.A. 7 vols. 1865. 8vo. *Price reduced to* 1*l.* 10*s.*

Councils and Ecclesiastical Documents relating to Great Britain and Ireland. Edited, after Spelman and Wilkins, by A. W. Haddan, B.D., and W. Stubbs, M.A. Vols. I. and III. 1869-71. Medium 8vo. each 1*l.* 1*s.*

> Vol. II. Part I. 1873. Medium 8vo. 10*s. 6d.*
>
> Vol. II. Part II. 1878. Church of Ireland; Memorials of St. Patrick. Stiff covers, 3*s. 6d.*

Hamilton (John, Archbishop of St. Andrews), The Catechism of. Edited, with Introduction and Glossary, by Thomas Graves Law. With a Preface by the Right Hon. W. E. Gladstone. 8vo. 12*s. 6d.*

Hammond (C. E.). Liturgies, Eastern and Western. Edited, with Introduction, Notes, and Liturgical Glossary. 1878. Crown 8vo. 10*s.6d.*

> An Appendix to the above. 1879. Crown 8vo. paper covers, 1*s. 6d.*

John, Bishop of Ephesus. The Third Part of his Ecclesiastical History. [In Syriac.] Now first edited by William Cureton, M.A. 1853. 4to. 1*l.* 12*s.*

—— Translated by R. Payne Smith, M.A. 1860. 8vo. 10*s.*

Leofric Missal, The, as used in the Cathedral of Exeter during the Episcopate of its first Bishop, A.D. 1050-1072; together with some Account of the Red Book of Derby, the Missal of Robert of Jumièges, and a few other early MS. Service Books of the English Church. Edited, with Introduction and Notes, by F. E. Warren, B.D. 4to. half morocco, 35*s.*

Monumenta Ritualia Ecclesiae Anglicanae. The occasional Offices of the Church of England according to the old use of Salisbury, the Prymer in English, and other prayers and forms, with dissertations and notes. By William Maskell, M.A. Second Edition. 1882. 3 vols. 8vo. 2*l.* 10*s.*

Records of the Reformation. The Divorce, 1527-1533. Mostly now for the first time printed from MSS. in the British Museum and other libraries. Collected and arranged by N. Pocock, M.A. 1870. 2 vols. 8vo. 1*l.* 16*s.*

Shirley (W. W.). Some Account of the Church in the Apostolic Age. Second Edition, 1874. Fcap. 8vo. 3s. 6d.

Stubbs (W.). Registrum Sacrum Anglicanum. An attempt to exhibit the course of Episcopal Succession in England. 1858. Small 4to. 8s. 6d.

Warren (F. E.). Liturgy and Ritual of the Celtic Church. 1881. 8vo. 14s.

ENGLISH THEOLOGY.

Butler's Works, with an Index to the Analogy. 2 vols. 1874. 8vo. 11s.   **Also separately,**

    Sermons, 5s. 6d.   *Analogy of Religion,* 5s. 6d.

Greswell's Harmonia Evangelica. Fifth Edition. 8vo. 1855. 9s. 6d.

Heurtley's Harmonia Symbolica: Creeds of the Western Church. 1858. 8vo. 6s. 6d.

Homilies appointed to be read in Churches. Edited by J. Griffiths, M.A. 1859. 8vo. 7s. 6d.

Hooker's Works, with his life by Walton, arranged by John Keble, M.A. Sixth Edition, 1874. 3 vols. 8vo. 1l. 11s. 6d.

—— the text as arranged by John Keble, M.A. 2 vols. 1875. 8vo. 11s.

Jewel's Works. Edited by R. W. Jelf, D.D. 8 vols. 1848. 8vo. 1l. 10s.

Pearson's Exposition of the Creed. Revised and corrected by E. Burton, D.D. Sixth Edition, 1877. 8vo. 10s. 6d.

Waterland's Review of the Doctrine of the Eucharist, with a Preface by the late Bishop of London. Crown 8vo. 6s. 6d.

—— *Works,* with Life, by Bp. Van Mildert. A new Edition, with copious Indexes. 6 vols. 1856. 8vo. 2l. 11s.

Wheatly's Illustration of the Book of Common Prayer. A new Edition, 1846. 8vo. 5s.

Wyclif. A Catalogue of the Original Works of John Wyclif, by W. W. Shirley, D.D. 1865. 8vo. 3s. 6d.

—— *Select English Works.* By T. Arnold, M.A. 3 vols. 1869-1871. 8vo. 1l. 1s.

—— *Trialogus.* With the Supplement now first edited. By Gotthard Lechler. 1869. 8vo. 7s.

HISTORICAL AND DOCUMENTARY WORKS.

British Barrows, a Record of the Examination of Sepulchral
Mounds in various parts of England. By William Greenwell, M.A., F.S.A.
Together with Description of Figures of Skulls, General Remarks on Pre-
historic Crania, and an Appendix by George Rolleston, M.D., F.R.S. 1877.
Medium 8vo. 25s.

Britton. A Treatise upon the Common Law of England,
composed by order of King Edward I. The French Text carefully revised,
with an English Translation, Introduction, and Notes, by F. M. Nichols, M.A.
2 vols. 1865. Royal 8vo. 1l. 16s.

Clarendon's History of the Rebellion and Civil Wars in
England. 7 vols. 1839. 18mo. 1l. 1s.

Clarendon's History of the Rebellion and Civil Wars in
England. Also his Life, written by himself, in which is included a Con-
tinuation of his History of the Grand Rebellion. With copious Indexes.
In one volume, royal 8vo. 1842. 1l. 2s.

Clinton's Epitome of the Fasti Hellenici. 1851. 8vo. 6s. 6d.

—— *Epitome of the Fasti Romani.* 1854. 8vo. 7s.

Corpvs Poeticvm Boreale. The Poetry of the Old Northern
Tongue, from the Earliest Times to the Thirteenth Century. Edited, clas-
sified, and translated, with Introduction, Excursus, and Notes, by Gudbrand
Vigfússon, M.A., and F. York Powell, M.A. 2 vols. 1883. 8vo. 42s.

*Freeman (E. A.). History of the Norman Conquest of Eng-
land;* its Causes and Results. In Six Volumes. 8vo. 5l. 9s. 6d.

—— *The Reign of William Rufus and the Accession of*
Henry the First. 2 vols. 8vo. 1l. 16s.

Gascoigne's Theological Dictionary ("Liber Veritatum"):
Selected Passages, illustrating the condition of Church and State, 1403-1458.
With an Introduction by James E. Thorold Rogers, M.A. Small 4to. 10s. 6d.

Magna Carta, a careful Reprint. Edited by W. Stubbs, D.D.
1879. 4to. stitched, 1s.

Passio et Miracula Beati Olaui. Edited from a Twelfth-
Century MS. in the Library of Corpus Christi College, Oxford, with an Introduction and Notes, by Frederick Metcalfe, M.A. Small 4to. stiff covers, 6s.

Protests of the Lords, including those which have been ex-
punged, from 1624 to 1874; with Historical Introductions. Edited by James
E. Thorold Rogers, M.A. 1875. 3 vols. 8vo. 2l. 2s.

Rogers (J. E. T.). History of Agriculture and Prices in
England, A.D. 1259-1793.
> Vols. I and II (1259-1400). 1866. 8vo. 2l. 2s.
> Vols. III and IV (1401-1582). 1882. 8vo. 2l. 10s.

Saxon Chronicles (Two of the) parallel, with Supplementary
Extracts from the Others. Edited, with Introduction, Notes, and a Glossarial Index, by J. Earle, M.A. 1865. 8vo. 16s.

Sturlunga Saga, including the Islendinga Saga of Lawman
Sturla Thordsson and other works. Edited by Dr. Gudbrand Vigfússon.
In 2 vols. 1878. 8vo. 2l. 2s.

York Plays. The Plays performed by the Crafts or Mysteries
of York on the day of Corpus Christi in the 14th, 15th, and 16th centuries.
Now first printed from the unique MS. in the Library of Lord Ashburnham.
Edited with Introduction and Glossary by Lucy Toulmin Smith. 8vo. 21s.

Statutes made for the University of Oxford, and for the Colleges
and Halls therein, by the University of Oxford Commissioners. 1882. 8vo.
12s. 6d.

Statuta Universitatis Oxoniensis. 1885. 8vo. 5s.

The Examination Statutes for the Degrees of B.A., B. Mus.,
B.C.L., and B.M. Revised to Trinity Term, 1886. 8vo. sewed, 1s.

The Student's Handbook to the University and Colleges of
Oxford. Extra fcap. 8vo. 2s. 6d.

The Oxford University Calendar for the year 1886. Crown
8vo. 4s. 6d.
The present Edition includes all Class Lists and other University distinctions for
the five years ending with 1885.

Also, supplementary to the above, price 5s. (pp. 606),

The Honours Register of the University of Oxford. A complete
Record of University Honours, Officers, Distinctions, and Class Lists; of the
Heads of Colleges, &c., &c., from the Thirteenth Century to 1883.

MATHEMATICS, PHYSICAL SCIENCE, &c.

Acland (H. W., M.D., F.R.S.). Synopsis of the Pathological
Series in the Oxford Museum. 1867. 8vo. 2s. 6d.

De Bary (Dr. A.). Comparative Anatomy of the Vegetative
Organs of the Phanerogams and Ferns. Translated and Annotated by F. O.
Bower, M.A., F.L.S., and D. H. Scott, M.A., Ph.D., F.L.S. With two
hundred and forty-one woodcuts and an Index. Royal 8vo., half morocco,
1l. 2s. 6d.

Müller (J.). On certain Variations in the Vocal Organs of
the Passeres that have hitherto escaped notice. Translated by F. J. Bell, B.A.,
and edited, with an Appendix, by A. H. Garrod, M.A., F.R.S. With Plates.
1878. 4to. paper covers, 7s. 6d.

Price (Bartholomew, M.A., F.R.S.). Treatise on Infinitesimal Calculus.

Vol. I. Differential Calculus. Second Edition. 8vo. 14s. 6d.

Vol. II. Integral Calculus, Calculus of Variations, and Differential Equations. Second Edition, 1865. 8vo. 18s.

Vol. III. Statics, including Attractions; Dynamics of a Material Particle. Second Edition, 1868. 8vo. 16s.

Vol. IV. Dynamics of Material Systems; together with a chapter on Theoretical Dynamics, by W. F. Donkin, M.A., F.R.S. 1862. 8vo. 16s.

Pritchard (C., D.D., F.R.S.). Uranometria Nova Oxoniensis. A Photometric determination of the magnitudes of all Stars visible to the naked eye, from the Pole to ten degrees south of the Equator. 1885. Royal 8vo. 8s. 6d.

—— *Astronomical Observations* made at the University Observatory, Oxford, under the direction of C. Pritchard, D.D. No. 1. 1878. Royal 8vo. paper covers, 3s. 6d.

Rigaud's Correspondence of Scientific Men of the 17th Century, with Table of Contents by A. de Morgan, and Index by the Rev. J. Rigaud, M.A. 2 vols. 1841–1862. 8vo. 18s. 6d.

Rolleston (George, M.D., F.R.S.). Scientific Papers and Addresses. Arranged and Edited by William Turner, M.B., F.R.S. With a Biographical Sketch by Edward Tylor, F.R.S. With Portrait, Plates, and Woodcuts. 2 vols. 8vo. 1l. 4s.

Westwood (J. O., M.A., F.R.S.). Thesaurus Entomologicus Hopeianus, or a Description of the rarest Insects in the Collection given to the University by the Rev. William Hope. With 40 Plates. 1874. Small folio, half morocco, 7l. 10s.

The Sacred Books of the East.

TRANSLATED BY VARIOUS ORIENTAL SCHOLARS, AND EDITED BY
F. MAX MÜLLER.

[Demy 8vo. cloth.]

Vol. I. The Upanishads. Translated by F. Max Müller. Part I. The Khândogya-upanishad, The Talavakâra-upanishad, The Aitareyaâranyaka, The Kaushîtaki-brâhmana-upanishad, and The Vâgasaneyi-samhitâupanishad. 10s. 6d.

Vol. II. The Sacred Laws of the Âryas, as taught in the Schools of Âpastamba, Gautama, Vâsishtha, and Baudhâyana. Translated by Prof. Georg Bühler. Part I. Âpastamba and Gautama. 10s. 6d.

Vol. III. The Sacred Books of China. The Texts of Confucianism. Translated by James Legge. Part I. The Shû King, The Religious portions of the Shih King, and The Hsiâo King. 12*s. 6d.*

Vol. IV. The Zend-Avesta. Translated by James Darmesteter. Part I. The Vendîdâd. 10*s. 6d.*

Vol. V. The Pahlavi Texts. Translated by E. W. West. Part I. The Bundahi*s*, Bahman Ya*s*t, and Shâyast lâ-shâyast. 12*s. 6d.*

Vols. VI and IX. The Qur'ân. Parts I and II. Translated by E. H. Palmer. 21*s.*

Vol. VII. The Institutes of Vish*n*u. Translated by Julius Jolly. 10*s. 6d.*

Vol. VIII. The Bhagavadgîtâ, with The Sanatsugâtîya, and The Anugîtâ. Translated by Kâshinâth Trimbak Telang. 10*s. 6d.*

Vol. X. The Dhammapada, translated from Pâli by F. Max Müller; and The Sutta-Nipâta, translated from Pâli by V. Fausböll; being Canonical Books of the Buddhists. 10*s. 6d.*

Vol. XI. Buddhist Suttas. Translated from Pâli by T. W. Rhys Davids. 1. The Mahâparinibbâna Suttanta; 2. The Dhamma-*k*akkappavattana Sutta; 3. The Tevig*g*a Suttanta; 4. The Akankheyya Sutta; 5. The *K*etokhila Sutta; 6. The Mahâ-sudassana Suttanta; 7. The Sabbâsava Sutta. 10*s. 6d.*

Vol. XII. The *S*atapatha-Brâhma*n*a, according to the Text of the Mâdhyandina School. Translated by Julius Eggeling. Part I. Books I and II. 12*s. 6d.*

Vol. XIII. Vinaya Texts. Translated from the Pâli by. T. W. Rhys Davids and Hermann Oldenberg. Part I. The Pâtimokkha. The Mahâvagga, I-IV. 10*s. 6d.*

Vol. XIV. The Sacred Laws of the Âryas, as taught in the Schools of Apastamba, Gautama, Vâsish*th*a and Baudhâyana. Translated by Georg Bühler. Part II. Vâsish*th*a and Baudhâyana. 10*s. 6d.*

Vol. XV. The Upanishads. Translated by F. Max Müller. Part II. The Ka*th*a-upanishad, The Mu*nd*aka-upanishad, The Taittirîyaka-upanishad, The B*ri*hadâra*n*yaka-upanishad, The *S*veta*s*vatara-upanishad, The Pra*sn*a-upanishad, and The Maitrâya*n*a-Brâhma*n*a-upanishad. 10*s. 6d.*

Vol. XVI. The Sacred Books of China. The Texts of Confucianism. Translated by James Legge. Part II. The Yî King. 10*s. 6d.*

Vol. XVII. Vinaya Texts. Translated from the Pâli by T. W. Rhys Davids and Hermann Oldenberg. Part II. The Mahâvagga, V-X. The *K*ullavagga, I-III. 10*s. 6d*

Vol. XVIII. Pahlavi Texts. Translated by E. W. West.
Part II. The Dâdistân-î Dînîk and The Epistles of Mânûskihar. 12s. 6d.

Vol. XIX. The Fo-sho-hing-tsan-king. A Life of Buddha
by Asvaghosha Bodhisattva, translated from Sanskrit into Chinese by Dhar-
maraksha, A.D. 420, and from Chinese into English by Samuel Beal. 10s. 6d.

Vol. XX. Vinaya Texts. Translated from the Pâli by T. W.
Rhys Davids and Hermann Oldenberg. Part III. The Kullavagga, IV–XII.
10s. 6d.

Vol. XXI. The Saddharma-pundarîka; or, the Lotus of the
True Law. Translated by H. Kern. 12s. 6d.

Vol. XXII. Gaina-Sûtras. Translated from Prâkrit by Hermann Jacobi. Part I. The Âkârânga-Sûtra. The Kalpa-Sûtra. 10s. 6d.

Vol. XXIII. The Zend-Avesta. Translated by James Darmesteter. Part II. The Sîrôzahs, Yasts, and Nyâyis. 10s. 6d.

Vol. XXIV. Pahlavi Texts. Translated by E. W. West.
Part III. Dînâ-î Maînôg-î Khirad, Sikand-gûmânîk, and Sad-Dar. 10s. 6d.

Second Series.

Vol. XXV. Manu. Translated by Georg Bühler. 21s.

Vol. XXVI. The Satapatha-Brâhmana. Translated by
Julius Eggeling. Part II. 12s. 6d.

Vols. XXVII and XXVIII. The Sacred Books of China.
The Texts of Confucianism. Translated by James Legge. Parts III and IV.
The Lî Kî, or Collection of Treatises on the Rules of Propriety, or Ceremonial
Usages. 25s. *Just Published.*

The following Volumes are in the Press:—

Vols. XXIX and XXX. The Grihya-Sûtras, Rules of Vedic
Domestic Ceremonies. Translated by Hermann Oldenberg. Part I, Vol. XXIX,
nearly ready.

Vol. XXXI. The Zend-Avesta. Part III. The Yasna,
Visparad, Âfrînagân, and Gâhs. Translated by the Rev. L. H. Mills.

Vol. XXXII. Vedic Hymns. Translated by F. Max Müller.
Part I.

Vol. XXXIII. Nârada, and some Minor Law-books.
Translated by Julius Jolly. [*Preparing.*]

Vol. XXXIV. The Vedânta-Sûtras, with Sankara's Commentary. Translated by G. Thibaut. [*Preparing.*]

*** *The Second Series will consist of Twenty-Four Volumes.*

Clarendon Press Series

I. ENGLISH, &c.

A First Reading Book. By Marie Eichens of Berlin; and edited by Anne J. Clough. Extra fcap. 8vo. stiff covers, 4d.

Oxford Reading Book, Part I. For Little Children. Extra fcap. 8vo. stiff covers, 6d.

Oxford Reading Book, Part II. For Junior Classes. Extra fcap. 8vo. stiff covers, 6d.

An Elementary English Grammar and Exercise Book. By O. W. Tancock, M.A. Second Edition. Extra fcap. 8vo. 1s. 6d.

An English Grammar and Reading Book, for Lower Forms in Classical Schools. By O. W. Tancock, M.A. Fourth Edition. Extra fcap. 8vo. 3s. 6d.

Typical Selections from the best English Writers, with Introductory Notices. Second Edition. In Two Volumes. Extra fcap. 8vo. 3s. 6d. each.

　　Vol. I. Latimer to Berkeley.　　　　Vol. II. Pope to Macaulay.

Shairp (J. C., LL.D.). Aspects of Poetry; being Lectures delivered at Oxford. Crown 8vo. 10s. 6d.

A Book for the Beginner in Anglo-Saxon. By John Earle, M.A. Third Edition. Extra fcap. 8vo. 2s. 6d.

An Anglo-Saxon Reader. In Prose and Verse. With Grammatical Introduction, Notes, and Glossary. By Henry Sweet, M.A. Fourth Edition, Revised and Enlarged. Extra fcap. 8vo. 8s. 6d.

An Anglo-Saxon Primer, with Grammar, Notes, and Glossary. By the same Author. Second Edition. Extra fcap. 8vo. 2s. 6d.

Old English Reading Primers; edited by Henry Sweet, M.A.
　　I. Selected Homilies of Ælfric. Extra fcap. 8vo., stiff covers, 1s. 6d.
　　II. Extracts from Alfred's Orosius. Extra fcap. 8vo., stiff covers, 1s. 6d.

First Middle English Primer, with Grammar and Glossary. By the same Author. Extra fcap. 8vo. 2s.

Second Middle English Primer. By the same Author. Extra fcap. 8vo. *Just Published.*

The Philology of the English Tongue. By J. Earle, M.A. Third Edition. Extra fcap. 8vo. 7s. 6d.

An Icelandic Primer, with Grammar, Notes, and Glossary. By the same Author. Extra fcap. 8vo. 3s. 6d.

An Icelandic Prose Reader, with Notes, Grammar, and Glossary. By G. Vigfússon, M.A., and F. York Powell, M.A. Ext. fcap. 8vo. 10s. 6d.

A Handbook of Phonetics, including a Popular Exposition of
the Principles of Spelling Reform. By H. Sweet, M.A. Extra fcap. 8vo. 4*s*. 6*d*.

Elementarbuch des Gesprochenen Englisch. Grammatik,
Texte und Glossar. Von Henry Sweet. Extra fcap. 8vo., stiff covers, 2*s*. 6*d*.

The Ormulum; with the Notes and Glossary of Dr. R. M.
White. Edited by R. Holt, M.A. 1878. 2 vols. Extra fcap. 8vo. 21*s*.

Specimens of Early English. A New and Revised Edition.
With Introduction, Notes, and Glossarial Index. By R. Morris, LL.D., and
W. W. Skeat, M.A.

 Part I. From Old English Homilies to King Horn (A.D. 1150 to A.D. 1300).
 Second Edition. Extra fcap. 8vo. 9*s*.

 Part II. From Robert of Gloucester to Gower (A.D. 1298 to A.D. 1393).
 Second Edition. Extra fcap. 8vo. 7*s*. 6*d*.

Specimens of English Literature, from the 'Ploughmans
Crede' to the 'Shepheardes Calender' (A.D. 1394 to A.D. 1579). With Introduction, Notes, and Glossarial Index. By W. W. Skeat, M.A. Extra fcap.
8vo. 7*s*. 6*d*.

The Vision of William concerning Piers the Plowman, by
William Langland. Edited, with Notes, by W. W. Skeat, M.A. Third
Edition. Extra fcap. 8vo. 4*s*. 6*d*.

Chaucer. I. *The Prologue to the Canterbury Tales;* the
Knightes Tale; The Nonne Prestes Tale. Edited by R. Morris, Editor of
Specimens of Early English, &c., &c. Fifty-first Thousand. Extra fcap. 8vo.
2*s*. 6*d*.

—— II. *The Prioresses Tale; Sir Thopas;* The Monkes
Tale; The Clerkes Tale; The Squieres Tale, &c. Edited by W. W. Skeat,
M.A. Second Edition. Extra fcap. 8vo. 4*s*. 6*d*.

—— III. *The Tale of the Man of Lawe;* The Pardoneres
Tale; The Second Nonnes Tale; The Chanouns Yemannes Tale. By the
same Editor. Second Edition. Extra fcap. 8vo. 4*s*. 6*d*.

Gamelyn, The Tale of. Edited with Notes, Glossary, &c., by
W. W. Skeat, M.A. Extra fcap. 8vo. Stiff covers, 1*s*. 6*d*.

Spenser's Faery Queene. Books I and II. Designed chiefly
for the use of Schools. With Introduction, Notes, and Glossary. By G. W.
Kitchin, D.D. Extra fcap. 8vo. 2*s*. 6*d*. each.

Hooker. Ecclesiastical Polity, Book I. Edited by R. W.
Church, M.A. Second Edition. Extra fcap. 8vo. 2*s*.

Marlowe and Greene. Marlowe's Tragical History of Dr.
Faustus, and *Greene's Honourable History of Friar Bacon and Friar Bungay.*
Edited by A. W. Ward, M.A. 1878. Extra fcap. 8vo. 5*s*. 6*d*. In white
Parchment, 6*s*.

Marlowe. Edward II. With Introduction, Notes, &c. By
O. W. Tancock, M.A. Extra fcap. 8vo. 3*s*.

Shakespeare. Select Plays. Edited by W. G. Clark, M.A.,
and W. Aldis Wright, M.A. Extra fcap. 8vo. stiff covers.

The Merchant of Venice. 1*s*.   Macbeth. 1*s*. 6*d*.
Richard the Second. 1*s*. 6*d*.   Hamlet. 2*s*.

Edited by W. Aldis Wright, M.A.

The Tempest. 1*s*. 6*d*.   Midsummer Night's Dream. 1*s*. 6*d*.
As You Like It. 1*s*. 6*d*.   Coriolanus. 2*s*. 6*d*.
Julius Cæsar. 2*s*.   Henry the Fifth. 2*s*.
Richard the Third. 2*s*. 6*d*.   Twelfth Night. 1*s*. 6*d*.
King Lear. 1*s*. 6*d*.   King John. 1*s*. 6*d*.

Shakespeare as a Dramatic Artist; a popular Illustration of
the Principles of Scientific Criticism. By R. G. Moulton, M.A. Crown 8vo. 5*s*.

Bacon. I. *Advancement of Learning*. Edited by W. Aldis
Wright, M.A. Second Edition. Extra fcap. 8vo. 4*s*. 6*d*.

—— II. *The Essays*. With Introduction and Notes. By
S. H. Reynolds, M.A., late Fellow of Brasenose College. *In Preparation*.

Milton. I. *Areopagitica*. With Introduction and Notes. By
John W. Hales, M.A. Third Edition. Extra fcap. 8vo. 3*s*.

—— II. *Poems*. Edited by R. C. Browne, M.A. 2 vols.
Fifth Edition. Extra fcap. 8vo. 6*s*. 6*d*. Sold separately, Vol. I. 4*s*.; Vol. II. 3*s*.

In paper covers :—

Lycidas, 3*d*.   L'Allegro, 3*d*.   Il Penseroso, 4*d*.   Comus, 6*d*.
Samson Agonistes, 6*d*.

—— III. *Samson Agonistes*. Edited with Introduction and
Notes by John Churton Collins. Extra fcap. 8vo. stiff covers, 1*s*.

Bunyan. I. *The Pilgrim's Progress, Grace Abounding, Rela-
tion of the Imprisonment of Mr. John Bunyan*. Edited, with Biographical
Introduction and Notes, by E. Venables, M.A. 1879. Extra fcap. 8vo. 5*s*.
In ornamental Parchment, 6*s*.

—— II. *Holy War*, &*c*. Edited by E. Venables, M.A.
In the Press.

Clarendon. *History of the Rebellion*. *Book VI*. Edited
by T. Arnold, M.A. Extra fcap. 8vo. 4*s*. 6*d*.

Dryden. *Select Poems*. Stanzas on the Death of Oliver
Cromwell; Astræa Redux; Annus Mirabilis; Absalom and Achitophel;
Religio Laici; The Hind and the Panther. Edited by W. D. Christie, M.A.
Second Edition. Extra fcap. 8vo. 3*s*. 6*d*.

Locke's Conduct of the Understanding. Edited, with Introduction, Notes, &c., by T. Fowler, M.A. Second Edition. Extra fcap. 8vo. 2*s*.

Addison. *Selections from Papers in the Spectator*. With
Notes. By T. Arnold, M.A. Extra fcap. 8vo. 4*s*. 6*d*. In ornamental
Parchment, 6*s*.

Steele.   Selections from the Tatler, Spectator, and Guardian.
Edited by Austin Dobson. Extra fcap. 8vo. 4*s.* 6*d.* In white Parchment, 7*s.* 6*d.*

Pope. With Introduction and Notes. By Mark Pattison, B.D.

—— I. *Essay on Man.* Extra fcap. 8vo. 1*s.* 6*d.*

—— II. *Satires and Epistles.* Extra fcap. 8vo. 2*s.*

Parnell.   The Hermit. Paper covers, 2*d.*

Johnson. I. *Rasselas; Lives of Dryden and Pope.* Edited
by Alfred Milnes, M.A. (London). Extra fcap. 8vo. 4*s.* 6*d.*, or *Lives of Dryden and Pope* only, stiff covers, 2*s.* 6*d.*

—— II. *Vanity of Human Wishes.* With Notes, by E. J.
Payne, M.A. Paper covers, 4*d.*

Gray.   Selected Poems. Edited by Edmund Gosse. Extra
fcap. 8vo. Stiff covers, 1*s.* 6*d.* In white Parchment, 3*s.*

—— *Elegy and Ode on Eton College.* Paper covers, 2*d.*

Goldsmith.   The Deserted Village. Paper covers, 2*d.*

Cowper. Edited, with Life, Introductions, and Notes, by
H. T. Griffith, B.A.

—— I. *The Didactic Poems of* 1782, with Selections from the
Minor Pieces, A.D. 1779–1783. Extra fcap. 8vo. 3*s.*

—— II. *The Task, with Tirocinium,* and Selections from the
Minor Poems. A.D. 1784–1799. Second Edition. Extra fcap. 8vo. 3*s.*

Burke.   Select Works. Edited, with Introduction and Notes,
by E. J. Payne, M.A.

—— I. *Thoughts on the Present Discontents; the two Speeches
on America.* Second Edition. Extra fcap. 8vo. 4*s.* 6*d.*

—— II. *Reflections on the French Revolution.* Second Edition.
Extra fcap. 8vo. 5*s.*

—— III. *Four Letters on the Proposals for Peace with the
Regicide Directory of France.* Second Edition. Extra fcap. 8vo. 5*s.*

Keats.   Hyperion, Book I. With Notes by W. T. Arnold, B.A.
Paper covers, 4*d.*

Byron.   Childe Harold. Edited, with Introduction and Notes,
by H. F. Tozer, M.A. Extra fcap. 8vo. 3*s.* 6*d.* In white Parchment, 5*s.*

Scott.   Lay of the Last Minstrel. Edited with Preface and
Notes by W. Minto, M.A. With Map. Extra fcap. 8vo. Stiff covers, 2*s.* Ornamental Parchment, 3*s.* 6*d.*

—— *Lay of the Last Minstrel.* Introduction and Canto I.,
with Preface and Notes, by the same Editor. 6*d.*

[9]   C

II. LATIN.

Rudimenta Latina. Comprising Accidence, and Exercises of
a very Elementary Character, for the use of Beginners. By John Barrow
Allen, M.A. Extra fcap. 8vo. 2s.

An Elementary Latin Grammar. By the same Author.
Forty-second Thousand. Extra fcap. 8vo. 2s.6d.

A First Latin Exercise Book. By the same Author. Fourth
Edition. Extra fcap. 8vo. 2s. 6d.

A Second Latin Exercise Book. By the same Author. Extra
fcap. 8vo. 3s. 6d.

Reddenda Minora, or Easy Passages, Latin and Greek, for
Unseen Translation. For the use of Lower Forms. Composed and selected
by C. S. Jerram, M.A. Extra fcap. 8vo. 1s. 6d.

Anglice Reddenda, or Easy Extracts, Latin and Greek, for
Unseen Translation. By C. S. Jerram, M.A. Third Edition, Revised and
Enlarged. Extra fcap. 8vo. 2s. 6d.

Passages for Translation into Latin. For the use of Passmen
and others. Selected by J. Y. Sargent, M.A. Fifth Edition. Extra fcap.
8vo. 2s. 6d.

Exercises in Latin Prose Composition; with Introduction,
Notes, and Passages of Graduated Difficulty for Translation into Latin. By
G. G. Ramsay, M.A., LL.D. Second Edition. Extra fcap. 8vo. 4s. 6d.

Hints and Helps for Latin Elegiacs. By H. Lee-Warner, M.A.
Extra fcap. 8vo. 3s. 6d.

First Latin Reader. By T. J. Nunns, M.A. Third Edition.
Extra fcap. 8vo. 2s.

Caesar. The Commentaries (for Schools). With Notes and
Maps. By Charles E. Moberly, M.A.
Part I. *The Gallic War.* Second Edition. Extra fcap. 8vo. 4s. 6d.
Part II. *The Civil War.* Extra fcap. 8vo. 3s. 6d.
The Civil War. Book I. Second Edition. Extra fcap. 8vo. 2s.

Cicero. Selection of interesting and descriptive passages. With
Notes. By Henry Walford, M.A. In three Parts. Extra fcap. 8vo. 4s. 6d.
Each Part separately, limp, 1s. 6d.

Part I. Anecdotes from Grecian and Roman History. Third Edition.
Part II. Omens and Dreams: Beauties of Nature. Third Edition.
Part III. Rome's Rule of her Provinces. Third Edition.

Cicero. Selected Letters (for Schools). With Notes. By the
late C. E. Prichard, M.A., and E. R. Bernard, M.A. Second Edition.
Extra fcap. 8vo. 3s.

Cicero. Select Orations (for Schools). In Verrem I. De
Imperio Gn. Pompeii. Pro Archia. Philippica IX. With Introduction and
Notes by J. R. King, M.A. Second Edition. Extra fcap. 8vo. 2s. 6d.

Cornelius Nepos. With Notes. By Oscar Browning, M.A.
Second Edition. Extra fcap. 8vo. 2s. 6d.

Horace. Selected Odes. With Notes for the use of a Fifth
Form. By E. C. Wickham, M.A. In two Parts. Extra fcap. 8vo. *cloth*, 2s.
Or separately, Part I. Text, 1s. Part II. Notes, 1s.

Livy. Selections (for Schools). With Notes and Maps. By
H. Lee-Warner, M.A. Extra fcap. 8vo. In Parts, limp, each 1s. 6d.
Part I. The Caudine Disaster. Part II. Hannibal's Campaign
in Italy. Part III. The Macedonian War.

Livy. Books V–VII. With Introduction and Notes. By
A. R. Cluer, B.A. Extra fcap. 8vo. 3s. 6d.

Livy. Books XXI, XXII, and XXIII. With Introduction
and Notes. By M. T. Tatham, M.A. Extra fcap. 8vo. 4s. 6d.

Ovid. Selections for the use of Schools. With Introductions
and Notes, and an Appendix on the Roman Calendar. By W. Ramsay, M.A.
Edited by G. G. Ramsay, M.A. Third Edition. Extra fcap. 8vo. 5s. 6d.

Ovid. Tristia. Book I. The Text revised, with an Introduction and Notes. By S. G. Owen, B.A. Extra fcap. 8vo. 3s. 6d.

Plautus. The Trinummus. With Notes and Introductions.
Intended for the Higher Forms of Public Schools. By C. E. Freeman, M.A.,
and A. Sloman, M.A. Extra fcap. 8vo. 3s.

Pliny. Selected Letters (for Schools). With Notes. By the
late C. E. Prichard, M.A., and E. R. Bernard, M.A. Extra fcap. 8vo. 3s.

Sallust. With Introduction and Notes. By W. W. Capes,
M.A. Extra fcap. 8vo. 4s. 6d.

Tacitus. The Annals. Books I–IV. Edited, with Introduction and Notes for the use of Schools and Junior Students, by H. Furneaux,
M.A. Extra fcap. 8vo. 5s.

Terence. Andria. With Notes and Introductions. By C.
E. Freeman, M.A., and A. Sloman, M.A. Extra fcap. 8vo. 3s.

—— *Adelphi.* With Notes and Introductions. Intended for
the Higher Forms of Public Schools. By A. Sloman, M.A. Extra fcap.
8vo. 3s.

Virgil. With Introduction and Notes. By T. L. Papillon,
M.A. Two vols. Crown 8vo. 10s. 6d. The Text separately, 4s. 6d.

Catulli Veronensis Liber. Iterum recognovit, apparatum cri-
ticum prolegomena appendices addidit, Robinson Ellis, A.M. 1878. Demy
8vo. 16s.

—— *A Commentary on Catullus.* By Robinson Ellis, M.A.
1876. Demy 8vo. 16s.

C 2

Catulli Veronensis Carmina Selecta, secundum recognitionem
Robinson Ellis, A.M. Extra fcap. 8vo. 3s. 6d.

Cicero de Oratore. With Introduction and Notes. By A. S.
Wilkins, M.A.
Book I. 1879. 8vo. 6s.　　Book II. 1881. 8vo. 5s.

—— *Philippic Orations.* With Notes. By J. R. King, M.A.
Second Edition. 1879. 8vo. 10s. 6d.

—— *Select Letters.* With English Introductions, Notes, and
Appendices. By Albert Watson, M.A. Third Edition. 1881. Demy 8vo. 18s.

—— *Select Letters.* Text. By the same Editor. Second
Edition. Extra fcap. 8vo. 4s.

—— *pro Cluentio.* With Introduction and Notes. By W.
Ramsay, M.A. Edited by G. G. Ramsay, M.A. Second Edition. Extra fcap.
8vo. 3s. 6d.

Horace. With a Commentary. Volume I. The Odes, Carmen
Seculare, and Epodes. By Edward C. Wickham, M.A. Second Edition.
1877. Demy 8vo. 12s.

—— A reprint of the above, in a size suitable for the use
of Schools. Extra fcap. 8vo. 5s. 6d.

Livy, Book I. With Introduction, Historical Examination,
and Notes. By J. R. Seeley, M.A. Second Edition. 1881. 8vo. 6s.

Ovid. P. Ovidii Nasonis Ibis. Ex Novis Codicibus edidit,
Scholia Vetera Commentarium cum Prolegomenis Appendice Indice addidit,
R. Ellis, A.M. 8vo. 10s. 6d.

Persius. The Satires. With a Translation and Commentary.
By John Conington, M.A. Edited by Henry Nettleship, M.A. Second
Edition. 1874. 8vo. 7s. 6d.

Tacitus. The Annals. Books I-VI. Edited, with Introduction and Notes, by H. Furneaux, M.A. 8vo. 18s.

Nettleship (H., M.A.). Lectures and Essays on Subjects con-
nected with Latin Scholarship and Literature. Crown 8vo. 7s. 6d.

—— *The Roman Satura:* its original form in connection with
its literary development. 8vo. sewed, 1s.

—— *Ancient Lives of Vergil.* With an Essay on the Poems
of Vergil, in connection with his Life and Times. 8vo. sewed, 2s.

Papillon (T. L., M.A.). A Manual of Comparative Philology.
Third Edition, Revised and Corrected. 1882. Crown 8vo. 6s.

Pinder (North, M.A.). Selections from the less known Latin
Poets. 1869. 8vo. 15s.

Sellar (W. Y., M.A.). Roman Poets of the Augustan Age.
VIRGIL. New Edition. 1883. Crown 8vo. 9s.

—— *Roman Poets of the Republic.* New Edition, Revised
and Enlarged. 1881. 8vo. 14s.

Wordsworth (J., M.A.). Fragments and Specimens of Early
Latin. With Introductions and Notes. 1874. 8vo. 18s.

III. GREEK.

A Greek Primer, for the use of beginners in that Language.
By the Right Rev. Charles Wordsworth, D.C.L. Seventh Edition. Extra fcap.
8vo. 1s. 6d.

Easy Greek Reader. By Evelyn Abbott, M.A. In two
Parts. Extra fcap. 8vo. 3s. *Just Published.*

    The Text and Notes may be had separately, 1s. 6d. each.

Graecae Grammaticae Rudimenta in usum Scholarum. Auc-
tore Carolo Wordsworth, D.C.L. Nineteenth Edition, 1882. 12mo. 4s.

A Greek-English Lexicon, abridged from Liddell and Scott's
4to. edition, chiefly for the use of Schools. Twenty-first Edition. 1884.
Square 12mo. 7s. 6d.

Greek Verbs, Irregular and Defective; their forms, meaning,
and quantity; embracing all the Tenses used by Greek writers, with references
to the passages in which they are found. By W. Veitch. Fourth Edition.
Crown 8vo. 10s. 6d.

The Elements of Greek Accentuation (for Schools): abridged
from his larger work by H. W. Chandler, M.A. Extra fcap. 8vo. 2s. 6d.

A SERIES OF GRADUATED GREEK READERS:—

First Greek Reader. By W. G. Rushbrooke, M.L. Second
Edition. Extra fcap. 8vo. 2s. 6d.

Second Greek Reader. By A. M. Bell, M.A. Extra fcap.
8vo. 3s. 6d.

Fourth Greek Reader; being Specimens of Greek Dialects.
With Introductions, etc. By W. W. Merry, M.A. Extra fcap. 8vo. 4s. 6d.

Fifth Greek Reader. Selections from Greek Epic and
Dramatic Poetry, with Introductions and Notes. By Evelyn Abbott, M.A.
Extra fcap. 8vo. 4s. 6d.

The Golden Treasury of Ancient Greek Poetry: being a Collection of the finest passages in the Greek Classic Poets. with Introductory
Notices and Notes. By R. S. Wright, M.A. Extra fcap. 8vo. 8s. 6d.

A Golden Treasury of Greek Prose, being a Collection of the
finest passages in the principal Greek Prose Writers, with Introductory Notices
and Notes. By R. S. Wright, M.A., and J. E. L. Shadwell, M.A. Extra fcap.
8vo. 4s. 6d.

Aeschylus. Prometheus Bound (for Schools). With Introduction and Notes, by A. O. Prickard, M.A. Second Edition. Extra fcap. 8vo. *2s.*

—— *Agamemnon.* With Introduction and Notes, by Arthur Sidgwick, M.A. Second Edition. Extra fcap. 8vo. *3s.*

—— *Choephoroi.* With Introduction and Notes by the same Editor. Extra fcap. 8vo. *3s.*

Aristophanes. In Single Plays. Edited, with English Notes, Introductions, &c., by W. W. Merry, M.A. Extra fcap. 8vo.

I. The Clouds, Second Edition, *2s.*

II. The Acharnians, *2s.*   III. The Frogs, *2s.*

Cebes. Tabula. With Introduction and Notes. By C. S. Jerram, M.A. Extra fcap. 8vo. *2s. 6d.*

Euripides. Alcestis (for Schools). By C. S. Jerram, M.A. Extra fcap. 8vo. *2s. 6d.*

—— *Helena.* Edited, with Introduction, Notes, etc., for Upper and Middle Forms. By C. S. Jerram, M.A. Extra fcap. 8vo. *3s.*

—— *Iphigenia in Tauris.* Edited, with Introduction, Notes, etc., for Upper and Middle Forms. By C. S. Jerram, M.A. Extra fcap. 8vo. cloth, *3s.*

—— *Medea.* By C. B. Heberden, M.A. In two Parts. Extra fcap. 8vo. *2s.*

Or separately, Part I. Introduction and Text, *1s.*
Part II. Notes and Appendices, *1s.*

Herodotus, Selections from. Edited, with Introduction, Notes, and a Map, by W. W. Merry, M.A. Extra fcap. 8vo. *2s. 6d.*

Homer. Odyssey, Books I–XII (for Schools). By W. W. Merry, M.A. Twenty-seventh Thousand. Extra fcap. 8vo. *4s. 6d.*

Book II, separately, *1s. 6d.*

—— *Odyssey,* Books XIII–XXIV (for Schools). By the same Editor. Second Edition. Extra fcap. 8vo. *5s.*

—— *Iliad,* Book I (for Schools). By D. B. Monro, M.A. Second Edition. Extra fcap. 8vo. *2s.*

—— *Iliad,* Books I–XII (for Schools). With an Introduction, a brief Homeric Grammar, and Notes. By D. B. Monro, M.A. Second Edition. Extra fcap. 8vo. *6s.*

—— *Iliad,* Books VI and XXI. With Introduction and Notes. By Herbert Hailstone, M.A. Extra fcap. 8vo. *1s. 6d.* each.

Lucian. Vera Historia (for Schools). By C. S. Jerram, M.A. Second Edition. Extra fcap. 8vo. *1s. 6d.*

Plato. Selections from the Dialogues [including the whole of the *Apology* and *Crito*]. With Introduction and Notes by John Purves, M.A., and a Preface by the Rev. B. Jowett, M.A. Extra fcap. 8vo. *6s. 6d.*

Sophocles. For the use of Schools. Edited with Introductions and English Notes. By Lewis Campbell, M.A., and Evelyn Abbott, M.A. *New and Revised Edition.* 2 Vols. Extra fcap. 8vo. 10s. 6d.
Sold separately, Vol. I, Text, 4s. 6d.; Vol. II, Explanatory Notes, 6s.

Sophocles. In Single Plays, with English Notes, &c. By Lewis Campbell, M.A., and Evelyn Abbott, M.A. Extra fcap. 8vo. limp.

Oedipus Tyrannus, Philoctetes. New and Revised Edition, 2s. each.

Oedipus Coloneus, Antigone, 1s. 9d. each.

Ajax, Electra, Trachiniae, 2s. each.

—— *Oedipus Rex:* Dindorf's Text, with Notes by the present Bishop of St. David's. Extra fcap. 8vo. limp, 1s. 6d.

Theocritus (for Schools). With Notes. By H. Kynaston, D.D. (late Snow). Third Edition. Extra fcap. 8vo. 4s. 6d.

Xenophon. Easy Selections (for Junior Classes). With a Vocabulary, Notes, and Map. By J. S. Phillpotts, B.C.L., and C. S. Jerram, M.A. Third Edition. Extra fcap. 8vo. 3s. 6d.

—— *Selections* (for Schools). With Notes and Maps. By J. S. Phillpotts, B.C.L. Fourth Edition. Extra fcap. 8vo. 3s. 6d.

—— *Anabasis*, Book I. Edited for the use of Junior Classes and Private Students. With Introduction, Notes, etc. By J. Marshall, M.A., Rector of the Royal High School, Edinburgh. Extra fcap. 8vo. 2s. 6d.

—— *Anabasis*, Book II. With Notes and Map. By C. S. Jerram, M.A. Extra fcap. 8vo. 2s.

—— *Cyropaedia*, Books IV and V. With Introduction and Notes by C. Bigg, D.D. Extra fcap. 8vo. 2s. 6d.

Aristotle's Politics. By W. L. Newman, M.A. [*In the Press.*]

Aristotelian Studies. I. On the Structure of the Seventh Book of the Nicomachean Ethics. By J. C. Wilson, M.A. 8vo. stiff, 5s.

Aristotelis Ethica Nicomachea, ex recensione Immanuelis Bekkeri. Crown 8vo. 5s.

Demosthenes and Aeschines. The Orations of Demosthenes and Aeschines on the Crown. With Introductory Essays and Notes. By G. A. Simcox, M.A., and W. H. Simcox, M.A. 1872. 8vo. 12s.

Hicks (E. L., M.A.). A Manual of Greek Historical Inscriptions. Demy 8vo. 10s. 6d.

Homer. Odyssey, Books I–XII. Edited with English Notes, Appendices, etc. By W. W. Merry, M.A., and the late James Riddell, M.A. 1886. Second Edition. Demy 8vo. 16s.

Homer. A Grammar of the Homeric Dialect. By D. B. Monro,
M.A. Demy 8vo. 10s. 6d.

Sophocles. The Plays and Fragments. With English Notes
and Introductions, by Lewis Campbell, M.A. 2 vols.

    Vol. I. Oedipus Tyrannus. Oedipus Coloneus. Antigone. 8vo. 16s.

    Vol. II. Ajax. Electra. Trachiniae. Philoctetes. Fragments. 8vo. 16s.

IV. FRENCH AND ITALIAN.

Brachet's Etymological Dictionary of the French Language,
with a Preface on the Principles of French Etymology. Translated into
English by G. W. Kitchin, D.D. Third Edition. Crown 8vo. 7s. 6d.

—— *Historical Grammar of the French Language.* Translated into English by G. W. Kitchin, D.D. Fourth Edition. Extra fcap.
8vo. 3s. 6d.

Works by GEORGE SAINTSBURY, M.A.

Primer of French Literature. Extra fcap. 8vo. 2s.

Short History of French Literature. Crown 8vo. 10s. 6d.

Specimens of French Literature, from Villon to Hugo. Crown
8vo. 9s.

Corneille's Horace. Edited, with Introduction and Notes, by
George Saintsbury, M.A. Extra fcap. 8vo. 2s. 6d.

Molière's Les Précieuses Ridicules. Edited, with Introduction
and Notes, by Andrew Lang, M.A. Extra fcap. 8vo. 1s. 6d.

Racine's Esther. Edited, with Introduction and Notes, by
George Saintsbury. M.A. Extra fcap. 8vo. 2s. *Just Published.*

Beaumarchais' Le Barbier de Séville. Edited, with Introduction
and Notes, by Austin Dobson. Extra fcap. 8vo. 2s. 6d.

Voltaire's Mérope. Edited, with Introduction and Notes, by
George Saintsbury. Extra fcap. 8vo. cloth, 2s.

Musset's On ne badine pas avec l'Amour, and Fantasio. Edited,
with Prolegomena, Notes, etc., by Walter Herries Pollock. Extra fcap.
8vo. 2s.

Sainte-Beuve. Selections from the Causeries du Lundi. Edited
by George Saintsbury. Extra fcap. 8vo. 2s.

Quinet's Lettres à sa Mère. Selected and edited by George
Saintsbury. Extra fcap. 8vo. 2s.

Gautier, Théophile. Scenes of Travel. Selected and Edited
by George Saintsbury. Extra fcap. 8vo. 2s.

L'Éloquence de la Chaire et de la Tribune Françaises. Edited
by Paul Blouët, B.A. (Univ. Gallic.). Vol. I. French Sacred Oratory
Extra fcap. 8vo. 2s. 6d.

Edited by GUSTAVE MASSON, B.A.

Corneille's Cinna. With Notes, Glossary, etc. Extra fcap. 8vo.
cloth, 2s. Stiff covers, 1s. 6d.

Louis XIV and his Contemporaries; as described in Extracts
from the best Memoirs of the Seventeenth Century. With English Notes,
Genealogical Tables, &c. Extra fcap. 8vo. 2s. 6d.

Maistre, Xavier de. Voyage autour de ma Chambre. Ourika,
by *Madame de Duras;* Le Vieux Tailleur, by *MM. Erckmann-Chatrian;*
La Veillée de Vincennes, by *Alfred de Vigny;* Les Jumeaux de l'Hôtel
Corneille, by *Edmond About;* Mésaventures d'un Écolier, by *Rodolphe Töpffer.*
Third Edition, Revised and Corrected. Extra fcap. 8vo. 2s. 6d.

Molière's Les Fourberies de Scapin, and *Racine's Athalie.*
With Voltaire's Life of Molière. Extra fcap. 8vo. 2s. 6d.

Molière's Les Fourberies de Scapin. With Voltaire's Life of
Molière. Extra fcap. 8vo. stiff covers, 1s. 6d.

Molière's Les Femmes Savantes. With Notes, Glossary, etc.
Extra fcap. 8vo. *cloth,* 2s. Stiff covers, 1s. 6d.

Racine's Andromaque, and *Corneille's Le Menteur.* With
Louis Racine's Life of his Father. Extra fcap. 8vo. 2s. 6d.

Regnard's Le Joueur, and *Brueys and Palaprat's Le Grondeur.*
Extra fcap. 8vo. 2s. 6d.

*Sévigné, Madame de, and her chief Contemporaries, Selections
from the Correspondence of.* Intended more especially for Girls' Schools.
Extra fcap. 8vo. 3s.

Dante. Selections from the Inferno. With Introduction and
Notes. By H. B. Cotterill, B.A. Extra fcap. 8vo. 4s. 6d.

Tasso. La Gerusalemme Liberata. Cantos i, ii. With Introduction and Notes. By the same Editor. Extra fcap. 8vo. 2s. 6d.

V. GERMAN.

Scherer (W.). A History of German Literature. Translated
from the Third German Edition by Mrs. F. Conybeare. Edited by F. Max
Müller. 2 vols. 8vo. 21s.

Max Müller. The German Classics, from the Fourth to the
Nineteenth Century. With Biographical Notices, Translations into Modern
German, and Notes. By F. Max Müller, M.A. A New Edition, Revised,
Enlarged, and Adapted to Wilhelm Scherer's 'History of German Literature,'
by F. Lichtenstein. 2 vols. crown 8vo. 21s.

GERMAN COURSE. By HERMANN LANGE.

The Germans at Home; a Practical Introduction to German Conversation, with an Appendix containing the Essentials of German Grammar. Second Edition. 8vo. 2s. 6d.

The German Manual; a German Grammar, Reading Book, and a Handbook of German Conversation. 8vo. 7s. 6d

Grammar of the German Language. 8vo. 3s. 6d.

German Composition; A Theoretical and Practical Guide to the Art of Translating English Prose into German. 8vo. 4s. 6d.

Lessing's Laokoon. With Introduction, English Notes, etc. By A. Hamann, Phil. Doc., M.A. Extra fcap. 8vo. 4s. 6d.

Schiller's Wilhelm Tell. Translated into English Verse by E. Massie, M.A. Extra fcap. 8vo. 5s.

Also, Edited by C. A. BUCHHEIM, Phil. Doc.

Goethe's Egmont. With a Life of Goethe, &c. Third Edition. Extra fcap. 8vo. 3s.

—— *Iphigenie auf Tauris.* A Drama. With a Critical Introduction and Notes. Second Edition. Extra fcap. 8vo. 3s.

Heine's Prosa, being Selections from his Prose Works. With English Notes, etc. Extra fcap. 8vo. 4s. 6d.

Heine's Harzreise. With Life of Heine, Descriptive Sketch of the Harz, and Index. Extra fcap. 8vo. paper covers, 1s. 6d.; cloth, 2s. 6d.

Lessing's Minna von Barnhelm. A Comedy. With a Life of Lessing, Critical Analysis, etc. Extra fcap. 8vo. 3s. 6d.

—— *Nathan der Weise.* With Introduction, Notes, etc. Extra fcap. 8vo. 4s. 6d.

Schiller's Historische Skizzen; Egmont's Leben und Tod, and *Belagerung von Antwerpen.* With a Map. Extra fcap. 8vo. 2s. 6d.

—— *Wilhelm Tell.* With a Life of Schiller; an historical and critical Introduction, Arguments, and a complete Commentary, and Map. Sixth Edition. Extra fcap. 8vo. 3s. 6d.

—— *Wilhelm Tell.* School Edition. With Map. 2s.

Modern German Reader. A Graduated Collection of Extracts in Prose and Poetry from Modern German writers :—
 Part I. With English Notes, a Grammatical Appendix, and a complete Vocabulary. Fourth Edition. Extra fcap. 8vo. 2s. 6d.
 Part II. With English Notes and an Index. Extra fcap. 8vo. 2s. 6d.

Niebuhr's Griechische Heroen-Geschichten. Tales of Greek Heroes. Edited with English Notes and a Vocabulary, by Emma S. Buchheim. School Edition. Extra fcap. 8vo. *cloth,* 2s. *Stiff covers,* 1s. 6d.

VI. MATHEMATICS, PHYSICAL SCIENCE, &c.
By LEWIS HENSLEY, M.A.

Figures made Easy: a first Arithmetic Book. Crown 8vo. 6d.

Answers to the Examples in Figures made Easy, together with two thousand additional Examples, with Answers. Crown 8vo. 1s.

The Scholar's Arithmetic: with Answers. Crown 8vo. 4s. 6d.

The Scholar's Algebra. Crown 8vo. 4s. 6d.

Baynes (R. E., M.A.). Lessons on Thermodynamics. 1878. Crown 8vo. 7s. 6d.

Chambers (G. F., F.R.A.S.). A Handbook of Descriptive Astronomy. Third Edition. 1877. Demy 8vo. 28s.

Clarke (Col. A. R., C.B., R.E.). Geodesy. 1880. 8vo. 12s. 6d.

Cremona (Luigi). Elements of Projective Geometry. Translated by C. Leudesdorf, M.A. 8vo. 12s. 6d.

Donkin. Acoustics. Second Edition. Crown 8vo. 7s. 6d.

Euclid Revised. Containing the Essentials of the Elements of Plane Geometry as given by Euclid in his first Six Books. Edited by R. C. J. Nixon, M.A. Crown 8vo. 7s. 6d.

Sold separately as follows,

Books I–IV. 3s. 6d.

Books I, II. 1s. 6d.

Book I. 1s.

Galton (Douglas, C.B., F.R.S.). The Construction of Healthy Dwellings. Demy 8vo. 10s. 6d.

Hamilton (Sir R. G. C.), and J. Ball. Book-keeping. New and enlarged Edition. Extra fcap. 8vo. limp cloth, 2s.

Harcourt (A. G. Vernon, M.A.), and *H. G. Madan, M.A. Exercises in Practical Chemistry.* Vol. I. Elementary Exercises. Third Edition. Crown 8vo. 9s.

Maclaren (Archibald). A System of Physical Education: Theoretical and Practical. Extra fcap. 8vo. 7s. 6d.

Madan (H. G., M.A.). Tables of Qualitative Analysis. Large 4to. paper, 4s. 6d.

Maxwell (J. Clerk, M.A., F.R.S.). A Treatise on Electricity and Magnetism. Second Edition. 2 vols. Demy 8vo. 1l. 11s. 6d.

—— *An Elementary Treatise on Electricity.* Edited by William Garnett, M.A. Demy 8vo. 7s. 6d.

Minchin (G. M., M.A.). A Treatise on Statics with Applications to Physics. Third Edition, Corrected and Enlarged. Vol. I. *Equilibrium of Coplanar Forces.* 8vo. 9s. Vol. II. *Statics.* 8vo. 16s.

Minchin (*G. M., M.A.*).   *Uniplanar Kinematics of Solids and Fluids.* Crown 8vo. 7s. 6d.

Phillips (*John, M.A., F.R.S.*).   *Geology of Oxford and the Valley of the Thames.* 1871. 8vo. 21s.

—— *Vesuvius.* 1869. Crown 8vo. 10s. 6d.

Prestwich (*Joseph, M.A., F.R.S.*).   *Geology, Chemical, Physical, and Stratigraphical.* Vol. I. Chemical and Physical. Royal 8vo. 25s.

Rolleston's Forms of Animal Life. Illustrated by Descriptions and Drawings of Dissections. New Edition. (*Nearly ready.*)

Smyth.   A Cycle of Celestial Objects. Observed, Reduced, and Discussed by Admiral W. H. Smyth, R.N. Revised, condensed, and greatly enlarged by G. F. Chambers, F.R.A.S. 1881. 8vo. *Price reduced to* 12s.

Stewart (*Balfour, LL.D., F.R.S.*).   *A Treatise on Heat,* with numerous Woodcuts and Diagrams. Fourth Edition. Extra fcap. 8vo. 7s. 6d.

Vernon-Harcourt (*L. F., M.A.*).   *A Treatise on Rivers and Canals,* relating to the Control and Improvement of Rivers, and the Design, Construction, and Development of Canals. 2 vols. (Vol. I, Text. Vol. II, Plates.) 8vo. 21s.

—— *Harbours and Docks;* their Physical Features, History, Construction, Equipment, and Maintenance; with Statistics as to their Commercial Development. 2 vols. 8vo. 25s.

Watson (*H. W., M.A.*).   *A Treatise on the Kinetic Theory of Gases.* 1876. 8vo. 3s. 6d.

Watson (*H. W., D. Sc., F.R.S.*), *and S. H. Burbury, M.A.*

    I. *A Treatise on the Application of Generalised Coordinates to the Kinetics of a Material System.* 1879. 8vo. 6s.

    II. *The Mathematical Theory of Electricity and Magnetism.* Vol. I. Electrostatics. 8vo. 10s. 6d.

Williamson (*A. W., Phil. Doc., F.R.S.*).   *Chemistry for Students.* A new Edition, with Solutions. 1873. Extra fcap. 8vo. 8s. 6d.

VII. HISTORY.

Bluntschli (*J. K.*).   *The Theory of the State.* By J. K. Bluntschli, late Professor of Political Sciences in the University of Heidelberg. Authorised English Translation from the Sixth German Edition. Demy 8vo. half bound, 12s. 6d.

Finlay (*George, LL.D.*).   *A History of Greece* from its Conquest by the Romans to the present time, B.C. 146 to A.D. 1864. A new Edition, revised throughout, and in part re-written, with considerable additions, by the Author, and edited by H. F. Tozer, M.A. 7 vols. 8vo. 3l. 10s.

Fortescue (Sir John, Kt.). The Governance of England: otherwise called The Difference between an Absolute and a Limited Monarchy. A Revised Text. Edited, with Introduction, Notes, and Appendices, by Charles Plummer, M.A. 8vo. half bound, 12*s.* 6*d.*

Freeman (E.A., D.C.L.). A Short History of the Norman Conquest of England. Second Edition. Extra fcap. 8vo. 2*s.* 6*d.*

George (H.B., M.A.). Genealogical Tables illustrative of Modern History. Third Edition, Revised and Enlarged. Small 4to. 12*s.*

Hodgkin (T.). Italy and her Invaders. Illustrated with Plates and Maps. Vols. I—IV., A.D. 376—553. 8vo. 3*l.* 8*s.*

Kitchin (G. W., D.D.). A History of France. With numerous Maps, Plans, and Tables. In Three Volumes. *Second Edition.* Crown 8vo. each 10*s.* 6*d.*

    Vol. 1. Down to the Year 1453.

    Vol. 2. From 1453–1624.   Vol. 3. From 1624–1793.

Payne (E. J., M.A.). A History of the United States of America. In the Press.

Ranke (L. von). A History of England, principally in the Seventeenth Century. Translated by Resident Members of the University of Oxford, under the superintendence of G. W. Kitchin, D.D., and C. W. Boase, M.A. 1875. 6 vols. 8vo. 3*l.* 3*s.*

Rawlinson (George, M.A.). A Manual of Ancient History. Second Edition. Demy 8vo. 14*s.*

Select Charters and other Illustrations of English Constitutional History, from the Earliest Times to the Reign of Edward I. Arranged and edited by W. Stubbs, D.D. Fifth Edition. 1883. Crown 8vo. 8*s.* 6*d.*

Stubbs (W., D.D.). The Constitutional History of England, in its Origin and Development. Library Edition. 3 vols. demy 8vo. 2*l.* 8*s.*

    Also in 3 vols. crown 8vo. price 12*s.* each.

—— *Seventeen Lectures on the Study of Medieval and* Modern History, &c., delivered at Oxford 1867–1884. Demy 8vo. half-bound, 10*s.* 6*d.*

Wellesley. A Selection from the Despatches, Treaties, and other Papers of the Marquess Wellesley. K.G., during his Government of India. Edited by S. J. Owen, M.A. 1877. 8vo. 1*l.* 4*s.*

Wellington. A Selection from the Despatches, Treaties, and other Papers relating to India of Field-Marshal the Duke of Wellington, K.G. Edited by S. J. Owen, M.A. 1880. 8vo. 24*s.*

A History of British India. By S. J. Owen, M.A., Reader in Indian History in the University of Oxford. In preparation.

VIII. LAW.

Alberici Gentilis, I.C.D., I.C., De Iure Belli Libri Tres. Edidit T. E. Holland, I.C.D. 1877. Small 4to. half morocco, 21*s.*

Anson (Sir William R., Bart., D.C.L.). Principles of the English Law of Contract, and of Agency in its Relation to Contract. Fourth Edition. Demy 8vo. 10*s.* 6*d.*

—— *Law and Custom of the Constitution.* Part I. Parliament. Demy 8vo. 10*s.* 6*d.*

Bentham (Jeremy). An Introduction to the Principles of Morals and Legislation. Crown 8vo. 6*s.* 6*d.*

Digby (Kenelm E., M.A.). An Introduction to the History of the Law of Real Property. Third Edition. Demy 8vo. 10*s.* 6*d.*

Gaii Institutionum Juris Civilis Commentarii Quattuor; or, Elements of Roman Law by Gaius. With a Translation and Commentary by Edward Poste, M.A. Second Edition. 1875. 8vo. 18*s.*

Hall (W. E., M.A.). International Law. Second Ed. 8vo. 21*s.*

Holland (T. E., D.C.L.). The Elements of Jurisprudence. Third Edition. Demy 8vo. 10*s.* 6*d.*

—— *The European Concert in the Eastern Question,* a Collection of Treaties and other Public Acts. Edited, with Introductions and Notes, by Thomas Erskine Holland, D.C.L. 8vo. 12*s.* 6*d.*

Imperatoris Iustiniani Institutionum Libri Quattuor; with Introductions, Commentary, Excursus and Translation. By J. B. Moyle, B.C.L., M.A. 2 vols. Demy 8vo. 21*s.*

Justinian, The Institutes of, edited as a recension of the Institutes of Gaius, by Thomas Erskine Holland, D.C.L. Second Edition, 1881. Extra fcap. 8vo. 5*s.*

Justinian, Select Titles from the Digest of. By T. E. Holland, D.C.L., and C. L. Shadwell, B.C.L. 8vo. 14*s.*

Also sold in Parts, in paper covers, as follows :—

Part I. Introductory Titles. 2*s.* 6*d.*   Part II. Family Law. 1*s.*
Part III. Property Law. 2*s.* 6*d.*   Part IV. Law of Obligations (No. 1). 3*s.* 6*d.*
Part IV. Law of Obligations (No. 2). 4*s.* 6*d.*

Lex Aquilia. The Roman Law of Damage to Property: being a Commentary on the Title of the Digest ' Ad Legem Aquiliam ' (ix. 2). With an Introduction to the Study of the Corpus Iuris Civilis. By Erwin Grueber, Dr. Jur., M.A. Demy 8vo. 10*s.* 6*d.*

Markby (W., D.C.L.). Elements of Law considered with reference to Principles of General Jurisprudence. Third Edition. Demy 8vo. 12*s.* 6*d.*

Twiss (Sir Travers, D.C.L.). The Law of Nations considered as Independent Political Communities.

Part I. On the Rights and Duties of Nations in time of Peace. A new Edition, Revised and Enlarged. 1884. Demy 8vo. 15*s.*

Part II. On the Rights and Duties of Nations in Time of War. Second Edition Revised. 1875. Demy 8vo. 21*s.*

IX. MENTAL AND MORAL PHILOSOPHY, &c.

Bacon's Novum Organum. Edited, with English Notes, by
G. W. Kitchin, D.D. 1855. 8vo. 9s. 6d.

—— Translated by G. W. Kitchin, D.D. 1855. 8vo. 9s. 6d.

Berkeley. The Works of George Berkeley, D.D., formerly
Bishop of Cloyne; including many of his writings hitherto unpublished.
With Prefaces, Annotations, and an Account of his Life and Philosophy,
by Alexander Campbell Fraser, M.A. 4 vols. 1871. 8vo. 2l. 18s.

The Life, Letters, &c. 1 vol. 16s.

—— *Selections from.* With an Introduction and Notes.
For the use of Students in the Universities. By Alexander Campbell Fraser,
LL.D. Second Edition. Crown 8vo. 7s. 6d.

Fowler (T., D.D.). The Elements of Deductive Logic. designed
mainly for the use of Junior Students in the Universities. Eighth Edition,
with a Collection of Examples. Extra fcap. 8vo. 3s. 6d.

—— *The Elements of Inductive Logic,* designed mainly for
the use of Students in the Universities. Fourth Edition. Extra fcap. 8vo. 6s.

Edited by T. FOWLER, D.D.

Bacon. Novum Organum. With Introduction, Notes, &c.
1878. 8vo. 14s.

Locke's Conduct of the Understanding. Second Edition.
Extra fcap. 8vo. 2s.

Danson (J. T.). The Wealth of Households. Crown 8vo. 5s.

Green (T. H., M.A.). Prolegomena to Ethics. Edited by
A. C. Bradley, M.A. Demy 8vo. 12s. 6d.

Hegel. The Logic of Hegel; translated from the Encyclo-
paedia of the Philosophical Sciences. With Prolegomena by William
Wallace, M.A. 1874. 8vo. 14s.

Lotze's Logic, in Three Books; of Thought, of Investigation,
and of Knowledge. English Translation; Edited by B. Bosanquet, M.A.,
Fellow of University College, Oxford. 8vo. *cloth,* 12s. 6d.

—— *Metaphysic,* in Three Books; Ontology, Cosmology,
and Psychology. English Translation; Edited by B. Bosanquet, M.A.
8vo. *cloth,* 12s. 6d.

Martineau (James, D.D.). Types of Ethical Theory. Second
Edition. 2 vols. Crown 8vo. 15s.

Rogers (J. E. Thorold, M.A.). A Manual of Political Economy,
for the use of Schools. Third Edition. Extra fcap. 8vo. 4s. 6d.

Smith's Wealth of Nations. A new Edition, with Notes, by
J. E. Thorold Rogers. M.A. 2 vols. 8vo. 1880. 21s.

Wilson (J. M., B.D.), and T. Fowler, D.D. The Principles
of Morals (Introductory Chapters). 8vo. *boards,* 3s. 6d.

X. ART, &c.

Hullah (John). The Cultivation of the Speaking Voice.
Second Edition. Extra fcap. 8vo. 2s. 6d.

Ouseley (Sir F. A. Gore, Bart.). A Treatise on Harmony.
Third Edition. 4to. 10s.

—— *A Treatise on Counterpoint, Canon, and Fugue,* based
upon that of Cherubini. Second Edition. 4to. 16s.

—— *A Treatise on Musical Form and General Composition.*
Second Edition. 4to. 10s.

Robinson (J. C., F.S.A.). A Critical Account of the Drawings
by Michel Angelo and Raffaello in the University Galleries, Oxford. 1870.
Crown 8vo. 4s.

Ruskin (John, M.A.). A Course of Lectures on Art, delivered
before the University of Oxford in Hilary Term, 1870. 8vo. 6s.

Troutbeck (J., M.A.) and R. F. Dale, M.A. A Music Primer
(for Schools). Second Edition. Crown 8vo. 1s. 6d.

Tyrwhitt (R. St. J., M.A.). A Handbook of Pictorial Art.
With coloured Illustrations, Photographs, and a chapter on Perspective by
A. Macdonald. Second Edition. 1875. 8vo. half morocco, 18s.

Vaux (W. S. W., M.A.). Catalogue of the Castellani Collec-
tion of Antiquities in the University Galleries, Oxford. Crown 8vo. 1s.

The Oxford Bible for Teachers, containing supplementary HELPS TO THE STUDY OF THE BIBLE, including Summaries
of the several Books, with copious Explanatory Notes and Tables
illustrative of Scripture History and the characteristics of Bible
Lands; with a complete Index of Subjects, a Concordance, a Dictionary of Proper Names, and a series of Maps. Prices in various sizes
and bindings from 3s. to 2l. 5s.

Helps to the Study of the Bible, taken from the
OXFORD BIBLE FOR TEACHERS, comprising Summaries of the
several Books, with copious Explanatory Notes and Tables illustrative of Scripture History and the Characteristics of Bible Lands ;
with a complete Index of Subjects, a Concordance, a Dictionary
of Proper Names, and a series of Maps. Crown 8vo. *cloth,* 3s. 6d. ;
16mo. *cloth,* 1s.

———+———

LONDON: HENRY FROWDE,
OXFORD UNIVERSITY PRESS WAREHOUSE, AMEN CORNER,

OXFORD: CLARENDON PRESS DEPOSITORY,
116 HIGH STREET.

The DELEGATES OF THE PRESS *invite suggestions and advice from all persons*
interested in education; and will be thankful for hints, &c. addressed to the
SECRETARY TO THE DELEGATES, *Clarendon Press, Oxford.*